FRIEND ZONE HELL

The Hellman Brothers #3

MARIKA RAY

Friend Zone Hell

Ebook ISBN: 978-1-950141-47-0
Print ISBN: 978-1-950141-48-7

To my friend, Sandi Hatt, for her guidance in describing the medical issues someone with epilepsy must deal with on a daily basis. You are amazing.

FRIEND ZONE HELL

The town's most eligible bachelor just saved my life. I paid him back by puking on him.

Callan Hellman. Mr. Nice Guy paramedic. My best friend.

He buys my friends flowers when he knows they've had a hard day. Who does that? Callan's the guy every girl wants to date and take home to mama. Not me though. We're just friends. Have been since elementary school. I was the weird girl who kept him laughing with my antics, even when his father abandoned his family and Callan hid those scars behind his smile.

But due to my sudden medical diagnosis at twenty-four, Callan insists I move in with him. I accept and soon regret it. Since when did he grow all those muscles, and why is he allergic to wearing shirts? I'm getting white-picket-fences feelings I have no business feeling, and try as I might to suppress them, Callan makes a bold move that proves he's carried a love-shaped torch for me for years.

Turns out, best friends make the best lovers, but when Callan's daddy issues come between us, will his well-meaning brothers be able to patch us up and get our hearts beating together again? Or have I just lost the best friend I'll ever have?

CHAPTER ONE

allan

ACE AND ADDY'S wedding wasn't the place to cause a scene. I swore I wasn't going to react to every stupid-ass thing that came out of that guy's mouth today.

Turned out I was wrong.

As my fist went flying toward Alistair's pretty boy face, I had a momentary flicker of regret. Then my knuckles smashed into his nose, instantly squashing the flicker. Blood flowed, and even then, it only slightly mollified the beast in me that rose up to defend Cricket. In my defense, Alistair deserved it.

There I was at the wedding, standing to the right of Ace as he took his vows to love and cherish Addy forever. I could barely take my eyes off Cricket, standing to Addy's left, in order to focus on my big brother's big day. The front of her hair was pulled back in a tiny braid that somehow twirled around her head and left the rest of her pale blonde hair to cascade down her back in a riot of curls. The bridesmaids' dresses were of

Addy's choosing, making Cricket look like the angel I'd always thought she was.

Cricket had walked into kindergarten with a backpack that nearly eclipsed her. I'd taken one look at her blonde hair and slight frame and decided she was mine to protect. That moment was etched into my long-term memory. I ran over and hung her backpack on the hook on the back wall of the classroom. Introductions were made and we became fast friends.

Over the years I followed the rules and she blazed right past them. I picked up after her, never complaining because I liked to watch the petite hurricane that was Cricket. I was tall and strong, she was short and slight. We made absolutely no sense and yet I believed some spirit beyond the veil had planned for us to be joined at the hip. We just worked. BFFs and all that.

It was the tinkling of a giggle that finally pulled my attention away from Cricket as Ace slipped a ring on Addy's finger. A whole throng of family and friends were seated in the white wooden chairs on the lawn outside of the Peacock B&B in Auburn Hill, the town we'd all grown up in. There in the sixth row was Alistair, the latest asshat Cricket had been dating. His suit was so ridiculously tight I wondered if he bought it from the boys' section of the department store. There was fashionably fitted and then there was Alistair's fashion sense.

His nose was practically buried in the hair of a redhead Daxon had dated last year as he whispered in her ear. I didn't know her name. Sadly, Daxon didn't date women for long, so there was no sense in memorizing her name. She let out another giggle and I thought I might crack a molar with how tightly I was clenching my jaw. I glanced back at Cricket, whose face had just gone white.

Fuck. It wasn't enough that the shitstain had gotten drunk at the rehearsal dinner last night. He had to flirt with a woman right in front of Cricket's face. I clenched my hands into fists and willed myself to get through the ceremony without looking at Alistair. Cricket did the opposite, her gaze never leaving the scene that was unfolding in the audience.

The crowd let out a cheer and Ace swept Addy into a rated-R kiss that made me proud to be his brother. If you love a woman, who the hell cares what level of PDA you engage in, right?

Eventually, they made their way back down the aisle and I stepped forward to meet up with Cricket for our own walk through the audience. Her eyes held a sheen that made me want to barrel through the crowd and provide the beatdown Alistair had coming.

"He's not worth it," I managed to let slip past my clenched jaw.

Cricket gripped my elbow like a lifeline. "Not now, Cal."

I kept my pace slow, knowing her short legs and high heels needed extra time to make the trip to the back of the wedding venue. I waited with her there, purposely changing the subject and keeping her occupied so she wouldn't try to stare at the back of the head of the worthless guy she was dating.

"You did incredible work with everyone's hair, angel."

Cricket managed a smile. "Thanks. Hell of a lot better than doing wash and sets for the geriatric crowd." She twirled a lock of hair around her finger, her nervous tell. "Not that I'm not incredibly grateful to that crowd for keeping my salon in business. It's just that a girl likes to do a braid every now and again."

I smiled down at her. "I know. I'm just grateful my hair's short enough you can't braid it or else you'd have me in a french braid right now."

Cricket pursed her lips and my attention dropped down to take in what would never be mine. "Nope. Waterfall braid actually."

I frowned. "What the hell is a waterfall braid?"

She grinned and some of my anger slipped away. "Grow your hair out and I'll show you."

"No chance, angel. You already have my brothers giving me shit about the shampoo lightening my hair."

Cricket reached way up and trailed a finger through my hair, her touch light as a butterfly. "They're just jealous that it looks amazing."

"Okay, everyone! Let's gather over here for the wedding party pictures." The wedding coordinator was a no-nonsense woman who scared her clients into complying with her commands. The dark eyebrows that would wing up at the ends when she frowned at you were the thing of nightmares. Addy swore by her though, saying her pictures were worthy of being on the wall at the Louvre.

I swallowed down whatever I could have managed to say when Cricket was touching me and being sweet. Probably better for everyone that I didn't open my mouth. Cricket was my best friend, but I was keeping a huge secret from her.

I was head over heels, insanely in love with her and had been since senior year of high school.

It was an affliction I'd tried to talk myself out of as being ridiculous. When that failed I'd purposefully tried to put distance between us, a decision that backfired when she called me out on my icy countenance and I'd felt like an asshole for making her sad. That left me with denial as my go-to tactic for ignoring the feelings she stirred up in me. I was the master of denial at this point. Six long years of dating other women and trying and failing to compare them to Cricket. Six years of protecting Cricket at all costs, including protecting her from my ridiculous feelings.

"Okay, boys, you can go. Let me get the girls." The photographer waved the four of us away, pinning Ace with a look that made my balls tremble. The poor guy was stuck with at least another hour of pictures. My brothers and I all pulled at our collars as we made our way back to the reception. All the guests were eating and drinking, which seemed highly unfair.

"Dude, Alistair has his hand on that chick's ass." Ethan pointed behind us as we waited in line for a cocktail. My head whipped in that direction, zeroing in on the scene. The redhead was laughing at something Alistair had said. He was looking at her like he was seconds away from pulling her into an empty room in the B&B and dropping his trousers.

"Oh, hell no," I muttered, bumping shoulders with my brothers as I pushed through them. Rage was too calm a word for what spun through my system like a tornado.

"Oh shit," I heard Blaze grumble behind me.

I made a beeline for Alistair, politely moving the redhead a step away from him before I let my fist fly. The fucker had reflexes as dull as his life's story, just standing there as my fist connected with his face. I didn't even feel the blow, but I did watch the blood flow from his nose in satisfaction.

"What the fuck?" he bellowed, hands holding his nose as blood dripped between his fingers.

I shook out my hand and considered following it up with an undercut that would have him thinking of me every time he took a deep breath the next few days. Blaze's arm came around my shoulders and Daxon darted in between us, cutting off that thought. Ethan put his hand on Alistair's shoulder and spun him around, whispering in his ear as he steered him away from the crowd. Only then did I become aware of the silence around me. The wedding guests had all gone quiet, watching me lose my cool. I squeezed my eyes shut and tried to calm down.

"Show's over, friends!" Daxon said loudly with a jovial smile. "Did I mention cocktails are free?" He waved his arm toward the empty bar and successfully drew most people's attention there.

Only a few heads were still turned in my direction. Notably my mother's. She gave me a glare that made the photographer look like a fuzzy teddy bear. I gave her a shoulder shrug and she rolled her eyes before turning away. I knew that wasn't the end of it. We'd be having words later and it wouldn't be fun.

Also turned in my direction was Lucy Sutter. Her eyes narrowed as she watched me. I gave her a smile that was known to calm people even when they'd been in a car accident, but even that didn't get her calculating eyes off me.

"Well, you've fucked up now. You got Lucy eyeballing you." Blaze clapped me on the shoulder. "She smells a love story and she won't quit until she figures it out. Good luck on that."

Before I could comment on that frightful thought, Cricket's angry voice had me spinning around.

"What the holy hell did you do, Callan Hellman?" Her hands were jammed on her hips and I could have sworn there was steam coming out of her ears. "Alistair just peeled out of here with blood on his shirt."

Blaze backed off with comically wide eyes, leaving me alone with not quite a hundred pounds of fury.

"Now, angel—"

"Don't you angel me when I'm mad at you!" Cricket took another step closer, her eyes blazing at me.

I sucked in another breath and tried to be patient. I'd been telling her for weeks that Alistair was no good for her and she kept ignoring all the red flags. She didn't even seem all that into him, so I couldn't understand why she'd put up with his bullshit.

"He had his hand on the redhead's ass, Cricket. Maybe he's just really friendly, but I couldn't sit around and watch him cheat on you. Not when I could do something about it."

Her eyes lost some of the anger, and maybe I was imagining it, but embarrassment seemed to replace it. "That was for me to deal with. Not you."

I leaned down, softening the blow as much as I could. "But you never do, Cricket."

She sucked in a gasp, frozen as she soaked in the truth of my words. By the time she unfroze, the heat was gone from her words. "Fuck off, Cal."

She spun on her heel and marched off, getting lost in the sea of people milling about the lawn. My heart sank. I shouldn't have said anything. Should have just stuffed down my feelings on the subject like I always did. My brothers found me a little while later staring off into space. I'd have to thank them for backing me up with Alistair when I needed them.

Daxon opened his mouth and I beat him to it.

"Don't."

He snapped his mouth shut and smirked. "I wasn't going to state the obvious."

Blaze, the brother who'd just recently put a ring on Annie's finger, thought himself to be an expert on love now. "You need to tell her how you feel, man. It's past time."

"But what if she doesn't feel the same way?" Ethan asked, stroking his beard in thoughtful contemplation. "Would that ruin the lifelong friendship?"

"Isn't it already strained by unrequited love?" Blaze snapped.

"Guys!" I stood in the middle of their huddle. "I don't need you debating my love life right in front of me. There's nothing there, okay?"

See? Denial. I would deny those feelings that kept me up at night until I was blue in the face. There was simply a chemical that had gone haywire somewhere in my biology. Until I could get it straightened out, I wasn't going to damage my friendship with Cricket.

Blaze shook his head, obviously disappointed. "The bloodshed is only going to continue. You can't keep it bottled up. Take it from me."

"It might be your blood next, bro. Check out Cricket's face." Daxon pointed subtly and we all turned to see Cricket giving me a glare from across the wooden dance floor that had been erected once the chairs had been removed from the lawn.

I sighed. "Let me go talk to her."

"Hope you're wearing a cup," Daxon whisper-yelled to my back. I shot him the middle finger and kept going, darting around people I'd known my whole life. I got quite a few fist bumps and only a couple frowns, telling me most people hadn't like ol' Alistair either.

When I got to Cricket, she pretended not to see me, talking instead with her friends, Meadow and Annie.

"Cricket. Can we chat?" I interrupted, drawing a glare from

Meadow and an encouraging smile from Annie. She had a soft spot for us Hellmans, thank God.

"We were just going to get another round of drinks," Annie said, grabbing Meadow and dragging her away despite her protests about wanting to watch the fight.

Cricket wouldn't look at me, focusing instead on my right shoulder, that lower lip stuck out just enough for me to know she was more hurt than mad. Cricket had a lot of expressions and I knew them all.

"Angel, please," I whispered, cupping her face and stroking my thumb across her cheek. She finally shifted her gaze so that she was looking directly into my eyes. "I'm sorry for embarrassing you. I'm sorry for causing a scene. I'm sorry for stepping in your business. I just couldn't let him disrespect you like that."

Cricket's eyes closed, and when she opened them, I knew she'd forgiven me. "I know you're sorry. And I know he deserved it. I just..." She sighed, the sound laced with disappointment, discontent, and a whole layer of something I couldn't identify. "I just wish I'd been the one to do it."

"Why, Cricket, that's mighty violent of you." My lips tugged into a smile I hoped she'd reflect.

I wasn't disappointed. "I would have kicked him in the nuts, but the nose was good too."

I chuckled and she did too, letting me pull her into a hug. Her blonde head fit in the dip right between my pec muscles. "Dance with me."

She didn't answer, but her hands slid up my chest and onto my shoulders. My arms wound around her waist and held her to me, letting me relish the scent of her perfume as it surrounded us. I couldn't live with myself if Cricket was mad at me.

She kept her cheek against my chest, her fingers playing in the hair that met the collar of my shirt. If I closed my eyes, I could get lost in this moment. Get lost in her. I could imagine dances just like this in our kitchen as we aged together. Our children growing up watching their parents dance to an imaginary song, too in love to care there was no actual music. I could envision a whole life with her.

"You're such a good friend, Cal. What would I do without you?" Cricket whispered, her words instantly and painfully dissolving the vision in my head.

Good friend.

That was all I'd ever be with Cricket, and I'd do well to remember it.

Like a criminal stuck in a life sentence on Alcatraz, I was firmly imprisoned in the friend zone.

But if that was all Cricket could give me, I'd take it and be the most grateful man on the planet. I loved her, and that meant giving her what she wanted: her freedom to love someone else.

CHAPTER TWO

ricket

"THIS ISN'T WORTH IT," I mimicked Alistair in a high-pitched voice, kicking off my high heels and sighing at how good it felt to be flatfooted again, like nature intended. "As if asking him not to grab another woman's ass was just too much for him to handle."

I rolled my eyes so hard it made my head hurt. My tiny apartment over the salon didn't answer me. I was talking to myself again. I let my purse slip off my shoulder and fall to the rug I spent six months searching for. As I looked around my home, I realized that not one possession of Alistair's littered my couch, table, or bedroom. We'd dated for two months and yet he'd taken up zero percent of my personal space. There was wisdom there if I took the time to reflect on it.

Instead, I went into the kitchen and grabbed a glass of water. The champagne at the wedding had given me a headache. Or was it Alistair who had done that? I sighed, the sound filling my apartment with ease. This space was used to hearing my sighs.

Usually when I spied my appointment book, filled to the brim with perms and sets instead of the color and cuts I'd dreamed about during beauty school.

Hugging the glass of water to my chest, I wandered into the living room and sank onto the couch. Knowing how Auburn Hill worked, my parents had probably already heard about Callan and Alistair. Dad would be disappointed that a preselected future son-in-law had yet again bit the dust, and mom would shrug her shoulders and ask if I needed a day of pampering. They meant well, but sometimes I felt like neither of them really understood me.

I grimaced even thinking that thought. I was the center of my parents' world. I knew that, yet with that came a heavy responsibility that I didn't ask for. They bent over backwards to give me whatever I wanted, so complaining seemed a bit spoiled, even for me, an only child.

A knock on the door saved me from spiraling down into a pit of self-imposed doom and darkness. Setting down the glass of water as I went, I opened the door to find Callan on my doorstep, still in his wedding tux, minus the tie. The light outside my door highlighted the deep golden strands I was responsible for. His handsome, familiar face split into a smile.

"Care for some company?"

I opened the door wider and let him step through. Callan was always stopping by, which was a reversal of our childhood. Back then, I'd constantly stopped by his mom's house, craving the chaos that came with a house full of boys. I couldn't take one more second of listening to our grandfather clock tick away the time while my parents did adult things and I braided my hair for the thousandth time, bored out of my mind.

Callan shrugged out of his coat and laid it across the purple paisley chair in the corner that was more fashion than function. I sank back down to the couch, propping my throbbing feet on the rattan puff that served as a coffee table.

"Why are women expected to wear heels? Is it strictly a

torture device to hamper our speed should we have to run from wandering hands? Or is this about the female form on display for men's viewing? What is it exactly and how can I reverse this perpetuating form of torture?"

Callan sat on the couch next to me, his broad shoulders taking up every inch of space that was left. He leaned forward and grabbed my legs, spinning me around and depositing my feet in his lap. His thumbs began to dig into the balls of my feet, exactly where they felt bruised from my high heels.

I groaned and leaned my head back against the armrest, eyes closed. "God bless you and your magical thumbs, Cal."

He didn't answer, just huffed out a chuckle and kept rubbing.

"You should take your thumbs on the road. Women would auction off their left ovary for ten minutes with those things."

"I'll keep that in mind in case the paramedic thing doesn't work out," he answered dryly. "Though I'd hate to be responsible for women losing a perfectly good ovary."

I cracked open one eye and glared at him. "All you have to do is smile that Mr. Nice Guy grin and all the ovaries explode. If you only knew how many of my friends have lost an ovary over the years because of you."

His face took on the cocky smirk he'd had even when he was little. Only now it wasn't just a cute little boy face. The grown man smirk had the ability to make women stop in their tracks and forget where they were going. I'd seen it happen on more than one occasion. I sighed and closed my eye, wondering why I had to be best friends with a guy who made all my female friends lose their ability to speak. It was highly annoying.

"You'll be happy to know I spent the last hour getting an earful from my mother."

My eyes popped open again to see him smiling ruefully. "Ah, Nikki Hellman gave you a classic lecture, huh? Good for her."

Callan made a face. "Apparently punching a wedding guest in the face is poor form. Who would have guessed?"

"Everyone," I deadpanned.

His thumbs quit their massaging, and before I could complain, he began to tickle my feet instead. I yelped and nearly clipped him in the face while I struggled to get out of his grip while also not flashing him the ridiculous pair of silky underwear I'd put on under my dress in case Alistair and I had come back to my apartment after the wedding. I didn't have siblings to teach me how to wrestle, but Callan had taken me under his wing during our childhood. I could punch and kick with the best of them.

"Okay!" Callan shot me a look of innocence perfected after years of tussling with his brothers and then escaping the wrath of their mother. "No more tickling, I swear. I don't want to lose parts of my anatomy." His hands covered his balls, just inches from where my heel had landed on my latest jab.

I cleared my throat and sat up, swinging my feet to the floor. Callan was my best friend, but even so, I wasn't touching—physically or in conversation—his private parts. "Serves you right for all the ovaries."

Callan shifted on the couch, the scent of his familiar woodsy cologne setting me at ease. He began to tell me about the finer points of Nikki's lecture, but his words faded out and melted into the background. I felt myself staring at the tiny television on the opposite wall that I barely used. That feeling came over me. The one where I felt frozen in space. The world went on around me, but I was stuck in some kind of sticky fog that wouldn't let me go. I knew it was happening but there was nothing I could do to stop the daydream state that had caused me to get into so much trouble over the years with my teachers and parents.

"Cricket. Angel, talk to me."

I finally blinked, the room coming back into my awareness. My hands had balled into fists, but Callan pried my fingers open as I slowly came back. I turned my head to the left and saw him staring at me with concern. His golden-brown eyes were scanning my whole body, as if he was doing some sort of diagnostic check. Embarrassment swept through me. I hated that I had these moments. These space-outs that I couldn't seem to control.

"Hey, eyes up here, big guy." I went for humor. Anything to wipe the concern off Callan's face.

His gaze flew back to mine, but the concern didn't shift. "Have you eaten?"

I tried to think back over the evening. I'd had a few bites at the reception, but mostly I'd been juggling the Alistair issue and avoiding Callan.

Callan sighed and stood up, not waiting for my answer. "I'm making you a snack. Could be low blood sugar."

Once Callan had a maiden-saving idea in his head, there was no stopping him. He was the very definition of a knight in shining armor, saving people on their worst days. He'd become a paramedic straight out of high school, attending the required junior college classes the summer after graduation in his eagerness to get started. If he thought I needed a snack, I wouldn't be heading to bed unless I at least ate some of it.

I felt around under the couch until I came up with the television remote. I had to blow off the dust bunnies before I could turn it on. "Wanna watch a movie?"

"Sure." Callan emerged from the tiny kitchenette with a plate piled high with cheese and crackers and some of the grapes that weren't halfway to raisins already. "As long as you eat."

I sighed but motioned that I was zipping my lips when he gave me a hard look.

"You have to take better care of yourself, Cricket. Did you make an appointment with the doctor in Blueball?" Callan sat on the couch and the whole thing dipped, rolling me toward him and his plate of food.

To stall, I popped a cracker in my mouth and chewed slowly. We'd had this conversation multiple times before and every time I told him it wasn't necessary. Just because I spaced out sometimes or got low blood sugar didn't mean anything was wrong with me.

"Cricket..." The warning was clear in his tone. Bossy best friend I had.

"No. I haven't! Have you considered the crazy price of a doctor visit these days? Who has the money for that on top of tests?"

Callan set the plate on my lap and put his hands on my arms. "Make the appointment or I'll make it for you. I'm sure your parents would be all too happy to pay for it."

I sighed and grabbed another cracker. "I don't want to keep asking them for things, Cal. I'm twenty-three years old. I should be able to stand on my own two feet."

Callan sat back with a sigh. "You're stubborn as a mule."

"You're ugly as a mule," I shot back.

"I may be ugly, but at least I have common sense," he replied.

I gave him side-eye right before he shoved his shoulder into mine and we both laughed.

"What movie are we watching?"

"We were just at a super romantic wedding so..."

Callan smiled. "Horror flick it is."

We both settled into the couch, finished off the plate of crackers, and cringed over the cheesy film we selected. I should have been jumping every time that freaky doll's eyes moved, but I was getting tired. My head ended up on Callan's shoulder and I felt myself being sucked down into dreamland.

Next thing I knew, I was blinking my eyes open to the first stream of sunlight. I looked down at myself in the same dress I wore to the wedding. I was in my bed but had no recollection of climbing in. Callan must have put me to bed when I fell asleep on him on the couch. Hopefully I didn't drool on his dress shirt. I had a habit of doing that, something he teased me about mercilessly.

I yawned and stretched my arms overhead. Sitting up I

noticed a note on the tiny end table next to my bed. There, in Callan's chicken scratch, were my instructions for the day.

Good morning, angel. EAT.

I huffed out loud but couldn't stop the grin. He was a nagging little bestie. Tossing off the covers, I slid out of bed and finally took the bridesmaid dress off. It was horribly wrinkled, but then again, who wore a bridesmaid dress after the big day? Once in my stretchy jeans and tank top, I padded to the kitchen to grab some fruit before heading down to my salon, Curl Up & Dye.

A knock on my front door had me veering off my path. Pulling open the door, I saw a teenager our town's coffee shop, aptly named Coffee, had hired just a week or so ago. She shifted from foot to foot, looking highly uncomfortable.

"Hey. Jasmine, right?"

She flashed a shy grin. "Yeah. I, uh, have your breakfast order."

I leaned on the doorframe. "Oh, I didn't order anything."

Jasmine frowned and read the receipt stapled to the white bag in her hands. "Are you Cricket?"

"Yes..."

She shoved the bag and the iced latte at me. "Then these are yours. Callan came by."

"Ah." Now it all made sense. I turned to grab my purse. "Well, thanks for the delivery. Let me get you a tip."

"No, it's all good. Callan tipped me already." She skipped back down the wooden stairs that led down to the sidewalk out front while I shook my head.

Using my foot, I closed the door and eyed the toasted bagel with cream cheese inside the white bakery bag. "Ah, Callan..."

I'd have to thank him later. The guy was always doing sweet stuff like that. Even if it was a bit heavy handed. If he wanted me to eat, I'd try. Just for him.

Not that I'd ever tell him that.

The guy didn't need an even bigger ego.

CHAPTER THREE

allan

THE RIG WAS FUELED up after the transfer calls earlier this afternoon and we were posting under the huge scrub oak out on the coast. My partner, Xavier, was busy texting his girlfriend about not wanting to go furniture shopping again this coming weekend. They'd just taken the big step to move in together, and according to him, she was taking things too far.

"Ah man, come on," he grumbled, turning to me like I was some sort of referee between him and his girl. "She wants me to pick out towel colors. I don't give a fuck what color they are, man! I just need them to dry my ass when I get out of the shower."

I checked my watch. Shit. Still had a few hours left on shift. "Sounds like the color is important to her."

He shook his head, expressionless. "Don't do that, man. Don't take her side."

"I'm not taking her side!" I laughed. "Just pick your battles wisely. That's all I'm saying."

He stared at me and I wasn't sure if he wanted to punch me or hug me. "Fine. Blue. There."

His thumbs flew over the screen and then he leaned his head back, staring out at the expanse of the ocean before us. Wasn't a bad place to wait for our next call. His phone buzzed and he looked back down at it before chucking it up onto the dashboard.

"Turquoise or royal?" he shrieked, getting a little more worked up than was strictly necessary if you asked me. Which he didn't.

My own phone buzzed in the console and I took it out, glad to leave Xavier to the rest of that conversation. Although I was certain whatever my brothers were texting in our group chat would be just as irritating.

Daxon: How's that hand feeling, Callan?

Me: Fine. Barely even feel it.

Ace: Tone it down at Blaze's wedding, would you? Addy thought you punching that turd was hot. And I really don't need to hear my wife call my little brother hot.

Ethan: I think you just like saying "my wife."

Ace: Fuck, yeah, I do. My wife is currently soaking in the bathtub in our honeymoon suite looking out at the ocean. Otherwise I wouldn't even be talking to you losers.

Blaze: I can't wait for honeymoon sex.

Daxon: Jesus, that's TMI. Can we get back to the fact that Callan clocked a guy in Cricket's honor?

Me: What about it? He's an asshole.

Daxon: Most definitely. His name's fucking Alistair. He had no chance but to grow up to be an asshole.

Ethan: I think what Daxon means is that there seems to be some underlying feelings toward Cricket that need to be discussed.

I sighed and rested my head back against the seat, wishing for the millionth time that I could come right out and say how I truly felt about Cricket. But the day that happened, it would be to Cricket's beautiful face, not my brothers.

The radio crackled to life, notifying us of a situation just a few miles down the coast. Xavier rattled off something in Spanish that sounded a lot like a prayer of thanks before radioing back that we were on our way.

Me: Gotta go. Life-and-death emergency and all that.

I put my phone in the console and hurried to get back on the road. My phone buzzed repeatedly as I took the curves quickly but safely, probably from my brothers thinking I was full of shit. Sometimes the timing of these calls was terrible, but then there were times like now, when the job took my focus off other things in my life that I didn't want to examine.

The dispatcher informed us the incident appeared to be an electric bike crash. Someone had called it in as they zoomed down the coast highway. I shook my head. We were getting more and more calls for electric bike crashes. Most people were dumb enough to get on a moving object that surpassed twenty miles an hour without a dang helmet. Not only was that illegal, it was rolling the dice with their own safety.

I saw two women off to the side of the road up ahead, one lying on the ground, the other sitting next to her. We put on the flashers and pulled to the side of the road behind them. Xavier grabbed our medical bag and we both ran to their sides. I was relieved to see both of them had helmets on.

"Good evening, ladies. Is everyone okay?" Even in an emergency, Xavier oozed charm.

The brunette sitting on the ground waved to her friend. "Yeah, she's fine. Said the world was spinning, so she had to lie down."

She looked up at me and gave me a lopsided smile. Her eyes were unfocused. I crouched down to assess her. Could be a concussion or maybe alcohol was involved. She shivered, but that probably had more to do with the cool evening breeze and the fact that she was in a tank top and skirt.

"May I?" I asked, pulling out my penlight. She looked down at it and nearly fell forward onto my leg. I grabbed her shoulder and held her upright. She looked oddly familiar, but I couldn't place her.

"Sure, go right ahead, schmexy doctor guy."

Yep, definitely alcohol involved. I put a hand on her forehead and lifted one eyelid while Xavier checked on the blonde lying in the dirt. "Paramedic, actually. Look left. Your other left. Good."

She was fine. Eyes tracked normally, if a little slow. Pupils were round and equal in size, reacting to the light.

"Anything hurt?"

She hiccuped and swung her leg at me, whacking me in the shin and flashing me in the process. Her panties matched the pink flowers on her skirt. "My leg hurts."

I pasted on a smile and assessed her leg, seeing a large bump forming over the shin bone. "You're going to have a nice goose egg, but putting ice on it might help. You live around here?"

I realized my mistake when her face lit up in an even bigger grin. "Just a few miles that way." She pointed toward Auburn Hill, then frowned. "No. That way." She pointed straight out into the ocean.

"You from Blueball, maybe?" She nodded semi-coherently, so I kept trying to get more information. "What's your name?"

"I'm Audrey. What's your name, nurse-doctor-PA-paramedic guy?" She tried to wink at me, but after the fifth flutter of her lashes, I thought maybe she just had something in her eye.

My stomach dipped and sunk like a boulder falling into the ocean. There was someone I knew by the name of Audrey and this girl was just about the right age. And now I knew why she looked so familiar.

"Do you have someone you can call to take you and your bikes back home?"

I wasn't interested in flirting. Not when I was face to face with my half sister whom I'd never met.

When Richard Hellman—Dick as we oh-so-affectionately liked to call our father—left our family, he stepped right into the other one he'd had a few towns over. Audrey was one of two daughters that he spawned with another woman while he left our mother to raise five boys. We'd never reached out to each other, and as far as I knew, these ladies didn't even know we existed.

"Hmm...maybe," Audrey answered slowly. Her hand landed on my shirt, her finger tracing over my name tag. "Callllllaaaaannn H."

I pulled her hand away from me, searching her face and finding features that reminded me of my dad. Fuck. *Our* dad.

"Maybe you could take us home, doctor cowboy." She shot me a lopsided grin and then froze. Before I could jump to my feet, she bent over and hurled all over my black boots.

"Whoa," Xavier called, backing away from the other girl in case she followed suit. "Everyone looks okay. Gonna be sore when they wake up hungover tomorrow though."

Audrey let out a groan, head bent. All the flirtation was gone now. My boots were gone too. I'd be tossing them out and buying a new pair. I couldn't leave her though. Whether I liked it or not, we were related.

"Give me the bag, would you?" I asked Xavier. He shoved the bag across the dirt, careful to miss the mess Audrey had made. I took out the saline IV and asked her permission to administer it. She nodded her head, but wouldn't look at me. The least I could do was make sure she was hydrated so the hangover wouldn't be so extreme tomorrow. I got the line started and moved away.

"Xav, will you call Clyde? See if he can come pick up the girls and get their rental bikes back before they close?"

He gave me a funny look, probably wondering why I was going the extra mile for two strangers, one of whom ruined my shoes. I usually went the extra mile for people, but this was at least twenty extra miles.

"Sure, boss." He walked back to the truck to grab his cell phone and call Clyde, the local tow truck driver. He was close to retirement age and was a good guy. I could trust that he'd get them both home safely.

While we waited for him, I grabbed a towel in the back of

the truck and tried to wipe down my boots. The smell alone made me gag. As a paramedic I came across a lot of vomit, which to me was worse than blood. By the time Clyde came by and the IV was done, my boots were as good as they were going to get and the girls were back on their feet and apologetic. We, of all people, knew that accidents happened, though I hoped they'd forgo the alcohol next time they got on some electric bikes.

I could feel Xavier's stare as we drove away from the scene, knowing Clyde had it handled. Our shift was over and there was nothing I wanted to talk to him about. Not the color of towels. Not why I went deathly quiet back there. Or why I couldn't stop staring at Audrey. My brain was on overload and there was only one thing that would calm me down.

Cricket.

By the time I made it to her salon, the place was empty and I found her sweeping the floor. The little bell above the door let out a jingle as I opened the glass pane. Just seeing her slight frame, white-blonde hair stacked on top of her head in a messy bun, and the smile that broke on her face when she saw me calmed me down instantly. My shoulders dropped from where they'd been pressed to my ears.

"I swear I ate today!" she called out, putting the broom aside and coming to greet me.

I didn't even answer her, I just swept her up in my arms and held on tight. I was a grown man who didn't need a lot of pampering but sometimes a human just needed a hug, you know? After a quick moment of hesitation, she gave it to me, wrapping those arms around my waist and nestling into her spot on my chest. I breathed her in and let some of the hurt and anger go. Something about seeing Audrey had knocked me off-center and Cricket was the only one who could push me back upright.

"I love you, dude, but you stink," she said, the words muffled against my chest.

I let her go instantly. "Oh shit. Sorry. I got puked on." I went back outside and toed off my boots, coming back into the salon in my socks. "That should be better."

She looked at my face longer than normal, studying me, instinctively knowing something was off. Then she broke out into a mischievous smile, the one that made me nervous and happy all at the same time.

"Follow me." She waved me over to one of the bowls, giving me a stern look that was hilarious on her angel face. I didn't put up a fight though. I sank into the tiny black chair made for someone her size and not mine. "Lean back."

She guided my head back and turned on the water. She stood so close I could have turned my head and kissed her stomach. I didn't though, knowing that would be completely out of line. Instead, I closed my eyes and lost myself in the ecstasy of her washing my hair, her fingers and nails providing me the kind of head massage that both relaxed me and made me so horny I might have embarrassed myself if anyone else had been there observing the front of my pants.

"Well, Dad called me today. I knew he would." Cricket sighed, talking about her day as if I wasn't struggling to keep myself from leaping from the chair and professing my feelings for her. "He wasn't too happy about Alistair breaking things off, but I guess Mom told him she didn't really like him, so Dad was ultimately fine with the breakup. As if he has a say in it." Cricket scoffed.

I frowned, hating how much of an influence her parents had over her. They kept setting her up with guys who were all wrong for her. Cricket was like a dream catcher with so many colors it made your eyes rejoice. The men her dad set her up with were vanilla-colored corporate drones who would slowly and systematically destroy her dream catcher as something frivolous and stupid.

"Dad apparently met a new client who has a son our age and wants us to meet."

My hands gripped the armrests of the chair. "What did you say?"

I could feel Cricket shrug and then flip on the water to rinse my hair again. "What could I say? I said maybe, which he takes as a yes."

This was the point in the conversation where I usually bit my lip and commiserated with her, despite the screaming voice in my head that wanted to tell her to stand up to her dad. I could normally control that voice, but something about seeing Audrey tonight had destroyed the filter.

"Just say no, Cricket," I bit out, voice hard with frustration.

Her hands stilled on my scalp before she went back to rinsing my hair. "It's not that easy, okay? They have expectations of me and I don't want to let them down."

I huffed and she stiffened. Then she flipped off the water and threw a towel at my face. The scalp massage was over apparently.

I stood and tried to dry my hair with the towel, seeing the closed look on her face as she gathered her things. Here she was trying to do something nice for me and I stuck my nose in her family business. I grabbed her arm and spun her to me.

"I'm sorry." And I meant it. I was only her friend, which meant I should be supporting her, not making her feel bad. I had no right to try to tell her what to do.

She crossed her eyes and stuck her tongue out at me, which in Cricket-speak meant I was forgiven. I still thought what I said was good advice, but she wasn't ready to hear it.

CHAPTER FOUR

ricket

"I DON'T KNOW, Polly. Science hasn't found a way for humans to procreate without the male species yet. I think we still kind of need them." I turned off the warm water and carefully placed a towel over her hair, making sure nothing dripped in her ears. Polly sat up, lips pursed.

"Well, I think we're close. Even though my own daughter insists she couldn't live without her man."

We walked back to my chair. Secretly, I wondered how Lucy Sutter had grown up with Polly as her mother and turned out relatively normal. In fact, she was quite the matchmaker in town, which was maybe in direct opposition to the way she'd grown up. She'd set my friend Meadow up with her current boyfriend, Judd, and they couldn't be happier.

A pinch low in my stomach had me grimacing while I towel dried Polly's hair. It was all gray these days, but she had a ton of it. It would take longer than most to blow dry and curl.

"You okay, honey?" Polly asked, eyeing me in the mirror.

I smiled and tossed the towel in the dirty bin. "Yeah, just starting to get cramps. Might be that time."

Polly bared her teeth. "I'm so glad I crossed over into the glorious blood-free land of menopause."

I cracked a smile. "God willing, I've got quite a few years left before that happens." Hell, my twenty-fourth birthday was just a few weeks away. I'd barely begun my trek through womanhood.

"Can you fit in another wash and set after lunch, Cricket?" Kennedy called out from the front desk where she had a phone jammed between her ear and her shoulder.

I'd hired her straight out of high school, and while she was very organized and had energy to spare, her professionalism could use some work. I'd have to show her how to put a client on hold before screaming across the whole salon.

"Sure thing," I answered, thankful at least that the interruption had halted talk of menopause with Polly.

Great. Another wash and set. I'd already done three of them this morning and now it looked like my afternoon would be more of the same. Didn't anyone around here want a streak of color? A balayage? I'd even go for some heavy '90s highlights right now.

I got the last curler in Polly's hair when I felt the telltale sign of my period arriving. Dammit. I hated not having a regular cycle. Periods always took me by surprise. "Give me one second to run to the bathroom."

Polly waved me away and picked up the latest gossip rag that we kept in the salon. I did the funny walk all women mastered soon after puberty to the tiny bathroom in the back of the salon. Once the door was locked, I dipped my hand into the basket on the back of the toilet, coming up empty.

"Shit, shit, shit." I could have sworn I asked Kennedy to keep it full of tampons. I spun and had a seat on the toilet before I messed up my light-colored jeans. Of all the days not to wear black.

I pulled my phone out of my pocket and debated who to call.

I couldn't have Kennedy run to the store. She was the only one holding down the fort while I hid out here in the bathroom. Meadow would be stuck at work in the jail all day. Addy was mid downward dog in her forest yoga class right now. And Annie probably had a line of pet owners waiting on her to treat their precious furballs.

I hesitated, landing on the one person I knew would drop everything to help me. In the end, I fired off a text anyway and tried not to be embarrassed.

Me: *Soooo...any chance you have time to drop off some tampons at the salon?*

The bubble immediately appeared, and while my face felt like it was on fire, I was desperate enough to hope he'd come through for me.

Callan: On my way. Should I use the siren?

I rolled my eyes, but huffed out a laugh.

Me: *I've got Polly in the chair and I'm hunkered down in the bathroom.*

Callan: Definite emergency, then. See you in five.

I shoved toilet paper in my underwear like girls do in emergencies and answered the sturdy knock that arrived exactly six minutes later. Callan stood there as I cracked the door open, a sheepish smile on his face.

"Did you get the goods?" I asked in my best mafia voice.

He schooled his face and played the part. "Got it, boss." He handed me a shopping bag that was far heavier than I expected.

"Jeez. Did you buy out the store?" I looked inside and saw at least four boxes of tampons of various brands and absorbencies.

Callan shifted on his feet, his hand going up to mess with his hair. "I, uh, didn't know which kind, so I got one of each."

I looked up at him, a smile growing on my face as I saw how uncomfortable he was. "That was very smart. And sweet."

Callan wouldn't meet my eyes. He just backed up and dipped his head. "At your service, m'lady." And then he was gone, headed back into the main salon where I was sure the ladies would accost him. You didn't send a Hellman brother into a ladies' salon and not expect an ambush.

I did my business and stored the rest of the tampons for future emergencies. I'd have to bake some brownies or something to thank Callan. Not many men would agree to buy out the tampon aisle.

I came back into the salon and saw Yedda clinging to one of his biceps. The snicker was entirely involuntary. Callan shot me a look over Yedda's gray head. Considering how kind he'd been, I'd have to save him from her clutches.

"You're my hero!" I proclaimed loudly, coming between the two of them and throwing my arms around Callan's shoulders. His huge hand held my back in an embrace that felt like wearing my favorite sweats and curling up on the couch while it rained cats and dogs outside.

Yedda let out a "whooooohiieeee" that had us breaking apart. She shook her head and nearly blinded us with her neon-pink lipstick. "In my day, men didn't go around buying feminine products unless they were married. Hell, not even then sometimes."

"What are you saying, Yedda?" Callan asked, sticking close to my side in case of further clinging from the geriatric lady.

Yedda smacked her forehead dramatically, her dentures half slipping out of her mouth at the jolt. She sucked them back in and carried on as if that wasn't the most jarring thing I'd seen in months.

"I'm saying that maybe y'all aren't just friends!" Yedda nearly shouted.

Callan stiffened next to me, which was a surprise to me. This was Yedda. Of course she said ridiculous things. No reason to get upset. I laughed out loud before Callan opened his mouth.

"He's my best friend, Yedda. Of course he'd buy me tampons. I'd buy him condoms. Times have changed."

"Times haven't changed that much," Polly muttered from behind us.

Yedda shrugged. "You say friends, I say soul mates."

Callan huffed and turned to me, effectively blocking out the old lady. "All right. I gotta go. Dinner after you close up?"

I made a face. "You just want to make sure I eat."

"Darn right. Meet you at Forty-Diner?"

"Sure. See you around seven?"

"It's a date," he said with his signature smile. Then he tipped his head to both Yedda and Polly, and walked out of the salon whistling under his breath.

All of us watched him go. The Hellman boys were worth watching. They were all handsome, sure. But it was more the swagger they all had that held a female's attention. We knew a confident man when we saw one and it made us wonder things. Like, what would it be like to have one kiss you? Or rock your world in the bedroom?

I mean, not *me*, of course. But most women.

After he was out of sight, I took the cooled curlers out of Polly's hair and got to styling it. Yedda hovered, not one to sit quietly and wait.

"I don't care what you nitwits say. That boy is perfect for you."

"Thank you?" I answered carefully. "But we are just friends. I assure you."

"Men and women *can* be friends, you know. Not everything needs to be about sexual attraction," Polly interjected.

Yedda flapped her lips. "Have you seen that man? Why the hell wouldn't it be about sexual attraction?" Then she gasped and swung my way. "Unless you're batting for the other team!"

I shook my head and prayed for patience. "I'm not gay, Yedda."

She shimmied over to the shampoo bowl and had a seat like she was a queen returning to her throne. "Wouldn't matter if you were, I just need to know these things if I'm to match you properly."

I put my hands on Polly's shoulders and looked over her head into the mirror. "All done, Polly. See you next week?"

She patted her newly coifed hair. "You bet. You know, I was thinking. Maybe we could try out a new color?"

I sucked in a sharp breath. "I'd love to. Maybe look through some magazines for inspiration and bring in any that interest you?"

She shot me a wink and went up to Kennedy to pay her bill and schedule for next week. I nearly skipped over to Yedda, my brain swirling with ideas of what would look fabulous on Polly. I really hoped she'd give me some creative license to do what I thought would look best.

By the time I got done with Yedda's hair and trying to convince her I did not need help from cupid, a headache was brewing. Picking at my lunch and then getting through my afternoon appointments didn't improve things. By the time I shut off all the lights and locked the front door, I was tempted to bail on Callan and just head upstairs to my couch and comfy sweats. Then again, he dropped everything to bring me tampons today. Canceling would be poor form.

As I walked down Main Street to Forty-Diner, I waved to Shelby. She was closing up her shop a few doors down. Annie's vet clinic was already dark, so she must have gone home early. I didn't see as much of her recently as she was caught up in her romance with Blaze, one of Callan's older brothers. I was happy for her. She was crazy in love and planning their wedding, which I'd be a part of again. All my friends were marrying Hellmans and it was getting weird. I'd have to keep Kennedy away from Daxon. He had a penchant for the young ones. Sure, she was legal, but way too inexperienced for Daxon.

I saw a flash of Callan's hair up ahead by the diner. He saw me too, lifting his arm to wave at me down the sidewalk. A weird tingling sensation rolled through my stomach. I ignored it since it was either hunger pains or cramps and waved back, making my way to his side. As soon as he was a few feet away, the weirdest thing happened. My whole body felt like it froze. My feet wouldn't move and my brain had gone sluggish. I opened my mouth to say something was wrong, but nothing came out.

The vision of Callan before me tipped to the side and the concrete seemed to snatch me up. I saw a glimpse of Callan above me, his eyes wide and concern etched across his handsome face. And then everything went delightfully black.

I woke a second later, something jostling me as I lay on an uncomfortable surface. Confusion and that familiar sticky fog made it hard to process where I was or what exactly had happened. I blinked repeatedly, happy to see that I could at least do that. I tried to lift my head and I groaned at the pain that shot through my skull. Somehow I'd aged fifty years and everything hurt.

Callan appeared above me in an instant, my hands in his. "Cricket?"

My eyelids felt like they had little weights on them. They were hard to keep open. "What happened?" My voice was more of a croak.

Callan squeezed my hands and I held them back like a tether to the here and now. I hoped he didn't let go. "You fell down outside Forty-Diner. I caught you, but you were out for awhile. We're in an ambulance, headed for the hospital. How do you feel?"

"Tired." I felt more than that but I was having a hard time processing everything he said. Disoriented was an understatement. Callan's normal smile was gone, replaced by the kind of worry that ages a person. "Everything hurts."

Callan nodded and swallowed hard. "Sounds about right. I think you had a seizure, angel."

CHAPTER FIVE

allan

SEEING Cricket crumble to the ground was the single most terrifying moment in my life. Thank God she was close enough that I could catch her before her head hit the pavement. She didn't even put her hands out to catch herself which alerted me to this being a true medical event. Then the convulsions started and I knew what we were dealing with. As I held her hand and made sure she didn't hurt herself mid-seizure, I knew those space-out moments she'd always had weren't about her head being in the clouds or even about low blood sugar. I'd bet money that Cricket had epilepsy.

The ER had admitted her and I was sitting on an uncomfortable chair next to her bed in the hospital room while she dozed. The door cracked open and her mom and dad crept in, fear lining their faces.

I stood immediately and shook their hands. "Mr. VanHunting. Mrs. VanHunting." I nodded my hellos. "She's okay. Just resting. The doctors said they plan to run some further tests in the morning."

"It's Debbie, you know that." Cricket's mom gave me a hug, her watery gaze never leaving her daughter. "What happened, Callan? Don't leave anything out."

I led her to the chair by Cricket and told them everything I could remember from the second I saw Cricket walking down the sidewalk toward me. Mr. VanHunting paced the room, his rubber-soled Top-Siders squeaking as he went. Even on a random Tuesday night the guy had on a collared shirt and slacks.

Debbie finally sighed when I finished recounting the evening. "We should have pushed her to get checked out before this. This is my fault."

I put my hand on her shoulder and she reached up to grip it tight. "I asked her to make an appointment too, but never pushed hard enough. This is on me, not you."

Debbie stood, finally looking me in the eye. "Just wait until you have kids someday, Callan. You'll know what I mean. My world doesn't turn if Cricket isn't okay."

"Why don't you go home? Get some rest." Mr. VanHunting had stopped pacing to finally speak, but he looked haggard. I knew he had heart problems from what Cricket had shared with me over the years. This worrying couldn't be good for him.

"Thank you, sir, but I plan to sleep right here. I'm no doctor but I understand enough. If anything happens, I plan to be here for it."

Debbie launched herself at me, squeezing me tight despite how slight she was. Cricket took after her in stature, but had Mr. VanHunting's coloring. "You're a good man, Callan Hellman."

Mr. VanHunting wouldn't say anything so effusive, but he did give me a head nod before taking his wife from the hospital room and promising to be back first thing in the morning. After they left, I settled into the small chair and prepared for a long night. Thankfully I knew the staff around here and they wouldn't make me leave overnight. Wild horses couldn't have dragged me away from Cricket's side. The little clock on the wall ticked away the seconds, each sweep of the minute hand settling a bit of the deep anxiety that had taken hold the second Cricket went down.

"Callan, honey. The doctor's coming in soon."

I blinked myself awake at the sound of my mother's whispered voice and immediately groaned. My neck felt like I'd slept wrong, which was an understatement in this ridiculous chair. Sunshine was just beginning to peek through the blinds.

"Hey, Mom." I tried to rotate my head and loosen up my neck. I saw that Mom had brought a huge bouquet of flowers and set it on the little table on wheels.

"They really ought to do better with rollaway beds in hospitals, huh?" She put her arm around my shoulders and squeezed, providing the kind of comfort only a mother can. "You okay, son?"

I nodded, staring at Cricket while she slept on. She looked so small in a hospital gown. So pale against the white sheets. She had always been so slight that I worried about her, but seeing her in a hospital bed had made every instinct in me to protect her roar to the surface. "Yeah. Just worried."

"Christine VanHunting may look like a fragile angel here on earth, but she's built sturdy where it counts. Don't you worry."

Cricket's eyes began to flutter and finally opened. A smile lit her face immediately upon seeing us. Mom rushed over to the bed and fussed over her. She'd always treated Cricket like a daughter growing up. The door opened behind me and the VanHuntings arrived, looking like a night at home in their own bed hadn't given them much more rest than I'd gotten in the chair.

"Cricket!" Her mom rushed forward and Mom stepped out of the way. She came to stand by me, and we watched her parents treat Cricket like she was as fragile as a single pane of glass in a hurricane.

Mom leaned into me and lowered her voice. "Have patience. You'll get time alone with her soon."

I glanced down to see a knowing smile. I'd never told Mom about my true feelings for Cricket, but moms knew things. She'd taken one look at my face senior year and deduced that things had changed on my end. Thankfully, she'd never divulged my secret or pressed me to do anything about it.

The door banged open and a guy in a white coat, followed by three others, came into the room. His nose was buried in a chart. I didn't know him as he wasn't an ER doc.

"Hello, Christine. I'm Dr. Blodgett. We've looked through your blood test results and have ruled out genetic conditions or infections for your seizure last night. We'd like to have you come in for further testing as soon as possible. Notably an EEG, MRI, and a PET scan."

He finally looked up, seeing us all staring at him as if he was talking in another language. I knew exactly what he was saying, but I didn't like how he didn't address Cricket directly. Or even ask how she was feeling. He cleared his throat and looked back down at the chart in his hands. The three colleagues behind him didn't make a peep. Probably interns.

"So, once we get those tests scheduled, you're free to go."

He turned, as if he was going to walk away. I stepped forward, hands balled into fists at my side. "Wait. Does she have any restrictions? Things she should do to prevent further seizures?"

Dr. Blodgett frowned at me, but I didn't care. A little more information and a dash of compassion was the least he could do.

"Sure. Um, eat frequent meals, lower stress, limit alcohol, and avoid flashing lights. Until we get those tests run, we won't know if we're dealing with epilepsy or just your run-of-the-mill seizure. Oh, and I'd avoid driving a car." With that he spun on his heel and left, the interns scrambling to follow him.

There was silence in the room as we all processed that dump of information. Debbie was the first to break the silence with what we were all thinking.

"Let's get you a new doctor, sweetie. That man may be smart but he's missing the human component."

"Mom, it's fine. He's just doing his job."

"It's not fine," Mr. VanHunting interrupted. "His job is to make his patients feel better, pumpkin. Barking out instructions and leaving isn't cutting it. We'll find you a specialist."

"He's right. There's a really great neurologist in Blueball I think you should see." Everyone's gaze swung to me.

"Great idea, Callan. Cricket, you need to move back in with us so we can monitor you." Debbie patted Cricket's hand.

"Whoa. Slow down." Cricket tried to scoot up in the bed, her pale blonde hair a messy riot around her shoulders. "I have my own place. He didn't say anything about needing supervision."

"Christine," her dad said in a stern voice.

"How about we all just get some coffee and discuss every-thing while the nurses work on the discharge papers?" Mom interrupted, putting her hand on Mr. VanHunting's arm. "I heard the coffee shop downstairs is actually quite good. Shall we?"

Debbie nodded aggressively, pulling her husband out of the room. Mom tossed me a wink over her shoulder and I'd never felt so lucky to call her mom.

"Ugh!" Cricket threw back the covers, exposing her bare legs.

I lurched forward to steady her, sitting down on the bed and putting my hand on her back. The gown opened in the back, meaning my entire palm was on her bare skin. She felt like the finest silk. Here she was in the hospital and my pants were getting tight. Clearly, I was a complete asshole.

"They're ridiculous! I don't need to move in with my parents! I've worked too hard to have my own place." Cricket looked up at me, her blue eyes swimming in tears. "Cal."

And there it was. The look that stopped me in my tracks. The pleading emotion that meant I would flay my skin open just to give her a moment of happiness.

"Move in with me, then."

It was the worst idea in the world. Asking my best friend—

the one I had a full-blown crush on—to move into my personal space. That was like being diagnosed a diabetic and opening a fucking donut shop.

But Cricket's face lit up, right before she threw her arms around me and buried her face in my chest. I held her tight and told myself to suck it up. Temptation was no stranger to me. I'd simply have to keep a tight lid on myself and do what was best for Cricket. Same as always.

"Oh my God, Callan. Yes!"

Immediately my brain swung to other scenarios in which I wanted to hear her say my name just like that. I squeezed my eyes shut.

This was going to be hell.

Cricket froze in my arms, her head coming up to peer at me. "What?"

"You stink, dude." She wrinkled her nose and it took everything in me not to bend my neck and kiss it.

I shrugged. "You vomited on me last night."

Cricket sat upright, pulling out from under my arm. She looked more shocked by that than the possible epilepsy diagnosis. "I did what?!"

I didn't understand why she was freaking out. "Lots of people vomit when they have a seizure. I rolled you to your side so you didn't choke. Only a little bit got on my shoes and pants."

Cricket shook her head back and forth and then threw her hands in the air dramatically. "No. Nope. Just no. Kill me now!"

I chuckled, reaching up to pull her arms down before any more of her back was exposed in the hospital gown. "Calm down."

She spun on me and I cut her off before she could let me have it.

"I know, I know. Never tell a woman to calm down."

She narrowed her eyes, but took a deep breath. "I'm a hot mess, you know. You're asking for absolute frustration by letting me move in temporarily."

I folded my arms across my chest. "How long have I known you, angel?"

She twirled a lock of hair so violently the knots were multiplying at an alarming rate. "A few years."

I put my hand on hers to stop her. "Almost your whole life, woman. I am well aware of your brand of 'hot mess.' And I'm not afraid."

"Well, you should be! I forget to go grocery shopping until there's one wilty apple in the fridge that would make a killer science experiment. I leave my clothes on the floor, right where you'll be most likely to trip on them. I—"

"Cricket," I interrupted, trying not to shout at her ridiculousness. "You're moving in. Period."

She snapped her mouth shut and stared at me. "Fine."

I nodded. "Fine."

We both sat there in silence. I was giving myself a lecture on keeping my head out of the gutter with this new arrangement. I had no idea what she was thinking.

She began to kick her legs, swinging them back and forth since her feet didn't even touch the ground. "I've decided, since you want me to move in so badly, you can feed me grapes. Rub my feet every night. Maybe even engage in a pillow fight or two. It'll be like a long-term sleepover!"

I pressed my knuckles to my mouth to keep in the groan.

She had no idea how badly I wanted to do all of those things.

And much, much more.

CHAPTER SIX

ricket

"OH MY GOD, you little freaks! What are you doing here?"

Meadow, Addy, and Annie met us outside the sliding glass doors of the hospital with flowers, smiles, and one giant mylar balloon in the shape of a dick. Mom muttered something under her breath, Dad looked sharply away, and Nikki cheered them on. My besties really were crazy.

Sadly, I had to return the stiff gown with a constant draft in the back. I was back in my regular clothes, but the hospital staff insisted on getting me out of the building in a damn wheelchair like an invalid. You have one little blackout seizure and everyone freaks out.

"We couldn't let you leave without an entourage," Meadow said as she leaned down to give me a hug.

Addy and Annie followed suit, tying the balloon around my wrist. Everyone reached for me as I pushed out of the wheelchair to stand on my own two feet.

"Careful, honey," Mom called from behind me.

I rolled my eyes and batted my hands through the air until everyone stepped back. "I'm fine, y'all. Honestly. Never felt better."

Callan's palm settled on my back, guiding me toward his truck in the parking lot. Everyone followed us, the balloon drafting behind me and hitting Dad in the face when a breeze kicked up. I almost burst out laughing but the angry look on his face stopped me. My father was the last person who would understand that a giant inflatable dick hitting him in the face was the funniest thing I'd seen in weeks. As it was, I heard Nikki snickering and that was enough to make me wonder how I hadn't been born into her family instead.

"She's got tests scheduled for next week," Mom was explaining to my friends.

"No alcohol," Dad piped in, as if my friends were responsible for coercing me into drinking. I mean, they were, but he didn't need to call them out like that.

"She's got to keep the stress low, so we might want to look into managing your appointments." I hated when Mom started using "we," as if my schedule was something she had anything to do with.

"And she needs to eat." This from Callan, the food-pusher.

"Guys," I said, pausing at the door to Callan's truck. "Please don't fuss. That just makes my stress worse. I'm fine. Okay?"

"Maybe you need to take a vacation. That would destress you." Addy nodded, looking tan and relaxed from her honeymoon. I had a feeling her relaxation had more to do with Ace's magical appendage and less to do with lounging poolside.

"She's staying with me for now, so I'll make sure she gets plenty of rest and relaxation." Callan lifted an eyebrow at me, daring me to argue. I rolled my lips in and shrugged my shoulders. I was fine with Callan's version of relaxation. We'd already discussed his talented thumbs and only an idiot would turn down more of that.

Mom pushed through the crowd and gave me a hug. "Call me every day and I'll be stopping by to check on you."

"I'm okay, Mom," I reassured her for the millionth time.

Dad patted my back and looked like he wasn't sure if he should leave. It was weird to see him look uncertain. He was usually the most confident person I'd ever met.

"Callan's got me."

That seemed to be what they needed to hear. All the parents left, and after more hugs and plans to bring me food, my friends finally left too. Callan helped me up into his truck, batting at the balloon dick until it floated into the back seat, and then we were off.

I groaned, burrowing into the seat as Callan drove us to my place. "I hate all that attention."

Callan shot sideways glances at me while he drove. "I know. You handled it well though. Everyone just loves you and wants to see for themselves that you're okay."

"Ugh. So tough to be so loved," I whined teasingly.

Callan parked right outside my salon. My two designated parking spots were empty since Kennedy had cancelled all my appointments for today. Oddly enough, I already missed work. Even all those wash and sets. I climbed the stairs to my apartment over the salon and dug around for my keys in my handbag. Callan pulled out his own set of keys and unlocked my door faster than I could find mine.

I'd given him an extra key the same day I moved in, but I had no idea he kept in on his keyring. Maybe that should have made me feel uncomfortable, but it didn't. I liked knowing he had access to my place in case of emergency. Or you know, in case I couldn't find my keys fast enough.

I slipped the ribbon off my wrist and left the balloon dick to bounce around the ceiling in my kitchen. I had a feeling Callan wouldn't want me to bring that to his place.

"Where's your duffle bag?" Callan asked, all business now that we'd gotten here.

In my bedroom, I pulled a black bag out of my closet and tossed it on the bed. Then I stared at my clothes. "I have no idea how much to pack."

"Just pack it all." Callan opened my top drawer and grabbed a handful of underwear in his big hand to toss in the bag.

"Hey!" I leaped over to grab it out of his hands, but that just resulted in us having a tug-of-war over a pair of deep red G-string underwear. My face felt like it might match the panties.

Callan finally let go, but not before a smirk of epic proportions took over his face. I shoved the undies in my bag and shot him a dirty look. He just laughed and kept opening drawers to throw clothes in my bag.

"You know, that stuff was folded nicely before you just threw them."

He shrugged his massive shoulders and kept right on pillaging my clothes. "I'll refold them when we get to my place."

With a huff, I turned my back on him to pull out shoes from the closet. I heard the scrape of another drawer and only realized belatedly that it was the sound of my bedside table drawer. The one that held the romance novels I read late at night as I dreamt of my own hero swooping in to knock me off my feet.

And my vibrator collection from The Hardware Store.

"No!" I spun around and watched in horror as Callan ran his finger over each colorful silicone toy, as if making a mental note of which ones I owned.

I ran over and slammed the drawer shut, nearly taking off his finger while I was at it. My heart was pounding right out of my chest, supplying all ten units of blood to my cheeks.

I had an impressive catalog of sex toys. A twenty-three-year-old woman was allowed to express herself sexually, especially when the boyfriends were few and far between. Except I didn't feel like a confident, sexual woman standing in front of my drawer of toys with Callan looking at me with something I couldn't define in his golden-brown eyes. I felt shaky. Maybe even a little like I felt last night before the world went dark.

The silence ticked away, awkward not a strong enough word for how I felt. Words were stacked up and strangled in my throat. Callan finally raised his hand and pressed his fist against his mouth.

His voice came out low and raspy from behind his fist, sending a tingle of something dancing over my skin. "We're going to talk about that later, angel. When you don't look like you're ready to pass out."

And then he spun on his heel and whistled as he roamed around my house doing God knew what. When my lungs finally unfroze and the blood began to drain to my extremities, I moved away from the drawer and tried to zip my duffle bag. I had no idea what had been packed, and frankly, I didn't give a damn. I needed to get the hell out of here before Callan began to dig any deeper into shit I didn't want to share with my male bestie. Some things were only shared with my female friends for good reason. I did not need the mental imprint of Callan Hellman fingering my vibrators.

I came out of the room with the duffle bag slung over my shoulder. The damn thing was nearly as heavy as me. Callan came hustling over and whisked it off my shoulder.

"I grabbed the tea you like and the chocolate bars you hide behind the multivitamins you never take."

My jaw dropped. Did he know *all* my secrets?

Callan looked back at me when he realized I wasn't following him to the front door. "Your face." He burst out laughing, the kind of laugh that fills all the available air in the room and requires you to join in or die trying to stop yourself.

I drilled him in the gut with my finger and he brought it down a notch. "After you, angel." I swept through the door with my head held high as if I hadn't been humiliated while he went through my drawers. He shut the door and locked it with his key before nudging me down the stairs.

Callan kept up a steady stream of conversation as we drove over to his place, a little three-bedroom, two-bathroom house a few miles away from the downtown area. His chatter helped fizzle out any of the residual embarrassment I harbored, and by the time I peeked my head into the guest bedroom where I'd be sleeping, I could admit that I was exhausted. Seizures were, apparently, a tiring thing to go through.

Callan put my bag on the bed and then pushed me down the hallway, his arm slung over my shoulders. I caught a glimpse of the third bedroom as we passed. It was set up with a bench press and more weights and equipment than he'd had last time I was here. Just thinking about Callan working out and getting sweaty in there made me feel faint again.

What the hell was wrong with me? Oh yeah, that's right. I had my first major medical event.

"How about an afternoon on the couch, watching your favorite movies?"

Reluctantly, I ducked under Callan's arm and had a seat on the couch. "Don't you have work?"

Callan snagged a blanket from the back of the recliner and spread it over my legs, following up with a pillow below my feet as I rested them on the coffee table. I was set up like a queen.

"Nope. Took the day off."

I tilted my head. That little shit took the day off for me. I should feel guilty he had to adjust his schedule, but all I felt was relieved. And safe. And a whole lot spoiled.

He handed me the remote. "You pick out the movie. I'll be back with snacks."

"You're determined to make me fat, aren't you?" I shouted after him as he whistled his way to the kitchen. He was like a cat with a bell around its neck. If you ever wanted to find him, you just had to listen for the whistling. I flipped through the movie offerings and found a '90s romantic comedy I'd seen at least thirty times.

He came back in the room, armed with a tray. "I don't care what you are, as long as you're healthy and happy."

My heart swooped and melted into a puddle. "Do you practice these lines?"

Callan set the tray on the coffee table and had a seat next to me. "I'm not Daxon."

I thought of Daxon's smooth flirtation. I'd been around the triplets enough growing up to have had a front-row seat to his flirting on more occasions than I cared for. The guy knew all the lines and delivered them with such confidence, a girl didn't even realize she was being served up something less than genuine.

"Definitely not Daxon, thank God."

Callan smirked as he handed me a pint of my favorite ice cream. The one with the brownie core. Callan didn't care for chocolate, though I tried to forgive him for such a significant flaw.

"When did you have time to run out and grab this?"

Callan shrugged and grabbed the remote from me, hitting play on the movie I'd chosen. "I always have your favorite on hand."

I peeled off the lid and tried to decipher why that comment lodged in my brain and poked at me. Like it was a notable statement that needed to be dissected and ruminated on.

"Like, just in case I come over?"

Callan shoved a huge bite of boring vanilla ice cream into his mouth, talking around it. "Yeah."

I stared at him, ignoring the opening credits of the movie. I didn't have a pint of his favorite at my place. Maybe I was a bad friend. Callan was more of a planner than me, but even so, it seemed like he was always going way out of his way for me.

I put the ice cream on the coffee table and launched myself at him. My arms wrapped around his broad shoulders and he nearly fell to the side on impact. He smelled like hospital disinfectant and cologne, a scent that should have been gross but wasn't.

"Jesus, Cricket," he muttered grumpily.

I rained down kisses across his cheek and he finally broke out into a smile and pushed me away.

"Watch the movie, weirdo."

I let him go and grabbed my ice cream, determined to finish the whole pint before the movie was over. Callan eventually put our empty ice cream containers on the table and wrapped his arm around me. I snuggled into his side and felt myself get sleepy.

Yesterday had been scary, but everything was as it should be again.

CHAPTER SEVEN

allan

IF MY DICK got any harder, I could use it as a bat in a baseball game. Definitely could pitch a tent with it. The pipes under my kitchen sink were fluffy cotton compared to this thing. I could even win a world record for hardest, longest erection if there was such a thing. Shit, maybe there was.

I could have sworn I'd been sporting some degree of erection ever since I woke up one morning as a budding teenager experiencing his first wet dream. The fact that the dream had centered around Cricket was something I'd take to my death bed, though now that I was most definitely in love with the grown-up version of her, I was thinking maybe that dream had simply been an omen. A vision of the future.

"I swear I'll kick you out if you're drooling on me, angel."

It was an empty threat. I'd never kick her out and I already knew she was drooling on me. She always did. Every single one of my shirts had at some point in time held a little wet spot from her, a fact that should irritate me, but didn't. It was cute and it showed me she really truly let her guard down around me.

As the credits rolled, Cricket lifted her head, her eyelids heavy with sleep. She ran her fingers over the corner of her mouth. "I would never."

"Mhm. What did you think of the movie?"

She'd been dozing off for most of it. She knew that I knew it. But I wanted to see if she'd own up to it.

The fire that was never far from the surface lit up her blue eyes. "I think the hero's character was amazing. I mean, a forty-year-old virgin is funny, right?"

I shrugged, liking how she hadn't sat up yet. Her whole body weight lay against my side and I'd be lying if I said it didn't make me feel like a real-life hero.

"I don't know. A virgin that old? Pretty unrealistic."

Cricket frowned and pushed off my chest to sit up. "Why is that unrealistic? All kinds of people are virgins. Of all ages. Not everyone lost their virginity to Stacy Peterson in the back of his truck while his two brothers were snickering in the woods."

Ouch. Her description wasn't wrong exactly, but I'd like to think it was a little better than that. My brothers had been far enough away I knew they didn't see or hear anything. And Stacy had been the one to make the first move. When she grabbed my dick through my jeans the second I parked and asked if I had a condom on me, I got the impression she wasn't looking for a hotel room with rose petals strewn across the bed.

"I'm just saying most people lose their virginity in high school and definitely by the end of their twenties." I leaned over to pick up our empty ice cream containers.

"I'm a virgin."

My brain shorted out and my hand overshot the ice cream. The empty pints rolled off the table, spoons clanking to the ground in a chaotic mess. I turned back to Cricket to see her arms folded across her chest and one eyebrow lifted in challenge.

Holy fucking shitballs.

"You...you're what?"

Her cheeks were pink, but my girl didn't back down. "I said, I'm a virgin. And I'm in my twenties. Not unrealistic at all."

My mouth was flopping open and then closed and then open again. Surely I looked like an idiot, but I honestly could not wrap my brain around this new information. My dick, however, was rejoicing to this news by sending further blood flow to the appendage least necessary in this delicate conversation.

"But...how?"

Cricket huffed, pulling her legs off the coffee table and flinging off the blanket I'd draped over her. "Simple. I haven't let a penis into my vagina, Callan."

I grimaced, squeezing my eyes shut. Could a dick actually explode if too much blood pumped into it? I never, ever wanted to hear the words penis or vagina coming out of Cricket's mouth unless she was naked and willing to let me show her exactly what I could do with those two body parts.

"But...what about Logan?"

I was referring to her boyfriend senior year. The guy that I reluctantly had to admit was a decent person, if a little lame due to his obsession with golf. I didn't remember the exact conversation that one late spring night, but it had something to do with Cricket kicking me out of her house because she had to get ready for her date with Logi—the ridiculous nickname she gave him that made me want to put my fist through his face. She had to get ready because she planned to sleep with him that night. I didn't remember much else from that evening because I convinced Ethan and Daxon to score some beer and head down to the beach for a bonfire where I proceeded to drink my weight in alcohol. I avoided Cricket for several days afterward until I could convince myself that I didn't care if she gave up her virginity to some douchebag named Logan.

Cricket stood up and came around the coffee table to pick up the remnants of our ice cream binge. Her long blonde hair swung in her face and it killed me that I couldn't look her in the eye as she imparted this well-kept secret.

"Logan was nice, until he wasn't. He was more interested in impressing everyone at mini-golf with his hole-in-ones instead of trying to get in my pants. So, I went home alone, V-card still in my wallet. And I've kept it there ever since." She straightened with her hands full and practically ran to the kitchen.

I stared after her, my palm coming down to press against my erection, begging it to calm down. Her being a virgin didn't change anything. Nope. Not at all.

Let's be real, it totally did. Somehow it shifted everything I thought I knew about her, only amplifying my already out-of-control feelings. Which was stupid. How many people she did or didn't sleep with had nothing to do with the person she was, but yet there was some primitive aspect of my ego that wanted to be the one and only male to know this intimate detail about her. To be the one that changed her status and set the bar for every man to enter her life.

Cricket stepped back into the room, jolting me from my stupor. I jerked my hand off my dick, backhanding the throw pillow like an idiot. Jesus. I needed to calm the fuck down.

"Now that we're talking about the elephant in the room, how many people have *you* slept with?" She had her hands on her hips, still not meeting my eye, but at least looking in my general direction.

"Does it matter?"

She shrugged. "Only as much as my virgin status matters."

Well, shit. If I said it didn't matter, it would look like I was trying to get out of answering the question. If I said it mattered, I sounded like an asshole who valued women only for their virginity.

"Five," I blurted out. Maybe a simple honest answer would move this conversation along. Or I could just find a cliff and jump off of it. That might be easier.

Cricket blinked, her blue-eyed gaze drilling into mine as she studied me. Her hands dropped away from her hips. "Five?"

I swallowed hard. That cliff was sounding better and better. "Are you asking five as in, wow, that many? Or five, as in, that's it?"

Cricket licked her lips. "The last one."

I stood also, edging around the couch to keep my lower half hidden. "Well, it's kind of something not to take lightly, right? I want both me and the woman to be all in." Fuck, that didn't even make sense in my own head, but I couldn't seem to string a coherent sentence together. And the real answer was that none of the women I'd dated had been her. I'd tried to move my heart along a few times, but had failed miserably.

Cricket's head nodded, seeming to pick up steam with each nod. Pretty soon she was just a blonde bobble-headed blur. "Yep. Sure. Of course."

Silence filled the room. I couldn't think of a single time when things between Cricket and me had been this awkward. I needed to leave. I needed to be away from her flowery scent, the one that clung to the very air around her no matter the day, time, or location. Needed to be far, far away from this conversation and all the roads my brain went down that it shouldn't.

"Okay, well, I'm beat. I think I'll head to bed," I muttered, backing out of the room. Jesus. Cricket was still nodding. Or maybe she was simply nodding again. "I'll, ah, get those clothes folded for you tomorrow, but clean sheets are on the guest bed."

And like the biggest chicken in all of Auburn Hill, I retreated to my room, leaving Cricket on her own. As just punishment, I couldn't sleep, instead tossing and turning in my bed and straining to hear sounds of Cricket in the house. When my alarm went off the following morning, I was more tired than when I'd climbed in bed the night before.

Quickly dressing in my paramedic uniform, I headed for the kitchen and started scrambling some eggs. I wasn't sure if Cricket was headed into work today—something I could have asked if I didn't run away from our conversation last night—but I had every intention of making sure she ate breakfast. While her medical issues probably didn't stem from low blood sugar like I may have thought, it certainly helped to be as healthy as possible so no further seizures were triggered.

"Please tell me you have hot water going," Cricket croaked from behind me. I turned to see her rubbing her eyes, her short tank top riding up her flat stomach. I turned back around with a silent groan and tried to pay attention to the eggs.

"Sure do. Pot's over there." I flung a hand out toward the electric kettle and oversized mug I kept on hand just for her. I'd placed her favorite teabag in the mug already so she just had to pour and let it steep. I didn't drink that weak shit. Give me a full-bodied coffee over plant water.

"Mpht."

I plated the eggs and slid them onto the bar area of the counter. I knew from years of experience not to try to engage Cricket in conversation until she'd had her first few sips of tea. I watched her fix the tea, squeeze in honey, taste test, yelp over how hot it was, and then squeeze in some more honey. By the time she had a seat and picked up a fork, I'd finished my eggs and toast.

"Didn't realize living with you came with breakfast," she mumbled around the eggs.

She was adorable. Her eyes looked puffy from sleep and her left cheek was still slightly pink. What I wouldn't give to be able to slide my hands into her hair, tip her head back, and wake her up with a kiss that coaxed her right back into bed.

"Well, you did promise me you'd eat, so I figured I'd just make it easy for you to fulfill your promise." I slammed the rest of my coffee and stood up from the barstool. "And you can make dinner."

Her gaze flew up to mine, a rebuttal on the tip of her tongue. When she saw my smile, she stuck her tongue out at me instead.

"I'm just so tired still." The statement was made with such an exaggerated whine, I knew she was just teasing me to get out of making dinner, but I worried about her just the same.

I put my dishes in the sink and came back over to her side. "Which is why I think you should take a few more days off from work. Get some rest, angel."

She was shaking her head before I quit talking. Stubborn little thing.

"I have a full day of washing and setting, but I promise I'll sit down lots and even eat a decent lunch."

I kissed her on the cheek. If I didn't hurry up, I'd be late to work. "Good. I'll call Kennedy and see if she can order you a lunch delivery."

"Has anyone told you what an overbearing brute you are?" she yelled after me as I found my keys and grabbed my backpack.

"You tell me every day!" I shouted back as I left the house and locked it after me.

My phone pinged before I'd even gotten in my truck. I pulled it out of my pocket, seeing a text from Cricket. The smile was on my face before I read it.

Angel: You stocked my expensive shampoo and conditioner???

I slammed the door after I got behind the wheel, putting the backpack on the passenger seat.

Me: I didn't want to hear you bitch and moan about my drugstore brand.

Angel: You should really try this stuff. Smells so good!

I groaned and cranked over the engine, pulling away from the house before I went back inside and explained to Cricket that I knew exactly how good it smelled. I'd been smelling that flowery scent of hers for several years now. It was imprinted on my brain. I could be ninety years old and still pick out that scent in a busy crowd.

My phone kept pinging but I didn't look down at it. I

couldn't tell you how many accidents I'd gotten called to over the years because of people texting and driving. No text was important enough to risk my life, even if it was from Cricket. When I pulled up to the station right on time, I gave myself a minute to read through the texts, all from my brothers.

Daxon: Really, Callan? Living in sin?

Daxon: You won't even answer? Too busy dicking down Cricket finally?

Ethan: That's vulgar, Dax.

Daxon: Oh come on. You know he's been wanting to do that for years.

Ace: Is that what the kids are calling it these days?

Daxon: Yes, grandpa.

Ethan: I, for one, am very happy for my brother. It only took a medical emergency to get his girl to move in with him.

Blaze: Careful, man. Living together can be tricky.

Ace: Only if there's mutual attraction. Is there, Callan?

Daxon: Of course there's mutual attraction. Have you seen Cricket? Like an angel fell down from heaven and is walking amongst us mere mortals. And Callan's a Hellman.

Ethan: Jeez. Ego much, Dax?

Daxon: Just spittin' facts.

I rolled my eyes so hard I almost lost conscious. My thumbs flew over the screen and I tried not to snap their heads off for talking about Cricket like that.

Me: Yes, she's living with me temporarily. No, there's nothing going on. She's my best friend. Full stop.

Before I could turn my phone off and head into work, Daxon pinged me back.

Daxon: Sure...

Irritation had me nearly kicking the truck door open and stomping over to the ambulance where Xavier was waiting for me.

"I don't like that look on your face, bro. Did Cricket ask you to pick out colored towels too?" Xavier looked horrified on my behalf, which made me crack a smile.

Maybe, just maybe, I could get through my work shift without being distracted by the topic of Cricket.

Sure...

CHAPTER EIGHT

ricket

I DID NOT, in fact, have an easy day of resting between appointments. Apparently, spending the night in the hospital did not conjure sympathy from the geriatric set of Auburn Hill. They showed up in force today to get the gossip directly from the horse's mouth. And oh, hey. Since I'm here, can I get a wash and set?

I stumbled through Callan's door a little after seven, dead on my feet. Kennedy had given me a ride home, saying Callan had texted her earlier today that he didn't want me driving nor walking home on my own. I could have been irritated that he went to my receptionist about my own travel plans—and I was for a little while—but now that I only had to climb the three steps to his door, I was thankful for the door-to-door service.

"Cricket?" he called from the kitchen.

"Yeah, it's me," I called back, kicking off my shoes and making my way to the kitchen, which was where his voice seemed to come from. I slumped into a barstool and laid my cheek down on the cool granite with a sigh.

Callan's hand was on my back in an instant, rubbing away the sore and tired muscles. I was totally drooling on his counter and it was all his fault. Those stupid, incredible thumbs.

"Thought you'd be home hours ago," he chided gently.

"Mpht," I grumbled against the countertop, refusing to crack an eye open or move a muscle lest he quit his massaging.

"I don't want to nag at you, angel, but rest is really important until you get those tests run."

I did blink my eyes open at that. Even sat up and wanted to cry when his hands dropped from my shoulders. Callan was still in his paramedic uniform, looking far more handsome than someone should after a full day of work. How was it fair I looked like I got run over repeatedly by Clyde's tow truck and Callan looked like he should star in a paramedic calendar for skeezy old ladies? And by old ladies, I meant every woman of legal age. I was convinced there wasn't one living woman who would look at Callan and think he wasn't gorgeous.

"I did that space-out thing three times today."

I didn't mean to say that out loud. Especially to Callan. His jaw hardened and I rushed to explain.

"I'm sure it's nothing, but like an idiot, I Googled that symptom and now I think I'm dying. Probably tomorrow."

That got his jaw muscle to calm down. He almost cracked a smile even. "Doctor Google is an idiot, not you."

I shrugged and shot him a smile. "Yeah, I know. Just couldn't help myself."

Callan pointed to the living room. "Go put your feet up and I'll be in with dinner in just a minute or two."

"I thought I was making dinner?"

He shot me a look that said if I didn't follow orders in the next three seconds, he was going to flip into "angry Callan" mode. He didn't do it often, but when he did, it had an effect on people. For example, when he told me at the hospital that I was moving in with him, his deep voice left no room for arguing. Again, it should have pissed me off that he ordered me around, but it didn't. If anything, it made my stomach feel weird. Like I had indigestion, the kind that you looked forward to, which was straight crazy.

I hopped off the barstool and made it almost out of the kitchen before I stuck my tongue out at the back of his head.

"Cricket, I swear to God..." he grumbled without turning around.

My eyes widened and I hoofed it over to the couch, tucking the blanket around my legs. I hadn't even gotten fully settled and Callan was back, setting a loaded plate of chicken fajitas on my lap. The smell alone was enough to have me drooling.

"Dang. I might never move out."

Callan made a strangled noise and I looked up sharply. He was busy spreading a napkin on his coffee table before putting his own plate down. Shit. Maybe I shouldn't joke about that. Surely having someone live here with him while he had to wait on them hand and foot wasn't his idea of a good time.

Silence stretched out as we both ate our dinner. When he was halfway done, Callan started talking about his day. Apparently he'd had to help Ace and his crew rescue a peacock that had tried to fly away from a fight with a flamingo at Peacock B&B. The peacock got as far as a large shrub and then went down, its beautiful feathers getting caught in the thick bush.

"Shouldn't you have called Annie?" My friend was the local vet here in Hell and would have been better suited to deal with a live animal.

"We probably should have, but Ace thought he could get the thing out quickly." Callan started chuckling and the lighthearted sound made me smile. "Ace fell over backwards when he freed the bird. And then when he went to get up, the peacock spread its feathers and knocked him on his ass again. It was amazing."

I shook my head. Only in Hell. "The flamingo was okay?"

Callan set his empty plate back on the coffee table. "Yeah, he was over on the side watching the whole thing standing on one leg. Didn't even bat an eyelid."

He stood quickly, the couch rolling in his wake. I held onto my plate and waited it out. "I'm going to hit the shower while you finish."

He was down the hallway before I had a chance to swallow my food and answer him. He was acting weird lately. All talkative like normal and then in the next second he wouldn't make eye contact and he was rushing from the room. Thankfully, his chicken fajitas were so good, I was able to distract myself from second-guessing my decision to stay here with him. Not that there was much of a decision. Callan barked out orders and I followed.

"Oh God," I groaned, leaning back on the couch with my eyes closed after finishing my plate. I practically licked the damn thing it was so good. Callan was going to get his wish and get me to gain weight while I stayed with him.

"Are you okay?"

I popped my eyes open to see a wet Callan Hellman rushing over to my side, a tiny white towel around his waist and barely able to cover the muscle-laden landscape. My body froze, but my eyeballs didn't. They took a long trip across the undulations of Callan's chest, abs, and those lines that seemed to point to something even more interesting below the waistline. I had been around Callan every single day of my life, and yet somehow I'd missed his transformation from lanky youth to chiseled man candy.

"Wha—?"

Callan's big hand slapped to my forehead and tilted my head back. For one crazy second I thought he might be leaning down to kiss me and that thought did not repulse me like I thought it might. Instead, I got that indigestion feeling again, only stronger this time. So strong it tugged on my girly parts and made my head spin.

Sadly, he leaned in to inspect my eyes like he would a car

accident victim on the side of the road, his wet hair dripping into my face. I blinked hard against his finger tugging on my eyelid and sputtered. Water droplets were sliding off his body right into my face.

"You're drowning me!" I tried to push him away but my hands landed on a hot wet towel with something human-like underneath that did not feel like his leg.

I froze again, my eyeballs joining in this time as I stared at the exact spot I'd just had my hands on. It was moving, growing, tenting his towel. Like a metamorphosis in slow motion. Callan's hand came down to cover himself, blocking my view of maybe the most fascinating thing I'd ever witnessed.

"Jesus, Cricket," he grumbled, backing away, looking like he could be part of the Thunder Down Under crew. Or a Magic Mike headliner with all his muscles in perfect proportion. He just needed to put a baseball hat on backwards and I'd toss dollar bills at him. Nope. Twenties. This show was worth bankrupting myself.

I balled my hands into fists. Not because I was having a space-out moment, but because my fingertips itched to reach out and touch him again. And I had the distinct feeling that any touch right now would dramatically change things between us in a way I could never comprehend. In a way I'd never envisioned. But holy shitballs, was I envisioning now.

"I thought you were having a seizure."

I blinked hard and found I couldn't swallow. I think I mumbled something but it must not have been what Callan was wanting to hear. He stepped closer again, his hand still covering his junk. My cheeks felt like they were on fire.

"Cricket. Angel, look at me."

His hand cupped my chin and tilted my face up until I was looking into his golden eyes. "What's going on?"

If I knew the answer to that, I would have told him. But I didn't, so I kept my mouth shut. There was only one thought drifting through my head at the moment and I didn't think I should share it out loud.

Was I seriously perving on my best friend right now?

I felt blood pumping quicker than normal through my veins. The squeeze of my stomach. The way my thighs clenched together. The heat in my face. The way my eyes kept straying south.

"Okay, I'm taking you to the ER."

Callan let go of my chin and stooped to slide his huge arm under my legs. He picked me up before I had a chance to stop him. Then I was pressed against the wet expanse of his chest and any words I may have uttered out loud were lost.

I squeezed my eyes shut and found it instantly easier to breathe. Good. This was good. I could operate like a functioning human like this. "I'm fine! I was just stuffed from those fajitas!"

Callan stopped midway through the living room. Or at least I thought that was where we were. My eyes were staying closed for the next foreseeable future. Until I dropped this ridiculous new obsession with Callan's body.

"So, you're not having a seizure? Why are your eyes closed?" When I didn't answer right away, Callan gave my legs a squeeze. "Open your eyes, Cricket, or so help me, I will throw your ass in my truck and dump you at the ER where they'll take your temperature with an anal thermometer."

That had my eyes flying open. I pulled my hand back where it had somehow been caressing Callan's chest and let my fist fly. It bounced right off his pec muscle and probably hurt me more than him.

"Hey! I said I was fine. Put me down, you brute."

Callan smiled at me, his straight white teeth even looking hot. Had someone flipped a switch in my body? Could they switch it back, please? I did not need to be looking at my best friend like a buffet for my viewing pleasure.

He set me down slowly, and I didn't miss the way he had to

shift and rearrange his towel. Jesus. It was hot in here. I backed away from him and fell into the recliner. How did that get there?

Callan crouched down, and yep, my eyes betrayed me, immediately flying down to see if there was a gap where the towel barely met around his waist. Sadly, the gap was just enough to the right to block any good stuff.

I slapped my hands to my cheeks and tried to rein in my wayward thoughts. My gaze darted around the room, desperately trying to stay away from Callan.

"You say you're fine, but you're acting really weird and spacing out."

I sucked in a deep breath and chalked everything up to something Callan put in the fajitas. Yep. That was it. Simple indigestion. Happened to me that one time my parents took us on a vacation to Mexico. I came home with a three-day bout of stomach issues so bad I thought I was going to lose my colon. Spoiler alert: I didn't die. Or lose my colon.

Swinging my head back to Callan, I pasted on a smile. "I'm good. Promise. Just tired and probably need to head to bed."

His eyes, so caring and serious, studied me for several long moments. "Okay. You should probably get some rest. You have the EEG test tomorrow."

"Oh yeah." I'd actually forgotten about that. I was going to need a ride if everyone insisted on this no-driving rule. "I need to call my parents."

"I talked to your mom earlier today. They have a golf fundraiser tomorrow, but I promised to take good care of you."

I wrinkled my nose. "You talked to my mom?"

Callan stood and walked to the doorway. Indigestion or not, my gaze dropped to his backside. Why did wet white towels have to be so thin? My addled brain did not need to see the outline of his ass. I did not need to know that his glute muscles were thick globes of firm flesh. I definitely did not need to have that image imprinted on my brain. You know, because of the indigestion.

"Eggs and fruit in the morning?" he asked, turning the corner and heading down the hallway.

I blew out a breath and hoped he couldn't hear the relief in my voice now that he was out of sight. "Sure! Um, and thanks!"

I shook my head at myself, muttering quietly, "Smooth, Cricket."

I grabbed my phone off the coffee table and texted my friends.

Me: Girls. I need a night out. Preferably in Blueball.

Where there'd be no chance of running into one of those Hellman brothers.

Meadow: I'm in. What night works best?

Addy: Are you sure that's in your best interest right now, Cricket?

Annie: Yeah, didn't your dad say no drinking?

Dammit! Why did I have to have such responsible friends? Well, excluding Meadow.

Me: I'll be the designated driver. PLEASE?

Addy: No way. No driving, remember?

We settled on next week because that was the soonest we all had the same free night, and agreed to argue about the driving thing later. I took the plates to the kitchen and put them in the dishwasher before heading to my bedroom and getting ready for bed. Maybe the EEG tomorrow would show wonky brain waves and I could pin all this craziness with Callan on my brain. That was the only thing that made sense. I'd been friends with him since kindergarten. There was zero chance of me developing a crush on him now.

Right?

CHAPTER NINE

ricket

"WHAT IF IT HURTS?"

Callan squeezed my hand, which was saying something because I'd already lost feeling in the tips of my fingers from holding on so tightly.

"There's no pain. The electrodes don't pierce your skin at all."

"What if I can't relax enough for them to get a good reading?"

"They do this all the time. They're used to nervous people. Just take deep breaths."

My knee jiggled up and down and I could have sworn there was a hummingbird in my chest. For not having anything to eat or drink in the last twelve hours I was a hopped-up mess of energy. We were in the waiting room doing the dreaded waiting. The place was painted a drab buttery yellow with baby-poop-colored chairs and a single painting of a cat only Yedda would love. We'd checked in right on time and filled out all the forms.

Callan had been literally by my side all morning to make sure everything went okay with my first test.

My next question was the one I'd been afraid to ask, which meant it came out all soft and vulnerable. Which made me want to jump up and run from the room. "What if they find something horribly wrong with me?"

Callan let go of my hand and put his arm around my shoulders, pulling me into his chest. I'd been distracted by that muscled chest last night, but now all I could focus on was sucking up his good vibes. I needed my best friend.

"We'll handle whatever the test results say together." The breath I'd been holding finally whooshed out. And then he opened his mouth again, this time his tone one of teasing. "Besides, we already know there's something horribly wrong with you."

"Hey!" I pinched his torso, making him flinch and pull his arm back. The front desk lady gave us a look over her reading glasses that reminded me of every single one of my elementary school teachers. "Take that back!"

Callan swallowed a laugh. "Absolutely not. You know you're a sick puppy when you drink tea in the morning instead of coffee."

I opened my mouth to give him crap about his favorite ice cream choice—can you be more lame than vanilla?—when the door off to the side opened and a nurse in scrubs called my name.

"Christine VanHunting?"

The terror was back, acute anxiety seizing me in its icy grip and making my throat feel like it was closing. The room dimmed in my peripheral vision until Callan grabbed my hand and squeezed hard.

"Deep breath, Cricket."

"Trying," I croaked, standing up and eyeing the nurse as she stared at her clipboard, all business.

"Tell you what, angel. You get through this test and I'll let you dye my hair."

My neck nearly snapped in two I moved so fast to gape at Callan. "Really? Any color?" I'd been begging him for literal years to let me dye his hair. So far I'd only succeeded in getting him to use the lightening shampoo that had given his medium-brown hair a slight golden shine in just the right lighting.

He shot me that lopsided grin that somehow made the hummingbird in my chest stop flapping her little wings. "Any color you want." He stuck his pinky finger out and I wrapped mine around it before he could take it back.

The nurse cleared her throat and I turned toward her, something way more exciting and wonderful to look forward to than this silly little test.

"I'm ready."

"Oh good," she said dryly, turning to show me the way down the hallway.

"Can I come with her?" Callan asked over my shoulder.

The nurse didn't even turn around. "No, sorry. Only the patient."

I squeezed Callan's hand and then let go. "It's okay. I've got this. See you in a few." And crazily enough, I felt like I did have this. I was going to be just fine.

I could feel Callan's gaze on me until the door swung shut, separating the two of us. The nurse pointed to room number three and I went in, taking a seat on the padded table with that paper liner that every woman learns to hate. All it takes is one gynecologist appointment for you to realize that thin paper just sticks, tears, and does everything except create a hygienic barrier between you and the table.

She went through the directions for the test, proceeding to place at least a hundred little probes on my scalp with the help of some kind of gel that would probably make my hair one giant snarl. When it was time, I lay down on the table and closed my eyes, taking deep breaths like Callan had advised and envisioning what hair color would be best on him.

"All done," the nurse announced, startling me from my vision of Callan with highlights and lowlights. I'd taken a nap without realizing it.

She unhooked the probes and left the room to give me privacy to dress. I caught a glimpse of myself in the reflection of the metal paper towel dispenser and yelped out loud. My hair was indeed one giant snarl, but it also reminded me of those old pictures of girls in the '80s yearbooks. My hair had impressive height. I used the hair band around my wrist to try to wrestle it into submission in the form of a messy bun on the top of my head.

Following the nurse waiting outside the testing room, she opened the door to the waiting room and Callan took one look at me before cupping his hand across his face to hide a smile.

"Go ahead and laugh." I waved a hand through the air like a queen. "It's pretty bad, I know."

He slung his arm across my shoulders as I checked out. "Thank God you're a hairstylist and have all the tools to straighten this rat's nest out."

I rolled my eyes as the front desk lady snickered, batting her eyelashes at Callan. See? Ovaries exploded everywhere I went when I took this guy. By the time we got back home after a quick trip to the salon, Callan was more nervous than I was this morning. I had yet to describe what color I would be dyeing his precious hair. He helped me carry in the bottles, trying to read the names off them to find a clue.

"I can always just shave my head if it's really bad." He scratched the back of his neck, looking so cute and scared I took pity on him.

"Relax, Cal. I'm just going to put in some highlights to brighten up your face. You'll look exactly like you normally do at the end of summer when you've hit the beach every day you have off work." It was only October but he'd already lost those sun-bleached locks on the top of his head and I missed them.

I looked him up and down, cataloguing his dark blue T-shirt and jeans. He looked good, of course, but they had to go. "You may want to take your shirt off. I don't want to get bleach on it."

His eyes bugged out of his head. "Bleach? Is that really necessary?"

I shrugged and began organizing my bottles on his counter-top. "Only if you don't want your hair to turn out orange."

He sighed and grabbed a barstool to drag it closer to the sink. "Bleach it is."

I spun around to see him strip out of his shirt, muscles flexing every which way. No wonder my head fit just right in the center of his chest when he hugged me. His pec muscles were puffy pillows that begged a girl to snuggle up to them.

The hummingbird in my stomach was back, y'all.

"Um, have a seat." I turned away, focusing instead on mixing my potions just right. Now that the EEG test was behind me, all those weird feelings I'd discovered last night came back full force and I didn't appreciate it. I had no room in this friendship for an ill-advised crush.

Callan had a seat, leaned his head back, and gifted me with a stare so trusting I nearly melted on the spot. His voice came out low and soft. "I'm glad that test is over."

Tears hit the back of my eyes. In so many ways Callan cared about me more than I cared about myself. He was happy the test was over simply so I wouldn't be nervous. Here I was crushing over his naked chest and he was thinking about my emotional wellbeing.

"Me too," I managed to sputter back. I put the first piece of foil to his head and began to paint. All the while my heart beat a little faster and a little harder for the sweet man my best friend had become.

CHAPTER TEN

allan

WHY THE HELL did I agree to this?

That thought flickered through my brain on repeat as Cricket attacked my hair with a passion that only made her hotter. No wonder her new salon was so busy. She clearly loved what she did for a living. But not only was I worried about having my hair dyed a color that would inspire teasing from Xavier when I went back to work tomorrow, but I was also dealing with a certain situation.

When I offered to let her dye my hair, I was only thinking about wiping that terror from her face. There was nothing that hurt me worse than seeing Cricket's pale face. Or hearing the fear in her voice. I would move heaven and earth to replace that with excitement and joy. Unfortunately, I had not accounted for the full hour that I would spend with Cricket's body pressed up against me, her scent and heat filling my head with all kinds of ideas. Her fingers were all over my scalp, and I discovered that having a hot hairstylist could be quite the turn-on.

Of course, that thought made me frown and decide to ask Kennedy about their male clientele. I didn't want other men booking appointments with Cricket because they wanted her breasts pressed against them.

"All done!" Cricket proclaimed, stepping back and admiring her handiwork.

I couldn't see myself, but I felt like I might be able to pick up a radio station down in Los Angeles. Cricket was smiling so broadly it almost made up for how ridiculous I felt.

"Did you need to use the whole roll of aluminum foil?"

She nodded and a giggle escaped. "Sure did." Then she went over to the sink to strip off her black gloves. "I need a picture!"

"Oh, hell no," I grumbled, standing up and reaching for her phone on the countertop.

She reached for it too, getting there first. I didn't let go though and soon we were tussling around the kitchen, both of us laughing and equally determined to get our way. Two pieces of foil floated to the ground in the mayhem, but still she wrestled with me. I didn't want to hurt her but there was no way I was allowing photo evidence of this little hair appointment.

"Oh shit, I got some on your shirt." We both froze, staring down at the smear on her shoulder. I couldn't help the smirk that slowly formed on my face. Two could play this game. "You better take your shirt off so you don't get more bleach on it."

The room turned decidedly hotter when Cricket's gaze instantly dropped to my bare chest. That wasn't repulsion or even disinterest I saw on her face. If I had to guess, Cricket quite liked my chest. And wasn't that interesting to note?

She shoved away from me, letting me keep her phone. I slid it in my back pocket and crossed my arms over my chest. Her lips wobbled and I knew she was biting back a laugh. Her hands skated across the bottom hem of the loose-fitting T-shirt she'd worn to her doctor's appointment. My heart stilled in my chest, waiting to see if she'd take the bait.

Defiance flitted across her face and then the shirt was lifted, up and over her smooth stomach, over the hills of a lacy pink bra, and then snagged on her messy bun. Cricket gave it another yank and the shirt came free, fluttering to the ground and leaving her standing there in just a pair of ripped jeans and a bra.

I'd seen Cricket in a swimsuit every single summer of our whole lives. I'd spend all my teen years wearing sunglasses at the beach, not because the sun was so intense, but simply so I could stare at the expanse of creamy flesh on Cricket and not get caught. But never, not once, had I had the opportunity to stare at Cricket in a lacy bra with that look of defiance stamped across her dainty features. The vision of her stopped my heart from beating. It shook me to my core. If there was still oxygen left in the kitchen, I wasn't breathing it.

"Let's rinse you." Cricket's voice came out breathy, like maybe she was having issues breathing too. I wish I knew what she said, but I was mostly just trying to get my eyes to stop staring at her breasts, or the dusky peaks that were forming behind the lace.

Cricket moved, standing by the sink and gesturing for me to sit on the stool. I swallowed hard and somehow made it the two steps to the stool, sinking down to it and wincing at the tightness of my jeans. The water flipped on and Cricket's silky smooth hands were guiding my head back.

Her breasts brushed against my shoulder as she began to pull the foil from my hair. I almost leaped out of the chair. My hands balled into fists as I tried to control myself. I reminded myself that taking her shirt off had not changed anything between us. She got bleach on her shirt. Her removing it was simply practical. Her breasts being on display in that pink bra were not an invitation for my hands to reach out and cup her. Or for my mouth to water at the notion of tasting her skin.

Fingers sifted through my hair, sending a shiver down my back. Fuck, that felt good. Shampoo lathered and I was inundated with the scent of Cricket. She was using her shampoo on me, which meant I'd smell like her until I could wash it out. This was straight torture. The kind that bends a man's brain and makes him lash out inappropriately.

I needed to talk to my brothers. Maybe go out for a drink with them. Anything to distract myself from the impossible crush I had on Cricket.

"Okay, you're all done!" Cricket pulled her hands from my hair and stepped back, handing me a clean towel.

I dried my hair much longer than necessary, just to keep my eyes averted. I could hear Cricket moving around the kitchen, collecting her tools and washing them in the sink.

"Now all the ladies will be pounding at your door," she said brightly.

I snorted from under the towel. "I don't care about that." I pulled the towel from my head and ran my fingers through my hair to try to style it.

Cricket had her back to me while she washed out the little bowl that had held her secret bleaching potion. "Hey, whatever happened with what's her name?"

I worked hard to get my brain to function. "Amy?"

"Yeah. You never told me what happened there. Or why you haven't dated since then," Cricket asked over her shoulder without ever looking at me.

She wanted to have a conversation about the woman I dated six months ago while we both were shirtless in the kitchen?

"Uh, well, we dated for a bit and then both decided it wasn't working. We still chat occasionally, but I'm fairly certain she's dating a guy long distance now."

Cricket nodded, flipping off the water and beginning to dry the bowl. "Ah. Got it. And no one since then?"

This was edging into the awkward territory of a few nights ago when I found out she was a virgin. I couldn't very well tell her my dating life sucked because I'd already given my heart away to her.

"Nope. I guess I just haven't found someone I wanted to date long term."

"Why not?"

I was officially done with this conversation. "Hey, your birthday is next week, young grasshopper. What did you have in mind to celebrate?"

Cricket finally put the bowl down and turned around. I immediately wished she hadn't. Looking at her almost bare back was much easier than keeping my eyes from taking in the front.

"Ugh. Don't remind me. I have plans to curl up and watch a movie and forget it's my birthday."

"What?" That was ridiculous. Of course we were going to celebrate it. I took a step closer to her and she turned like she was going to head out of the kitchen. I caught her hip and held on to stop her. "That's unacceptable, Cricket."

She tilted her head back to gaze up at me, those blue eyes losing their usual fire and slowly turning hazy. It was fascinating to watch. Then her pink tongue darted out to lick her bottom lip and my gaze snagged on her mouth. Alarm bells clanged in the back of my head, but I ignored them. Easy to do when they'd been ringing incessantly for years.

My other hand joined the first, holding her small body just an inch away from me. Her hands landed softly on my biceps, not pushing me away like they should. If anything, she moved closer, her lacy breasts brushing against my stomach. I sucked in a lungful of air and prayed for the restraint I'd spent most of my life building until it was my superpower. Cricket slowly walked her fingers up my arms and then they were diving into my hair, rearranging the strands I'd tried to fix myself.

"There, that's better," she whispered, her body now plastered against mine as she stood on her toes.

Just a slight dip of my head and my lips would be on hers. Just a small separation of space that got smaller with each rushed inhale. Soon we were sharing the same air, our lips so close if I licked mine, I'd brush against hers. This was it. The moment I'd spent my whole life waiting for.

Cricket was in my arms and had angled her head for my kiss.

"Yo, big brother, where are you?"

At the first sound of Daxon's obnoxious voice from the front door, we broke apart, gazes slithering to all corners of the kitchen. Before I could rearrange my face from the intense pain of losing my chance, or my pants where my dick was now holding them up better than a belt, Daxon and Ethan burst into the kitchen.

"There you are! You've been ignoring our texts." Daxon didn't stop to read the room, but Ethan did. A little smile formed on his face as he took in Cricket's hot cheeks and her frantic movements as she gathered all those bottles in her arms.

Shit. She didn't have a shirt on. The bottles covered most of her, but still. I didn't need my brothers getting a free view of what I'd spent my whole life waiting for.

"Hey, Cricket. Did I miss the dress code?" Daxon whipped his shirt off and circled it in the air over his head. The fucker.

"Everybody out!" I shouted, pushing Ethan and Daxon out of the kitchen.

"It's fine. I was on my way to my room anyway," Cricket said, squeezing past my idiot brothers to head into the living room and then down the hallway to the bedrooms.

Daxon snickered, looking at the doorway where she disappeared. "Did we interrupt something?"

"Dude, your hair looks amazing," Ethan said in wonder, reaching up to touch it. I smacked his hand away.

"What the hell are you doing here?" I usually loved my brothers but they'd just epically cock-blocked me and I wasn't going to pretend I wasn't pissed.

Daxon put his shirt back on. "Well, like we said, you weren't answering in the text string, so we thought we'd stop by to check on you."

Ethan winced and flung a hand toward the side of the house with the bedrooms. "We didn't realize we'd be interrupting something."

"Yeah, since you swore you were just friends. Remember?" Daxon piped in helpfully.

Someone really needed to punch him in the face one of these days. He was obnoxious. I folded my arms across my chest to keep myself from being the one to do it.

Ethan nudged Daxon aside. "Anyway, we're planning boys' night out this Friday. Be there or be the brother we bitch about behind your back."

While I normally enjoyed a night out with my brothers, I wasn't particularly happy about this one. They'd probably spend the whole night grilling me about Cricket. Especially after finding her with red cheeks and shirtless in my kitchen. Then again, if I didn't show, they'd spend the whole night in my business anyway, probably planning an intervention that would piss me off even more.

"Yeah, I'll be there."

Daxon clapped me on the back. "Excellent. Bring Cricket if you want. Had no idea she had those..." He gestured like he was holding melons against his chest and it took every ounce of self-control I had not to put a bump in that perfectly straight nose of his. Ethan pushed him out the door and shot me an apologetic look over his shoulder.

Silence stretched out in the house. I wondered if I should knock on Cricket's door and address what almost happened in the kitchen. Or should I ignore it and pretend it wasn't what we both thought it was? Or give her the night to calm down and address it tomorrow?

I sighed and slumped to the couch all alone. See? This was why you didn't develop a crush on your best friend. Because when things went sideways, who could you turn to for advice?

CHAPTER ELEVEN

ricket

"IT SHOULDN'T TAKE this long to get results back, don't you think?" Mom said with no small amount of worry in her tone.

I put the broom back in the closet and grabbed the rag out of Dad's hands before he cleaned the countertops in the salon for the fifth time. They meant well, wanting to help me close up at the end of the day, but their questions were just ramping up my anxiety. Maybe that had more to do with not getting much sleep the last two days.

To say I was blindsided by developing feelings toward Callan was putting it mildly. After that moment in the kitchen, that had yet to stop playing in a loop in my head, I spent most of the night staring at the ceiling and wondering what in the hell was happening to me. Maybe my attention to his body the past week was just a passing infatuation with a man who had a physique that was ridiculously perfect. So many of my female friends had certainly gone crazy over his body over the years. But then why did it feel like I might actually die right there on the wood floor if he didn't kiss me? That was more than a preoccupation with muscles.

"Cricket? Honey, did you hear me?"

"Yes, Mom. Sorry." I quit rearranging the bottles at my station and turned to address her. She was literally wringing her bony hands. "They said it could take several days for the neurologist to take a look. Add in the weekend, and it might be Tuesday before we hear anything."

I came over to put my arm around her. She was worried about my EEG results and I was over here obsessing about my best friend. My priorities were all messed up.

A thought hit me so suddenly I squeezed Mom too hard and she squeaked. Maybe the anxiety over my possible medical condition was causing me to look for other things to distract me. Maybe this sudden interest in Callan was simply my subconscious's way of providing distraction.

Well, shit. I felt better.

"Has Callan been driving you everywhere?" Dad's gruff voice cut off my internal celebrating from discovering I wasn't going crazy and that this obsession would be short lived. Once I figured out my medical situation, my focus on Callan would naturally fade.

"Yes. Mostly. I did walk here this morning and last, but Kennedy is giving me rides too." I didn't mention that I'd only walked here the last two days because I was waking up before sunrise and getting out of the house before Callan was even up. Avoidance and I were becoming friends.

"Is Kennedy old enough to drive?" Mom thought anyone south of fifty was a mere toddler.

"Yes, Mom. She just graduated high school." I let go of her to grab my purse and flip off the lights. Mom and Dad trudged over to the door, clearly trying to stay longer and interrogate me further.

Dad held the door for us, ever the gentleman. "I have a new client who's looking to buy some commercial property here in

Auburn Hill. I was hoping to have him over for dinner next week. Would you join us?"

The streetlights on Main Street had flipped on as soon as the sun started to make its descent. A cool breeze off the ocean made my hair dance and curl. The weather was starting to change, feeling more and more like fall with each passing day. It was nights like these that made me miss living above the salon. One wouldn't think living in the hustle and bustle of downtown would be nice, but then they didn't know Hell. This place shut down around eight, even on weekends.

"Sure, Dad," I replied absently, scanning the sidewalk for anyone I knew. In a town this small, it was inevitable.

Dad opened the passenger car door of his sedan for Mom. "Good. His son will be there too."

I halted with one foot off the sidewalk, shooting him a glare he didn't have the decency to pay attention to. "Dad."

He got in the car, still ignoring me. I climbed in the back and launched into it. "I'm not interested in dating anyone right now. Client or no client. And I really don't need you setting me up with someone, Dad."

He pulled away from the curb and shot me a stern look in the rearview mirror. "I wasn't setting you up. I just thought it would be nice for you to meet a young man your age."

I snorted, not believing that for a second. We'd been down this road too many times. How do you think I ended up with Alistair, the cheating bastard extraordinaire?

"Hank," Mom chided softly. "Cricket meets plenty of men on her own."

"Yeah? Like who?"

Mom's gentle tone got decidedly less gentle. "Like Callan! They have a great relationship."

Dad grunted and I discovered that, apparently, I was no longer needed in this conversation about my dating life.

"Callan," he said with a level of dismissal I didn't care for.

"He's her *friend*. You won't get grandchildren barking up that tree, Debbie."

I opened my mouth. "I don't—"

"How do you know?" Mom shot back, talking right over me. "They'd have adorable babies."

I sat back and let that thought stew in my brain. We *would* have beautiful babies. My cheeks flooded with heat and I was back to the recent obsession I couldn't seem to let go of.

"Callan is her childhood friend. Not husband material. Period."

Dad's voice interrupted my train of thought that had left friendship central and wound its way through white picket fences and babies galore. Probably for the best. That thought train was destined to derail. I blinked my eyes to see that we'd pulled up to Callan's house.

"Okay. Well, thanks for the dating advice and I'll have to get back to you about dinner. I might be working late that night."

"I haven't told you which night." Dad lifted an eyebrow as he swiveled to the back seat.

I lifted mine right back. "Might be working every night." I climbed out and scanned the area for Callan's truck. All clear.

Dad sighed so loud the neighborhood heard it. Mom leaned over to wave out the window. "Bye, dear!"

I waved back and hustled to get inside before Dad found yet another eligible bachelor to set me up with. I had a best friend to avoid and a girls' night out to get dressed for. Thankfully Callan never made it back home from work before Meadow picked me up an hour later. Addy and Annie were already in the back seat. I slid into the passenger seat and got hit with a wall of perfume and excited squeals.

"We've been needing to do this," Annie said with a mischievous grin.

Meadow whooped and pulled away from the curb with more enthusiasm than the little sedan's engine could give. Addy was even in a mood, managing the music with Meadow's phone, putting on songs that were several degrees peppier than her normal meditation music. I leaned my head back and grinned. I was tired, sure. But mostly I just wanted to hang with my girlfriends and forget all my troubles.

The chatter about all the recent Hell gossip kept us occupied all the way to the crappy little bar in Blueball. In order to prevent becoming part of the gossip grapevine ourselves, we had to head out of town. Personally, I was just glad to escape any Hellman brother sightings. I needed a break from that brand of pheromones.

"Only one light beer for me tonight, okay?" I told the group right before we piled out of the car.

"As long as your doctor thinks that's okay. We don't want to be the reason you have a setback." Addy snatched the keys from Meadow. "I'm the designated driver tonight, so I'll make sure you aren't served more than one."

Music spilled from the bar, every single dirt-smudged window sported at least one neon sign, most of which were blinking like they just might give up before the night was through. Even the parking lot was an advance apology for the state of the bar. Each pothole we had to walk around was like a warning for what lay ahead.

"The doctor didn't say much but I did some research and one beer isn't something to worry about," I promised Addy. And it was true. Now, if I really did have epilepsy, I probably wouldn't be able to have more than three drinks unless I was certain it wouldn't trigger a seizure, but I was never a big drinker. At barely a hundred pounds I was the quintessential lightweight.

Meadow pulled open the door and the smell of stale peanuts, sweat, and hops hit us in the face. Instead of grimacing like we probably should, we all let out a deranged whoop and raced inside to find a table. Preferably one that wasn't sticky, though all hope for that was dashed in short order.

I was halfway through my one beer and feeling all kinds of relaxed and happy when Meadow groaned.

"Seriously? You told them?"

I peeled my thighs off the sticky barstool and swiveled around to see five Hellman brothers come through the door. My heart took flight and my nose went numb. Of course, my gaze instantly zeroed in on Callan, easily the most handsome of the bunch. Even more so than Daxon. That boy was just too perfect. I liked the boy-next-door look that practically oozed from Callan's pores. His jeans molded to his muscled thighs, his shirt set off his tan, even skin, and then there was the easy grin that made him a people magnet. Callan was the man every woman wanted to date because you just knew he'd treat you like a queen.

"I didn't say anything!" Annie shouted, looking outraged even as a little smile danced around her lips.

Addy made the motion of zipping her lips, then gasped. "I didn't turn off my location on my phone though!" She winced. "Sorry, ladies. I only carry one so Ace doesn't freak out over my safety."

"You're telling me they tracked your ass and came all the way down here? For what? To flirt from across the room?" I watched as they swarmed like a pack of bees to a table across the wooden dance floor from us, pretending they didn't know we were here.

Meadow snorted. "I'm surprised Judd didn't get in on that action."

The door opened again and we all burst out laughing. Judd walked into the bar in one of his signature plaid shirts and flagged down the brothers. His beard had gotten even longer since I saw him last.

Staring at Callan greeting Judd, I could practically feel each hard muscle of his pressed against me. That almost-kiss had officially gotten under my skin. Heat flooded my core and made me so achy with need, it pissed me off.

"I think we should find some dance partners." I leaped off my chair onto my cowboy boots. The ones with the embroidered flowers along the top that made me feel like I could kick ass.

"And I don't mean any of those boys." I tossed my head in the direction of their table.

A new song came on over the speakers as if the universe was confirming what a great idea I'd had. It was fast paced with a deep beat that made me want to shake my ass. If those boys wanted to crash our girls' night out, they could watch exactly what we did. Dancing the night away after we got a good buzz going was our way of preventing a hangover. I was just moving up the timeline a bit.

"Come on, girls. Dance with me."

I turned and made a beeline for the center of the dance floor. Other couples and groups were already out there, but not so many we couldn't be seen. When I spun back around, my girls were with me, as I knew they would. Hands went in the air, hips were shaking, and sweat began to form. We danced through that song and the next until they all began to blend together. It felt good to move my body. Good to shake it out and set aside my health worries.

Big hands found my hips and suddenly there was a body behind me. Male, if the hard length pressing into me was any indication. The scent of familiar cologne hit, and after a quick second of hesitation, I kept dancing. Callan's hips kept time with mine, the song taking a decidedly sensual turn as his hands gripped me tight. I looked up and saw that Ace had pulled Addy into his arms. Blaze had wrapped Annie up and moved her clear across the dance floor like he needed some privacy. Judd and Meadow were reenacting Dirty Dancing right there for all to see, and hot damn, were they good.

I could have craned my neck to look for Daxon and Ethan, but I didn't care who they found to dance with. Not one little bit. Not when Callan turned me around and speared me with an intense golden-brown gaze that made our clothes seem to go up in flames. My body was an extension of his, his heartbeat keeping time with mine as the music and the bodies pressed in around us. One of his hands slid from my hip and found its way to my ass before he gave it a squeeze that did not scream friend zone in any shape or form.

Time stood still and everything faded away until it was just Callan's hot breath on my neck, the smell of cologne and sweat and something so carnal I found myself wanting to claw at him until his clothes were a thing of the past. I wanted Callan, and if I had any ability at all to read men, he wanted me just as badly.

"Angel," he moaned against my neck, his lips plucking the skin there and sending a shiver down my back.

CHAPTER TWELVE

allan

I SHOULD HAVE LET GO of Cricket. Should have at least put a millimeter of space between her body and mine. Anything to signal that we were, in fact, just friends as I'd spent the first ten minutes of the night professing to my brothers. But then I'd gotten my hands on her and she'd looked up at me with those eyes that were so familiar yet filled with something new.

I found I was plain out of restraint.

Every single male gaze in this place had been on Cricket and her friends as they danced. They were all beautiful in their own way, but no one was like Cricket with her small, ethereal body and white-blonde hair. When some jackass from the bar looked like he was making his way over to her with a cocky look in his eye that made my knuckles itch to connect with his face, I jumped up and slid in where I belonged: attached at the hip to Cricket.

There was no way to hide my erection. Not when her ass was pressed in tight and every beat of the music had her shimmying against me and making things tighter. I forgot where we were and all the eyes that could see us crossing that line. All that mattered was Cricket. My lips got a taste of her skin and I was lost.

"Angel," I breathed against her neck. My next sentence would have shattered any concept of just remaining friends, but a shove from a shoulder had me faltering and Cricket's skin slipped away.

I looked up, ready to push the intruder away and get back to whatever was happening between Cricket and me, but it was Ace and Addy. They danced next to us with a knowing look in their eyes. Cricket ducked her head and rested it in my chest, that special spot just for her.

"Could you dance any closer with your *friend?*" Ace asked, a taunt clear as day in his voice.

"Fuck off, Ace," I growled, knowing I'd have to apologize to Addy later for being an asshole.

Instead of heeding my warning, he burst out laughing, tossing his head back and pissing me off. I got a better grip on Cricket and tried to move away from them. When Ace finally calmed down, he had to steer Addy back in our direction to catch up.

"No more Mr. Nice Guy, huh?" he teased. Addy slapped him on the chest and addressed the side of Cricket's head, the only part visible as she hid in my chest.

"I assume Callan will be taking you home?"

Cricket nodded, still not lifting her head. Addy's laugh was lighter, less making fun and more just a friend finding joy in her friend's circumstances.

"I'll let the rest of them know. You kids get out of here."

"Thanks, Addy," I muttered, giving her a head nod and wondering how I was lucky enough to have a sister-in-law as understanding as her. I had only had brothers growing up, but I quite liked the soft touch of sisters.

"Come on, Cricket. Let's get you home." I tried to pull her off the dance floor, but she dug in her heels. Her cheeks were bright pink and she looked adorable.

"Wait. Let me at least finish my beer." She reached out and snagged her half glass of beer, tossing back her head and chugging it. She slammed it back down on the table empty and wiped her mouth with the back of her hand.

"That shouldn't have been hot, but it was." Like watching an angel take a shot of whiskey. A little bit innocent, a lot debauched.

Cricket shot me a saucy wink and I was officially done with being in the public eye. I ducked and grabbed her, tossing her over my shoulder and storming out of the bar with a few hoots and hollers from people I didn't know.

"What the hell? Callan! Put me down, you brute!" Cricket was beating her fists against my back but it felt like a nice massage.

"Nope. Not taking another chance that someone will interrupt."

I reached my truck and set her down, her hair a mess around her face and steam coming out her ears. She opened her mouth to rip me a new one, but I beat her to it. I tucked a lock of hair behind her ear and backed her up until she was against my truck and out of space to maneuver. I put my hands up on the top of my truck and crowded her. She lifted her chin, showing me she might be tiny, but she was strong. I'd always loved the fighting spirit in my girl.

"Say the word and I'll back off forever, Cricket. All it takes is a simple no and I'll never bring this up again, but I gotta tell you, I don't want to back off. I want to taste your lips and feel your body pressed against me. Preferably with less clothing." I leaned down and traced a kiss along her neck, seeing the way her breathing kicked up to that of a sprinter. "Tell me to stop, angel."

She swallowed hard and every cell in my body froze, waiting for an answer. No matter how much it pained me—and fucking hell would it pain me for the rest of my life—but if she said no, I'd honor that and never let her feel my disappointment.

That moment in the kitchen the other night had shown me a

tiny morsel of hope, that maybe, just maybe, Cricket felt the same heart-stopping excitement when we were together. If there was even a small window of chance, I had to take my shot. Watching my older brothers find love had taken those feelings I'd harbored for Cricket and given them an urgency I could no longer stuff down.

Her blue eyes were eating me up, the flush from earlier turning into a forest fire on her cheeks. Her voice came out on a barely there breath but I still fucking heard it. "I don't want you to stop, Cal."

Blood rushed through my veins, turning sound off and leaving my brain with one last thought. *Heaven.*

My head dropped and my lips were finally on Cricket's. A spotlight from the heavens could have shined down on this moment and I wouldn't have been surprised. Music from the clouds. Glitter thrown from friendly forest animals. This was magical.

Cricket softened, like each fiber in her body let go one at a time. My hand found its way to her jaw, tilting her head while I inhaled against her lips. My eyes were shut but I could see her just the same from the feel of her. Lips caressing, mouth moving until her lips parted ever so slightly.

I groaned into her mouth, my tongue brushing hers in an exquisite dance so intimate my insides turned to hot liquid. She tasted better than I imagined, and I'd imagined plenty. Her hand gripped my forearm and she reached up to pull me closer. I took the kiss deeper and she let me, diving into it with more passion than I could have hoped for.

Fuck, this was good.

Better than good. Better than any kiss I'd ever had. Where there might have been some doubt that things could go to the next level with my childhood best friend, this kiss blew that doubt into a million pieces.

I pulled back just slightly, my eyes popping open to see hers still closed. Her chest lifted and fell rapidly, her lips wet from my kiss. Her hand tightened on my wrist almost painfully right before her eyes fluttered open. They looked hazy. Lost.

"Holy shit," she whispered.

I nodded, a cocky grin growing, knowing she was just as affected as me. I fucking knew it would be this good with Cricket. "Should I keep going or take you home where I can kiss you like I want to in private?"

Her light eyebrows puckered. "There's more to that kiss?"

My hips pushed against hers against my will, seeking some sort of relief from the tension in my jeans. "Angel," I groaned. "Let me show you."

Cricket reached up and brushed a kiss against my lips, stunning me. I'd spent hours, maybe even weeks of cumulative time, thinking about Cricket kissing me and here it was in the flesh. "Take me home, Cal."

I didn't even waste a second breathing. If Cricket wanted me to take her home to take that kiss further, nothing could stop me. Not a forest fire, a downed tree, or a friendly townsperson who wanted to chat about the goddamn weather. I definitely wasn't going to let something like second thoughts stop us. I nearly threw her into the passenger side of my truck before rounding the hood and climbing in behind the wheel.

Before I pulled out of the parking lot, I hooked an arm around Cricket's waist and pulled her over to me, thanking the nameless soul who had the foresight to make bench seats. She let out a squeak, but buckled up next to me, her small hand landing on my thigh. I grit my teeth and pulled out onto the road. The sooner I got home, the sooner I could get her lips back on mine. I probably drove a little too fast, but I couldn't let the moment pass. I'd waited too long for this to drive the speed limit.

Headlights bounced over the front of my house as I came into the driveway hot. I killed the engine and unbuckled our seat belts. Cricket giggled as I practically sprang from the truck and turned back for her.

"In a hurry?" she teased.

"Fuck, yes, I am." I put my hands on her waist and helped her down, letting her slide against the erection that had been plaguing me since I started dancing with her. "A hot chick at the bar said I could kiss her again."

"A hot chick, huh? You pick those up often?"

I found her hand and slid our fingers together, pulling her to my door. "Nah. Why do that when I have the hottest one right here?" I pressed her up against my door and buried my hand in her hair, tilting her head back so I could lay another kiss on her. She was anticipating it, opening immediately with a breathy moan. I stepped between her legs, nudging them apart until I could press my erection against the heat of her, dry humping her like a desperate teenager.

"Fuck," I growled, pulling back and reaching around her to unlock the door. "Get inside, vixen."

Cricket giggled, but walked inside. "Demanding thing you are."

I laid my hands on her waist and twirled her back around, dead serious. "When it comes to something I want, absolutely. And I want you, Cricket."

Cricket raised her arms to rest her hands on my shoulders. "And as crazy as it sounds, I want you too."

I dipped my head to kiss her, but stopped just an inch away.

"This isn't the beer talking, right?" I asked, a morsel of doubt trickling in and trying to ruin my dream come true.

Cricket pulled back, fire spitting from her eyes. "I had one beer! I'm not that much of a lightweight."

I kissed the anger away, plucking at her lips until she was breathing hard for a different reason. When she opened her eyes again, I made sure she understood where I was coming from. This wasn't an experimentation. A momentary thrill of the forbidden. Not for me. This was something that would forever change our lives, and I needed to know she was on the same page.

"Just making sure. Because once you're mine, there's no going back, Cricket. Tap out now if you're not ready for that."

Her gaze held steady on mine. "I think I've always been yours, Cal."

I gave my head a shake, liking what she was saying but needing her to know there was so much more. "Not like it's been. I want everything from you, Cricket. And in return I'll give you all of me."

She swallowed hard. I didn't see doubt in her eyes so much as fear. "And what if all of me turns out to be a mess of medical issues that doesn't seem worth the effort?"

Anger burned against my skin. I hated that she saw herself as a mess. I didn't give two fucks what medical issues she had now or would have in the future. That had no bearing on loving the soul that she was.

"You don't need to worry about that. When I say I'm all in, I'm all in, angel. Nothing is too much."

Her eyes got wet, but still she didn't look away. "I'm in too," she said quietly.

I tapped my hand against my stomach, done with warning her. If she was all in, then she needed to know that the nice guy persona ended behind closed doors. I'd make sure she came at least three times for my every one, but I had some pent-up sexual urges to unleash first.

"Then jump up here and wrap your legs around my waist. I promised you a kiss."

Her face melted into a soft smile and then she jumped.

CHAPTER THIRTEEN

ricket

CALLAN had me up against the living room wall, an erection the size of the Titanic pressed between my legs, and his tongue exploring all corners of my mouth. I had a sea of wetness he could sink into but he seemed determined to take his time. Damn Callan and his thoroughness. There was so much to focus on here, my brain couldn't settle on any one thing. Mostly, I was just kissing the hell out of my best friend and enjoying the ride. Who would have thought the night would end up here? Certainly not me.

Callan growled and then pulled away, his hips still pinning me to the wall, but his hands leaving my body. I moaned and tried to pull him back in, but moving Callan was like trying to move a boulder. If he didn't want to, he wasn't budging. My eyes flew open and I saw his jaw looked a lot like that boulder too. His hands were in his hair, pulling and tugging at the strands like he was facing an internal battle.

Then he leaned in, wrapped his arms around my back and pulled me away from the wall.

"Where are we going?" I asked breathlessly, hoping with everything I had that we were headed to Callan's bed. I had a V-card I desperately wanted to turn in.

Callan didn't answer, but he did deposit me on the couch. I decided quickly that the couch would also work just fine. Hell, the floor or even the front driveway would be acceptable at this point. What was a little road rash for the orgasm of a lifetime? I reached for him, but he walked around to sit at the opposite end of the couch, eyeing me warily.

I wasn't an expert by any means, but this seemed like a detour from the normal pattern of events. Shouldn't clothes be coming off by now?

"Callan?"

"Shh," he practically snapped, flopping down on the couch.

"Did you just shush me?" I was starting to think that no matter how hot that man was, I was not handing over the goods after being shushed. Which was a goddamn shame because I had been seconds away from climbing him like a tree.

"We're not having sex, Cricket. Not yet."

I frowned. "Okay..."

He huffed and pressed down on his lap, shifting uncomfortably. Good. I hoped that erection plagued him all night long and stole his sleep. After the kisses he'd delivered tonight, I wouldn't be sleeping either.

He turned in my direction, those familiar brown eyes boring into mine. "I want to. Badly. You have no idea how badly."

I lifted an eyebrow and looked down at his lap. "I have an idea."

He put his hands out like he wanted to touch me and then let them drop to the couch. "No, that's just it. Yes, of course I want you. But I want so much more than that. I'm afraid that if we jump right into sex, that's all you'll think this is. I'm scared of messing this up, angel."

I sucked in a deep breath, the fog of intense attraction lifting enough to let the worry bleed in. Of course that was a concern for me too. I didn't want to change our relationship if it meant ruining our friendship. Callan and I had been fused at the hip for so long, I couldn't fathom a life without him in it.

"I'm scared too."

Callan reached for me then, pulling me into his side and wrapping his arm around my shoulders. I found that I craved the heat and weight of him, snuggling into his side to stave off the cold fear that had crept in.

"Then let's take this slow. Let's do this right. One small step at a time so we don't make a misstep."

I nodded against his chest. "Sounds super logical and practical."

Callan huffed out a laugh. "You hate it."

I grinned up at him. "I don't hate it. I think I might like seeing all your steps, Mr. Hellman. I just want to make sure we can throw in some non-practical things along the way so I don't get itchy."

Callan leaned down and chastely pressed his lips to mine, immediately causing my heart to tap out a faster rhythm. Yes, indeed, I would enjoy seeing how Callan moved us along the steps from best friends to lovers. Now that I'd had a taste, I wanted the full Hellman experience.

"Let's go to bed," Callan whispered. Then he kissed his way down my neck and everything in me melted. He could ask for anything right about now and I'd probably agree. In the back of my mind, I knew that should make me worried, but I couldn't muster the energy to care.

"I'm getting mixed signals," I whispered absentmindedly, shivers breaking out across my skin as his head moved lower. What my nipples wouldn't give right now for some attention.

Callan's head came back up with the sexiest smirk I'd ever seen from him. "You're sleeping with me. Fully clothed."

I stuck my bottom lip out. "When did you get so bossy?"

"When you agreed to date me." He winked and stood up, pulling me up with him.

"Did I agree to date you?" I teased him.

He halted and turned on me, that intense look in his eye that made something in my chest roar to life. "Hell yes, you did. There are no take-backs, Cricket."

I poked him in the stomach just to feel up his abs. I was dating those abs now. I felt a little delirious and a lot light-headed, to be honest. It was going to take my brain some time to wrap itself around this new arrangement.

"I'm just teasing. I'm in, remember? Now, let's go sleep together."

Callan grinned and led the way to his bedroom. "I'm going to regret this 'going slow' thing, aren't I?"

I laughed, kicking off my shoes and eyeing his big bed. "That's my objective, yes."

And then Callan pushed his jeans down to reveal tented navy-blue boxers. My mouth went dry at the sight. Sure, I'd seen Callan half naked before, but that had been when we were just friends. Now that my body had been introduced to his in a definite not-friend way, I was seeing things differently. Callan's thighs were the stuff that made a rugby scout take notice. Thick, muscled, and just a sprinkling of hair.

"You're staring, Cricket."

I looked up to see Callan smirking. I stuck my tongue out at him and forced myself to move into the adjoining bathroom to splash water on my heated cheeks. The man's ego was big enough already. I didn't need to be staring at him with my mouth hanging open, no matter how badly I wanted to.

When I came out of the bathroom, Callan was in bed already. I crawled in and hugged the side of the mattress, suddenly self-conscious. What was the protocol here? Did I snuggle up to him like I would if we were just friends still? Or did I give him space so we didn't skip over too many of his so-called steps?

"Get over here, Cricket."

Callan's velvety voice sent a shiver through me, but I was anything but cold. I rolled over, and as soon as I made contact with his side, his thick arm came to wrap around me, holding me tight.

"Good night, Cricket."

"'Night, Callan."

There was no fucking way I was falling asleep anytime tonight or even in the early hours of the morning. Too much had happened tonight. Too much hot, muscly man was pressed against me. My brain felt like it had consumed a gallon of nitro coffee right before bed.

"Go to sleep, Cricket," Callan whispered gruffly.

I snorted at his command—as if it was that simple—and he squeezed me tighter. I catalogued all the spots where we were touching, rejoicing in each one of them, allowing myself to settle into this new feeling that had bloomed between us. Before I knew it, the warmth from Callan's body had made me drowsy, and all the racing thoughts shifted into dreams that kept me asleep all night.

I woke slowly, taking a few deep breaths before I could recall all that had transpired the night before. A smile plastered to my face—even before my green tea caffeine—feeling Callan's arms still banded tightly around me. We'd shifted during the night and I was lying on my other side. Callan was a freaking heat rock at my back. If I wasn't mistaken, there was something pressing against my ass that told me Callan liked me very much, even in his sleep.

I tried to roll and get out of bed, thinking of the morning appointments I had to get to. Thankfully, it was Saturday and I only had a half day. But Callan's arms tightened around me and he wouldn't let me go. He groaned and kissed my shoulder. I wiggled my hips and earned myself a louder groan from behind me.

"Stop that, woman." His voice was rough and deep. It wasn't like his voice had suddenly changed since we decided to date a mere eight hours ago, but yet there was a quality to it that I could have sworn was different. An intimacy difference maybe? Whatever it was, I liked it. Very much.

"I have to work, mister." I tugged halfheartedly at his hands, but they didn't give an inch.

"No. Forget work. Just stay in bed with me all day." His voice was muffled from against my neck.

I snuggled in closer for just a moment. "As lovely as that sounds, I actually have a client today who wants to do a fun color."

I felt Callan's head lift. "Really?"

I nodded. "I'm actually pretty excited about it. If I do one more wash and set, I might scream."

He hummed against my shoulder, the sound more of a vibration I felt everywhere. "We can't have that. If you're screaming, it's going to be because of what I'm doing to your body."

Then it was my turn to groan. "Seriously? How am I going to leave now?"

Callan chuckled, rolling me over and climbing on top of me. I opened my legs and let him settle there. God, he felt good. His hair was messed up from sleep and yet I didn't think he'd ever looked better. He held himself up by his arms, those muscles flexing over and around me. Desire was like a tidal wave, crashing over me and making me crazy with it. My hips moved on their own, seeking out more of what was pressed against me. And for one glorious minute, Callan let me grind against him, taking what I wanted before he leaned down to kiss me quick and roll off.

"Go to work, woman. I can't have you missing your first opportunity for doing what you love."

I swore my eyes were crossed. "What if what I want to do is you?" I was not above begging. Not at all. No pride left here. Polly would understand if I was a little bit late because I was getting my rocks off with a Hellman brother. Wait, no she wouldn't. It was Polly, after all. She'd lecture me on the ways in which a man would simply distract me from reaching my full potential as a woman.

Callan slapped me on the ass and swooped out of bed. "Work, then play. As much as that pains me to say."

And before I could admire the sleepy look of my new boyfriend, he was in the bathroom, door shut, leaving me no choice but to get up and get dressed in the guest room. I flounced out of Callan's bedroom, feeling no more mature than a toddler with all the huffing and dramatics I was throwing around. By the time I got dressed and ran a brush through my hair, I was over my snit and excited to dye some color.

Callan hollered from the kitchen, "I've got breakfast ready!"

I sailed into the kitchen and admired the casual sweatpants and clean T-shirt Callan had on. "No work for you today?"

"Nope. Taking today and tomorrow off." He handed me a plate with scrambled eggs and one piece of perfectly toasted sourdough bread with melted butter. "My girlfriend has a birthday."

I took the plate from his hands, my brain pausing for one horrifying minute until I realized I was the girlfriend he spoke of. "Oh yeah." I'd actually forgotten about my birthday. Who could blame me with six feet and three inches of handsome in front of me?

He ate from his plate while I ate mine, both of us sitting at the bar like we were a real couple. Which we were. Damn. I really needed to get my head around this new development. I felt his gaze on me until I finished every last bite. In some ways, Callan was worse than my parents, yet I didn't feel annoyed by his attention. I felt cherished.

"Done, daddy," I teased, putting the fork down on my empty plate.

Callan growled and stood up to hover over me, his hands on

either side of the bar, pinning me in. "I like the way you call me daddy."

My cheeks went hot, realizing how he must have taken my statement. "Yeah?" I asked, quite out of breath. This was all uncharted territory to me. I'd had boyfriends, sure. But not one of them had inspired red cheeks, heart palpitations, and sincere contemplation of ditching my business for more time in bed.

He kissed my forehead and backed off, collecting our plates and heading for the sink. "I'll drive you in."

I was still catching my breath. "Thanks for breakfast."

He kept up a steady string of conversation the whole way to work. I answered appropriately, which I considered a win. I actually felt like I needed just a second without him polluting my airspace. Just a second to get my head screwed on straight and catch up to all the ways things were progressing.

When we got to the salon, he parked next to Polly's car and got out with me, holding the door and gesturing for me to walk in first. Kennedy was just putting her purse behind the front counter and Polly was perusing the magazines in the waiting area.

"Good morning, ladies!" I called brightly, hyper aware of Callan behind me.

All eyes were on me when Callan slid his arm around my waist and turned me around.

"See you in a few hours?" he asked quietly.

I didn't even care who was watching. Not when Callan was looking at me like he'd be counting the minutes until we were together again. "Yep."

He dipped his head and placed a kiss on my lips that was far more innocent than the ones before, yet affected me just as much. "Step one: make it public," he said against my mouth with a look of mischief that only added to his appeal.

Then he lifted his head and shot me a wink before walking to the door. "Good day, ladies," he called to Kennedy and Polly.

I watched him go, only pulling my gaze away when his truck

was out of sight. Kennedy's mouth was open, her eyes wide with shock. Polly was grinning like she'd caught a couple making out in the caves by the ocean.

I guess we were telling people about dating.

And as Polly pulled out her phone, thumbs dancing across the screen in rapid-fire, I knew the news would spread townwide by the time I closed up shop today.

CHAPTER FOURTEEN

allan

EVER HAD that feeling that everything in life was coming together exactly how it was destined to? That was me, bouncing along the road in my truck, the taste of Cricket still on my lips. This was it. The moment I'd been dreaming of and planning for. Nothing could bring me down from this high. Nothing could deter me from the course change that Cricket and I had implemented in the last twenty-four hours.

I was going to do every damn thing right so I didn't screw it up.

Which meant I was on my way to Mr. and Mrs. VanHunting's house to give them the news about Cricket and me dating. I wasn't asking permission so much as heading off the rumors. They deserved to hear it straight from my mouth and not some busybody.

Cricket's parents had generally been kind to me over the years, but I always got the sense that her father didn't fully approve of our friendship given that we were opposite sex.

While he mostly tolerated me, Debbie seemed to actually like me. My job was to convince Hank that, while I wasn't some country club kid like he kept setting Cricket up with, I was exactly right for his daughter.

Their large coastal house came into view right by the edge of the water. They'd always lived in one of the largest homes in Auburn Hill. The story was that Hank was an up-and-coming real estate investor in San Francisco when Cricket was just a baby. He'd had a cardiac-related event that scared him, prompting him to make drastic changes. They'd moved out here to the ocean, slowing their lives down and focusing on raising Cricket, which was probably why he was overly involved in her love life. He still sold real estate in the surrounding counties, but on a much smaller scale than before.

The sound of my truck door closing echoed between the trees that lined their driveway. If I held still, I could hear the crash of the waves below. When we were little, they'd had a hammock tied between two trees on the side of their yard. Cricket and I would play for hours and then collapse onto the hammock. That rope would dig into our skin, but we'd swing there together until we were so relaxed we were almost asleep. If anyone asked what my best childhood memory was, it would be that time spent swinging in the hammock with Cricket.

The front door swung open and Debbie filled the doorway. It was only nine o'clock on a Saturday but she was already dressed in a pair of slacks and colorful blouse. Her face split into a smile.

"Why, Callan, what are you doing here?" She hustled down the steps of the porch and threw her arms around me. Then she lurched back, a look of alarm written across her dark eyebrows. "Is Cricket okay?"

"Yes, totally fine," I reassured her. "Just dropped her off at work, but I wanted to talk to you and Mr. VanHunting."

She patted my chest. "It's Hank and Debbie. I've told you that more times than I've told Cricket to eat something. Come on in."

I followed her inside the house, settling on the couch when she led us into the front living room. Cricket always hated this room. Said the furniture wasn't meant for sitting. She preferred the puffy sectional in the playroom upstairs even though we'd dumped more snacks and drinks on it over the years than any one piece of furniture should have to endure.

"Let me just go get Hank." Debbie left the room, leaving me with the ticktock of the grandfather clock in the corner. Each second that passed ratcheted up my nerves. If it was just Debbie, I'd feel fine. It was Hank's reaction that had me concerned.

Hank and Debbie entered the living room, Debbie with a smile and Hank with a quizzical look above his slacks and polo shirt. Hank shook my hand and had a seat in the straight-back chair across from me. Debbie sat on the other end of the couch.

"What can I do for you, Callan?" Hank looked at his watch. It was a slight movement, but enough to signal that I didn't rank in importance. He had a busy day and I was intruding on it.

"I wanted to talk with you both before the rumor mill reached your door." Better to just jump right in. "Cricket and I are dating."

Debbie let out a yelp and pressed a hand to her mouth. Hank frowned, leaning forward to rest his elbows on his knees.

"Since when?" Hank asked.

"Since yesterday, sir."

He studied me as Debbie reached over to pat my arm. Based on the size of her smile, I guessed she was happy about this arrangement. Hank, on the other hand, looked far from impressed.

"And this is what Cricket wants?"

I nodded, feeling confident about that at least. "Yes, sir."

"Well, I'm just thrilled," Debbie interjected when Hank didn't say anything further.

"Settle down, Deb," he said quietly. Anger prickled at my skin. My mother didn't raise us boys to speak to a woman like that and hearing him say that to Cricket's mom was making me mighty uncomfortable.

Hank crossed his arms over his chest. "Cricket's young and fanciful. She needs a man to keep her grounded. I like you, Callan, but you just give her whatever she wants. She needs a stronger man than that."

That anger bubbling below the surface was threatening to blow. He had a lot of nerve saying I spoiled Cricket. First, there wasn't anything wrong with that, and second, he was one to talk.

"Seems a lot like how you treat her, sir."

"Excuse me?" Hank looked as pissed as I felt.

"You bought her the salon, the apartment, the car. You even find her dates. Maybe you spoil her more than me."

Hank's eyes narrowed. "I'm her father."

"I'm her best friend. And now her boyfriend." I may have been Mr. Nice Guy according to Cricket and my brothers, but this was one pissing match I didn't plan to back down from.

Debbie jumped off the couch and clapped her hands. "Well, now that we have all that settled, I'm so happy you told us, Callan. You know I hate to involve myself in town gossip, but Poppy and her friends don't seem to give one much chance to escape it. Did you know that when Cricket had her seizure, it was spread around town before we even got to the hospital to check on her?" Debbie shook her head, trying to change the subject and clear the tension in the room. "I don't like to hear about my own family's wellbeing from a stranger. Don't you agree, Hank?"

She smacked him on the shoulder. He blinked up at her and nodded, agreeing, though I was sure he had no idea what he was agreeing to.

"Didn't you say you had a conference call, Hank?"

Hank gave me one last glare and stood. I stood too, making sure he knew I beat him by three inches in height.

"Mr. VanHunting." I extended my hand, and after a second of hesitation, he shook it.

Without a single further word, he exited the room. Debbie and I watched him go, that damn grandfather clock in sync with his steps. When we heard the door to his office close, Debbie turned to me with an apologetic smile.

"I don't know what gets into him sometimes, but he is certainly protective of our little girl." She rubbed her hand up and down my arm, reminding me of all the times she stepped in to mother me when I visited this house years ago.

"I understand. But I also know Cricket wants to live her own life. Make her own decisions."

"He'll come around, Callan, don't you worry."

I gave Debbie a hug and excused myself. There wasn't much I could do right now to change Hank's mind. I did what needed to be done and now I had a birthday party to plan for my girlfriend. Debbie walked me out and waved until my truck turned out of their driveway.

I spent the drive back into town on the phone, telling my mom about Cricket and me. She screamed so loud I almost swerved off the road. Needless to say, she was happy for us. Then I made a few calls to set things in motion for Cricket's birthday. Considering it was tomorrow, I hadn't given myself much time to put it together. I'd been so focused on the change in our relationship, I'd failed to make birthday plans. Hopefully what I was able to get done would show her how much she meant to me.

Lastly, I parked on Main Street and swung by Shelby's place to pick up two bouquets of flowers. My phone started vibrating in my pocket, one notification after the other. While Shelby put Cellophane around the bouquets, I checked it. Just the brother text string blowing up. I'm sure Mom had called each of them to share the news. I rolled my eyes and stuffed the phone back in my pocket. I didn't have time for their nonsense. Not when I had a girl to woo.

I walked over to the salon with the flowers, earning myself a few whistles and even a squeal from Annie when she saw me through the window of her vet clinic and ran outside to thump me on the back. Guess the news had traveled.

Polly was exiting the salon with her normal gray hair on one side and a kaleidoscope of colors on the other side. She turned and saw me, her face lighting up at the sight of the flowers.

"Cricket gave me mermaid hair!"

I stopped and checked it out, amazed that Cricket was able to do that many colors and make it look good. "You look amazing."

Polly rang her fingers through her hair, looking years younger. "Cricket's amazing. Then again, you already know that, don't you, young man?" She pointedly looked at the flowers.

"Yes, ma'am, I do. Now if you'll excuse me, I have a birthday girl to celebrate."

Polly sighed and stepped aside to let me into the salon. "Ah, young love. So full of hope," she said wistfully.

Kennedy lifted her head at the front desk as I stepped inside. She gave me a shy smile and pointed over her shoulder. "She's just closing up."

"Hey, Callan," Cricket called from the back by the wash bowls where she was sweeping the floor. "Are those for me?" Her face lit up, seeing the flowers.

"Actually, they're for you," I handed one bouquet to Kennedy, whose mouth dropped open as she accepted the flowers. "And the other one is for you." I walked over to hand it to Cricket.

She took the bundle and buried her nose in it before reaching up to give me a hug. "You're good, Mr. Hellman. Very good."

"Step two in wooing my girl," I murmured in her hair.

Cricket pulled back. "Flowers for my front desk girl? That's next-level wooing."

I shot her a wink. "You deserve the best. And a happy front desk girl takes care of my girl when I'm not here."

The color in her cheeks was all the thanks I needed.

"Go have a seat. I'm almost done."

I leaned down to kiss her and then moved to the table and chairs in the front. There on the table was a page that looked like it had been ripped out of a magazine. I picked it up and read the advertisement. It was for some kind of hair contest in New York City.

"What's this?" I asked, holding it up.

Cricket squinted and then snorted. "Just Polly, thinking I should take my mermaid hair skills to New York."

I nodded, thinking that sounded amazing. "You should."

Cricket shot me a squint that smashed her lips together, but I could see the excitement in her eyes. "Nah, I'm good right here."

While she kept cleaning up, I took the ad and folded it, shoving it in my pocket for later. Cricket was always complaining about wash and sets and perms. Maybe trying out her skills in New York would be good for her creative side.

I had a seat and pulled out my phone, scanning through the texts I'd received.

Ethan: Congrats, Callan! We love Cricket.

Daxon: You and Cricket, huh? Who would have guessed? Oh, that's right. Everyone.

Ace: Addy is officially freaking out over this news. I'm super happy for you, bro.

Blaze: Lucky for you she has no brothers to give you shit...

Ethan: Ben came around eventually.

Blaze: True, but those two weeks of him hating me were torture.

Daxon: Maybe you shouldn't have slept with his sister in his bed, you dumbass.

Ace: Can we just focus on Callan for a second? He's literally been in love with this girl for years.

Ethan: Yeah, he even punched Alistair at your reception. That's love, man.

Daxon: You bought flowers for Kennedy too? BRO. Stop that shit. You're gonna make the rest of us look bad.

I rolled my eyes and stuffed my phone back in my pocket.

Gossip spread faster than pink eye around this town. Cricket flopped down on my lap and my attention was officially only on her.

"I'll let you take me to lunch," she said nuzzling her nose against my neck.

"Wait. Today's not your birthday." I was only teasing her. If Cricket wanted lunch, I'd take her wherever sounded good to her.

She slapped my chest and made to get off my lap. I held her there, liking the way she felt in my arms. "I'm just kidding. Where to, almost-birthday-girl?"

Cricket shot me a grin that lit up every single cell in my body.

This energy in my veins? This had to be joy.

CHAPTER FIFTEEN

ricket

THE COMBINATION of the very best chocolate truffle melting on my tongue, a massage by three European male models, and a limitless credit card for a trip to Target couldn't even top what was currently happening to my body. I shifted my hips, wanting more. So much more. My girlie parts had gone to heaven and I wasn't ever going to come back. Not even if Cosmo magazine named me their top hairstylist of the year.

But then everything started to fade away. I could feel myself whimpering, but I couldn't hear it through the misty fog. If this was only a dream, I didn't want to wake up. I clung to the sensations that had turned my skin inside out, but sleep abandoned me. Reality wrenched me back to the present and what a reality it was.

I was lying in Callan's bed. The ceiling fan above me oscillated on low, the gentle breeze cooling my burning skin. The man, the legend—my freaking boyfriend—was under the covers and between my legs.

"Callan!" I gasped, jolting violently. Lightning could have come down and struck my clitoris and I still wouldn't have been more electrified.

His facial scruff stung my thighs as he lifted his head and tented the sheets. I could only see one of his eyes, but it was positively burning. I guessed that made for two of us.

"You want me to stop, angel?" His voice was deep, dark, maybe even a little bit taunting.

"God, no," I managed to wheeze out on a single exhale.

"Tell me how much you like my tongue between your legs and I'll get back to work."

I swallowed hard. I wasn't a dirty talker. I didn't think. Hell, maybe I was and just didn't know it yet. "Um, so much?"

The sheet shifted as he shook his head. Disappointment bloomed in my chest. *Shit, come on, Cricket. You can do better.*

"You get one more try." Callan's quaking muscles vibrated the bed as he held himself above me, one quivering mass of solid muscle that looked ready to devour me if I could just spit out the right words.

I was desperate for more. Desperate for Callan in a way I didn't think was possible. In a voice I didn't even recognize, I let myself ask for exactly what I wanted. "Please go back to what you were doing to my pussy because if you don't, I really do think I'll die right this second, Callan."

That eye burned even hotter, and on a growl, he dove back under the covers and attacked me. His tongue flicked my clit so fast and furious I could have sworn he swiped one of my vibrators from my apartment. But it was all Callan as he pushed one finger inside of me. I whimpered again, not sure if I was going up in flames or having an electrical problem that was shorting out my brain. I couldn't think. Couldn't form words. Couldn't even remember my own freaking name. Little bright lights began to explode behind my eyelids. My breaths came in pants. And then the whole world went white as icy cold fire spilled across my skin.

Pretty sure I passed out for a few seconds, lost in some mystical land of orgasms. My whole body quaked like a newbie caught in the crosshairs of Poppy's attention. My brain flitted through the clouds while my extremities tingled. I only came back to reality when Callan pulled me into his side and shook the bed with his laughter.

"Shh," I moaned, still screwing my eyes shut to chase the last few zings of pleasure that were coursing through my body. "I'm still in orgasmland. It's like Disneyland, but way, way better."

His manly giggle made my lips turn up on the ends. Even interrupting my ride through orgasmland, Callan could make me smile with that laugh of his.

"Please tell me they don't have a rat mascot in orgasmland." Callan's voice was morning-time raspy, the laughter still detectible.

I didn't care if he was laughing at me. He could laugh at me all day long if he kept giving me orgasms like that. I wrenched one eye open and glared at him. His hair was a mess. I reached up and tried to pat it down, but he batted my hand away.

"I like my hair messed up from your hands gripping it tight."

The rumble of his voice, the fact that just minutes ago he'd been facedown between my legs, was giving me all kinds of weird shivers in my gut. Who would have thought that my best friend was capable of giving orgasms like that and I'd just been friends with him all these years? I could have been on the receiving end of that instead of dealing with snot buckets like Alistair.

I was such an idiot.

Before he could bat me away again, I darted below the covers, aiming for the erection that normally pressed against my ass during the night as he held me close as if he was afraid I'd get away while he slept. I only made the briefest of contacts with it before Callan's huge hands were lifting me back up.

"No way!" His chest bounced as he laughed again. He held me under the armpits like I was a wayward child.

I felt my lower lip roll down. "But I want to play too."

Callan reached up and plucked a kiss from my pout before laying me down on the bed and climbing out from beneath the covers. His erection was doing damage to his boxers. Why the hell wouldn't he let me help him out? I may still have my V-card, but I'd given a blow job here and there. I wasn't without *some* skills.

"Why can't—"

Callan leaned over me suddenly, cutting me off and bracketing me against the mattress. "Angel. It's your birthday."

My face lit up. I'd nearly forgotten. "Which means you have to give me what I want. I want to give you a blow job." I smirked up at him, feeling very proud of myself for my excellent logic.

Callan's jaw tightened and I could have sworn his eyes lit on fire. I squirmed on the bed, feeling like a powerful woman able to evoke such feelings from him. But then he opened his mouth and I lost all trains of thought except one.

"When I let you give me a blow job, I plan to make you gag on my cock, angel. So no. Not on your birthday." He bopped me on the nose with his finger and walked out of the room.

I lay there stunned, oddly turned on, and wondering what was wrong with me for wanting to gag on Callan's cock more than I wanted to celebrate my own birthday.

"Let's go, birthday girl!" Callan stuck his head back in the room, fully dressed.

I blinked and wondered how long I'd spaced out on that last thought. Based on the heat level of my cheeks, I'd have to guess it was longer than a minute or two. I'd have to come back to that thought later when I could go over it with a fine-tooth comb, or whatever was the brain equivalent for perseverating on a topic so incredibly foreign yet wildly stimulating.

I flung my hands in Callan's general direction. "Out, mister."

One light-brown eyebrow rose so wickedly on his handsome face that I froze in the process of climbing out of bed. "I can't watch you dress, angel? I just had my face between your legs."

And there went my face again. Flaming hot and so turned on

I couldn't think straight. He chuckled and left the room, granting me the reprieve I desperately needed to get myself together. I threw on a sundress, sandals, and then treated myself to an elaborate braid that tucked into the back of my hair, leaving the rest down in beachy waves. A few swipes of mascara later and I was ready to go. Definitely no need for blush with Callan around.

I found him by the door on his phone. When he heard me approach, he pocketed his phone and gave me a scorching hot look from head to toe and back again.

"Dammit, angel. You're stunning." He took me by the hands and pulled me in to place a kiss on my forehead. "Happy birthday," he whispered against my skin.

I smiled into his neck, not needing anything else to make this the most special birthday I'd ever had. No, it wasn't the trip to orgasmland. It wasn't even the look Callan gave me when he saw me in my sundress. It was the way I was his whole focus when I was in the room.

When I'd been with Alistair, and pretty much every other male before him, I'd always felt like a burden. Or an afterthought. Alistair would barely get off his phone to answer me. Callan dropped everything while in the middle of a work shift to buy me tampons. I wondered why the hell I'd ever put up with anything less.

"What are we doing today?" I asked as soon as Callan stepped back and opened the door for me, one hand remaining on my back.

He wasn't looking at me when he replied, which automatically made me suspicious. "Just a few things."

I narrowed my eyes, but allowed him to steer me toward his truck. When I finally looked away from him, I nearly tripped. His arm slid around my waist to steady me.

There in the driveway was his truck where we'd left it the night before, but there'd been a few modifications. Every window was decorated in multicolored chalk paint in variations of "Happy Birthday, Cricket!" or "an angel was born today." A crooked happy face, a heart that looked a bit like a round blob, and what might have been balloons (but looked like tiny sperm) were drawn badly around the words.

I sputtered, not able to get words out. It was the most hideously sweet thing anyone had done for me. His normally manly-looking truck looked ridiculous. And I fucking loved it.

"You—you did this?" I turned to peer up at Callan. He was watching me react, not looking at his truck. Because of course he was. The man always had his eyes on me.

He nodded, looking a touch embarrassed but owning it just the same.

I threw my arms around his waist and reached up to place a kiss on his collarbone, which was as high as I could reach without breaking out a ladder. "Thank you, Cal."

He didn't give me a chance to grab that ladder. He swooped down to wrap his arms around my waist and lift me clean off the ground. His mouth found mine and he devoured me right there in his driveway. Our tongues were exploring each other when the toot of a horn broke us apart. We both turned our heads to see James driving by in the postal service van. He gave a smirky head nod to Callan, as if giving him a mental high five for making out with a girl in broad daylight.

I shook my head as Callan reluctantly lowered me back to the ground. "That James is almost as bad as Poppy." The old woman had retired from the postal service, but she'd remained just as nosy in retirement. Seemed she even taught her protege, James, to interfere in personal things like driveway kisses. Nothing was sacred or private in a small town. Not when Poppy and her minions had their eyes everywhere.

"Hop in, birthday girl." Callan held the truck door open for me, helping me up and waiting until I'd buckled myself in. He shut the door and rounded the hood to climb behind the wheel.

"Where to?" I asked yet again, hoping he'd actually tell me what we were doing.

He shrugged and backed out of the driveway. "Just a simple picnic. Hope that's not too lame."

A picnic with my hot boyfriend? Not lame at all.

"I love that idea. Maybe if you pick a really private spot, I can work on giving that birthday blow job."

Callan jerked the wheel and I giggled. He shook his head at me and focused on driving through town.

"Still catches me by surprise."

I knew what he meant, maybe because we'd been finishing each other's thoughts for years already. "I know. I keep trying to pinch myself to see if this is real between us."

Callan reached over and laced our fingers together, squeezing me tight. "It's real, all right."

I looked off into the midday sun, smiling like only the girl with the hottest boyfriend in a fifty-mile radius could. I saw Shelby's flower shop up ahead. I leaned forward and squinted at the sign outside on the sidewalk.

"Hey! It says Happy Birthday, Cricket!"

I pointed to the sign, ecstatic that Shelby had thought of me. Then I saw Annie's vet clinic had something similar outside, except this sign had balloons attached.

I was so busy reading the birthday signs and gasping and pointing, I didn't realize until we hit my own salon that Callan was not acting the least bit surprised. Kennedy was on the sidewalk surrounded by several of the old ladies with matching curled gray hair. I knew them immediately since I did their hair every week, complaining about all the wash and sets I had to do. They saw our truck and waved their bony arms in the air. Kennedy shook her happy birthday sign and I felt so touched I honestly thought about giving her a raise I couldn't afford quite yet.

"Everyone's so sweet!" I gushed, leaning out the window to wave back. Callan finally made it to the other side of town, pulling into a parking space by the park. I turned to look at him, just then realizing that he'd had a hand in today's shenanigans. "Did you put this together?"

Callan shook his head, busy collecting his keys and wallet. "Nope. I just suggested it when a few people asked what they could do for your birthday."

I narrowed my eyes at him. He'd totally put it together. And I loved him for it. I leaned over to kiss him, but he moved back.

"Your parents," he whispered out of the side of his mouth.

I turned to see my mom smiling and waving just past the hood of the truck. My dad was there too, but he was busy glaring at Callan.

"Oh my God. My parents." There went the idea for the birthday blow job.

I jumped out of the truck and threw my arms around Mom and then Dad. I looked past them to see all kinds of people in the park, balloons and streamers chaotically decorated around the main pavilion. Meadow, Addy, and Annie put down the trays of food they'd been organizing and waved. Clients of mine stood around chatting in groups. I even saw Poppy and Yedda by the drink table adding who knew what to the punch bowl. Lucy Sutter was ushering a pack of little kids toward a bouncy house set up in the back. A piñata swung from the lowest branch of the oak tree next to the pavilion. Half the damn town turned out.

I looked back at Callan who stood there a bit awkwardly next to my parents. My heart felt a bit like it might burst.

"Happy birthday, Cricket," Callan said, his voice deep and solemn.

I walked back to his side and then launched myself at him at the last second, not giving two shits that Dad had to be shooting laser beams of disappointment at the back of my head. I crushed Callan to me and whispered in the general direction of his ear.

"Thank you for the birthday party." I wanted to say something far more eloquent, but that's all that came out. My throat felt like it might just close despite myself.

I felt Callan shrug even as he hugged me back, his voice low. "I remember you lamenting the adult dinners your parents always had for your birthday. Figured you were due for a real birthday party."

And that right there was when I fell for Callan. I didn't just love him. I'd spent almost my whole damn life loving him. But this was different. I was head over heels, screaming in giddy delight, in love with the man who remembered every little thing I said.

The whole time I talked and ate and played my way through my very first birthday party, I kept one eye on Callan. After all, he now held my heart in his capable hands.

CHAPTER SIXTEEN

allan

I MIGHT HAVE to move out of Hell.

Not because I wanted to leave my hometown, but more so because I was starting to identify with the town to the south of us. Blueball.

I'd never researched the effects of suppressing sexual urges to the point of constant pain, but I had to believe it wasn't good for your future ability to procreate. It wasn't doing good things to my mood either. My brothers were steering clear of me, which was a blessing in disguise. I didn't want to spend time with those assholes anyway. All my time and attention was focused on Cricket and I couldn't think of a better way to spend the rest of my life.

Except maybe with sex.

Without it, I thought I might just die.

"Callan? Hello?"

Cricket's voice interrupted my thoughts. I looked over to see her standing in front of me, looking up with blinking eyes and that little line between her eyebrows that appeared when she was thinking hard. She had on a purple sundress that left her silky white legs on display. I just wanted to smooth my palms over her skin and push that dress up over her waist and dip my finger inside her—

"Cal?"

I blinked again. The salon was bustling around me. Old ladies with the most perfectly curled white and gray hair were sitting around, pretending to read magazines.

I frowned and focused back on Cricket. "Are you sure you can leave? All those ladies are still here."

Cricket rolled her eyes, biting back a smile. "They're finished getting their hair done. They're just here to watch you."

I rubbed my bottom lip with my thumb, my cock springing into action before my brain had even fully formed the idea. "Better give them something to see, then, huh?"

Before Cricket could answer, I grabbed her and dipped her back, laying a kiss on her that had the old ladies whooping like they were at a strip show in Vegas. I tilted Cricket back up, turned her toward the door, and shot the ladies a wink.

"That ought to keep them satisfied for a bit," I whispered as we exited the salon.

Cricket shook her head at me. "Now you'll have them whispering about us all over town."

I shrugged and walked down the sidewalk with my hand on her back to my truck. "They would have been talking anyway. At least this way I had a good reason to lay one on you."

Cricket turned at my truck door, her hand landing on my chest as she gazed up at me. "You always have a reason to kiss me, you fool. The more the better."

I crowded her against the door, loving the way she felt against me. I loved control in the bedroom on any given day, but something about Cricket's tiny body made something wild in me lift its head with interest. She was driving me crazy. I was seriously regretting the comment about taking things slowly with her.

"Careful what you ask for, angel."

There was a bit of the devil in her eyes when she responded. "I've been asking for sex, or even just a blow job opportunity, but so far that hasn't manifested, so I guess it's safe to ask for anything, knowing I won't get it."

I thrust my hips not so subtly against her, oblivious to being out on the street where anyone could be watching. I was too far gone to care. "Maybe if you're a really good girl, we can make one of those wishes come true tonight."

Her skin took on a decided pink hue, from her chest to her neck and into her cheeks. She opened her mouth, but was cut off by her phone quacking like a duck.

"Oh! Sorry. That's my alarm to make sure I left in time for my appointment." She scrambled to find her phone in her purse, shutting it off while I opened the truck door.

Fuck. I was thinking about blow jobs when I was supposed to be taking her to her doctor's appointment to get the results of her tests. "I would never make you late." Except if I got sidetracked by thinking about sex constantly.

I helped her up into the truck and kept my hands to myself the whole way to the doctor's office. Cricket talked my ear off, which was fine by me. Gave me something else to think about besides my aching balls. Plus I knew it was her way of handling her nerves. When we parked, she cut herself off in the middle of a sentence. Shit. I needed to help her get through this.

I came around the truck to help her down and held her hand as we went into the waiting room. After checking her in, I sat in the chairs in the corner, the furthest away from everyone else waiting for the doctor. I tugged on her hands until she looked at me.

"No matter what this guy says, it doesn't change anything about me and you. You know that, right?"

Cricket's knee bounced up and down. "You say that now..."

I squeezed her hands tighter, wishing I could convey to her just how deep my feelings went. There was literally nothing on this earth that could get me to walk away from her. "I don't care about any of that, angel. I love you. No matter what medical jargon they throw your way."

Her eyes misted with tears, but she nodded her head. "Okay," she whispered.

The door to the right opened and a nurse in scrubs with little sea otters all over them called out her name. "Christine VanHunting?"

I stood up and pulled her with me. "Come on, Christine."

She stuck her tongue out at me for the use of her legal name and we both approached the nurse. Anything was preferable to the tears that had been in her eyes. The nurse gave me a look but turned and walked down the hallway without a word. Apparently, they were letting me go back with Cricket this time. I felt her take a deep inhale before going into the room the nurse indicated.

We got settled in one of those sterile exam rooms with the paper over the seat and a stiff chair in the corner for the patient's family. I joined Cricket on the paper.

"Hey! This premium paper seat is for me, you big oaf."

I nudged her with my elbow. "It's big enough for two if you'd quit squirming around."

She had a smile tugging on her lips. "What's the doctor going to say when he comes in and sees you trying to steal my limelight?"

I smirked. "He's going to congratulate me for hitting on the pretty lady in exam room seven."

Cricket gave me a cross-eyed look, but it quickly fled when the door to the exam room opened again. The doctor I'd suggested all those weeks ago when Cricket had been in the hospital walked into the room in a white coat and a bright smile.

"The chart says Christine, but at your first appointment I'm pretty sure you said you preferred Cricket, am I right?"

Cricket sat up straight, a genuine smile on her face. "That's right. Christine just makes me think I'm in trouble."

The worry that lined my gut seeing Cricket nervous eased a bit. This doctor had a way about him that deescalated what could be a tense situation. He held his hand out and shook mine, both of us doing formal introductions. I explained that I'd seen him before when bringing patients to the hospital.

"I thought you looked familiar." He sat in the uncomfortable chair. "I'm glad you're here, Callan. Always better to have two people to think of all the questions you want asked."

He turned to Cricket and got right down to business. "Looking at your EEG, we can safely say that you have epilepsy."

Cricket tensed beside me. I had been expecting that diagnosis, but I was eager to hear what else he had to say. There were many reasons for seizures and finding out why she had them would be important information.

"Now, your CT scan didn't show any abnormalities on the brain, which is a very good thing. I'd like to do an MRI though just to be certain. Barring anything physically amiss with the brain, we'll want to explore lifestyle modifications and medications to keep you from having further seizures. Let me stop there. What questions do you have for me?"

Cricket blinked a few times and then looked over at me. I could tell what she needed. This was Cricket's overwhelmed face.

"So a clear CT scan means there's no tumors causing the seizures, right?"

The doctor nodded. "That's right. The MRI will confirm that. There are other tests we could perform that could help us see where the seizures start in the brain. Surgeries are an option if you want to go that route, but we recommend starting with medication since it's much less invasive."

I turned to Cricket who was nodding absentmindedly. "There are quite a few medications you could try. Do you want to start with that?"

She swallowed hard. Then she straightened her spine and faced the doctor. "Yes. Let's do the MRI and also try medications. I don't think I want to talk about surgery yet. It was just the one seizure."

He nodded. "I think that's a great plan. But also know that it was just the one seizure where you lost consciousness. Your brain is having many of them in the background. Those moments of zoning out are actually mini seizures we call absence seizures. I don't say that to scare you, but to impress upon you that taking these medications and changing some lifestyle things will do a lot of good behind the scenes."

Cricket nodded. "Done. Tell me what to do and I'll do it."

The doctor brightened. "Okay, here's a prescription for a medication that's relatively mild and a good one to start with. I also want you walking or exercising. Something relaxing but also gets the blood flowing."

"How about yoga? My friend is a yoga instructor," Cricket chimed in.

"That's perfect actually. Start that a few times a week, plus getting good sleep. No pulling all-nighters for you." The doctor scribbled on a prescription pad and handed the paper to Cricket. "Get that MRI done this week and let's meet again in two weeks, after you've started the medication. Sound good?"

Cricket nodded and the doctor stood. He shook both of our hands and walked out. Cricket looked up at me as if in a daze. I gave her a hug, helped her gather her things, and made another appointment for two weeks from now at the front desk. She didn't say a word the whole time, not until we got in the truck and were headed back home.

"Well, fuck!"

I looked over at her, worried she might be having some sort of emotional breakdown. Instead, she looked like she'd break out into laughter at any second.

"You okay?"

Her hands flew through the air. "All this time I've been

labeled a daydreamer. You know how many times I was sent to the principal's office in school? I wasn't daydreaming or not paying attention to the teacher. I was having seizures! Take that, Mrs. Robertson!"

I chuckled. We all remembered Mrs. Robertson. She was a battle-ax of a woman who'd taught at the middle school until they forced her to retire. She'd had a particular thing with Cricket, always on her about staying focused. I'd put a hard-boiled egg in the back of Mrs. Robertson's desk on the last day of eighth grade. What I would have given to see her face when she opened up that desk after summer break.

"I think we should go TP her house," I muttered, still mad at the woman on Cricket's behalf.

Cricket barked out a laugh. "Nope. Can't pull all-nighters, remember? And you can't TP someone's house in the daytime."

I pulled into my driveway and turned off the engine. "Well, how about we go do something relaxing, then? A walk around the park?" Maybe I should think about getting a dog. Then we could take it for walks every day and get Cricket moving like the doctor wanted.

"I have a better idea." Cricket threw open the truck door and slid out, practically running to the front door. She waited there, hopping from one foot to the next while I got the door open and followed her inside.

She spun around in the middle of the living room and spread her arms wide. "Let's have sex!"

I tripped over my own damn feet and had to steady myself with a hand on the back of the couch. "What, now?" I was still thinking about medical diagnoses and evil middle school teachers and Cricket was thinking about sex. My balls sagged in relief. Finally it was their time to shine.

I shook my head. "I'm not so sure that's a good idea." I mean, she was in the middle of a health crisis and all I could think about was fucking her? That was messed up.

The smile slid from her face. In its place was an anger that promised I'd regret that statement. "Don't you treat me like some fragile flower, Callan Hellman." Her finger came up and she advanced on me, not stopping until the offending digit drilled me in the middle of my chest. "This epilepsy diagnosis doesn't change who I am. You swore to me just a mere hour ago that nothing they said at that appointment would change things between us. Did you lie to me, Callan?"

I held my hands up in the air. "I didn't lie at all. I feel the same way about you that I did when we woke up this morning. If you recall, I told you I wanted to take things slow."

Cricket took her finger from my chest and planted both hands on her hips. Shit. That was even worse. That was the woman's power pose that warned you she was going to let you have it.

"Because I'm a virginal epileptic, you don't want to have sex with me? Did I get that right, Mr. Hellman?"

I was done with this bullshit. I put my hands on her waist, picked her up, and spun her until her back was against the wall. She squeaked in surprise, but as she craned her neck to glare up at me, her eyes still held that fire that made every cell in my body want to strip her naked until she was screaming my name.

"Listen closely, *Ms. VanHunting*." I leaned down in her face and inhaled her perfume, letting it soak into the ache I felt every second since we kissed for the first time. "I want you more than I want to live one more day on this earth. I literally wake up in pain from holding myself back from you. I go to bed holding you and wishing I could climb inside your body and hold you tighter. I think about you when I'm supposed to be working. I envision what our future will look like in ten, twenty, fifty years from now. I am totally, one hundred and ten percent, completely, head over ass in love with you. So no, I'm not not having sex with you because you turn me off. I'm not having sex with you because you turn me on so damn much, I'm not sure I can be gentle once I finally get my fucking hands on you."

We stood there, chest to chest, both of us breathing hard and staring into each other's eyes. When more than a full minute had passed and I was sure I'd scared her off for good and fucked everything up in our friendship, Cricket wiggled her hands between us. I reached down and grabbed them, stilling her. If she so much as brushed against my dick right now, I might do something I regretted.

I dropped my forehead to hers. Why didn't she understand? "I want the best for you, angel. I don't want you stressed and making things worse medically."

Cricket wrenched her wrists out of my grasp and pushed on my chest. I stepped back. If she didn't want me touching her, it might kill me, but I'd step back. All the way back.

"You know what I heard, Callan?"

When I didn't answer, due to my heart feeling like it was being ripped in two right there in my chest, she continued.

"Sex is the very best release for stress."

She reached down for the hem of her dress and pulled it over her head, dropping it on the floor with a flourish. All she wore was a pair of strappy sandals and the tiniest scraps of lace for underwear. No bra to be found. Fuck me, she'd been braless all day. Her nipples were already pebbled hard, the most perfectly curved breasts aching for my hands to cup them.

I groaned, jamming my fist to my mouth.

Yep. I lived in my own personal hell called Blueball.

CHAPTER SEVENTEEN

ricket

MAYBE MOST PEOPLE would have been scared to slap a label on their illness. Unsure of the future. Frightened of the consequences. And to be fair, I'd probably be all of those things at some point, but right now all I could think about was living this life I'd been given to the fullest.

I finally had a diagnosis for what I'd been experiencing my whole life. I wasn't weird. Or flighty. Or even easily distractible like all my teachers had labeled me over the years. I had a medical condition that could be well managed with lifestyle and medication. I was alive and healthy and so sick of waiting when all I wanted to do was strip those clothes off Callan and have my way with him. Why were we waiting to have sex?

Callan let out a groan that made my insides quake in the very best of ways. Sure, stripping off my dress and standing before him practically naked was not exactly in my nature, but then again, I'd never had this powerful feeling that I had to live my life to the fullest. My brain begged the question, have you really lived if you haven't gotten Hellman cock?

"I want to experience life, Callan, and I'd really like to do it with you," I stated quietly, straightening my spine with every word. Callan was my best friend. I didn't want to experience this with anyone else.

Before I could blink, he was standing directly in front of me, the heat of him washing over me. His eyes alone could have burnt me to a crisp. His hand came up and hovered there in the charged air between us. Out of the corner of my eye, I could see it trembling. The steel that I'd had to line my spine with to proposition Callan melted in an instant. He wanted me just as badly as I wanted him.

"I don't know if I can be gentle," he whispered so hoarsely it was like hearing his voice for the first time. His hand finally touched down on my shoulder, light as a feather, hovering there as if he was afraid to touch me.

I leaned into him, my breasts aching to feel the broad expanse of this chest. My nipples got a brush of his T-shirt instead, enough friction in the cotton to have me biting back a moan.

"You can't break me, Cal. Do your worst."

Perhaps it was the permission he needed to hear because his arms banded around me as soon as the words left my mouth. He laid his lips on mine, nearly bending me in half as he coaxed my lips apart to plunder me with his tongue. There's knowing your boyfriend is holding back and then there's experiencing just how much he was holding back when he finally lets go. Callan was practically devouring me, his lips and tongue doing wicked things to my mouth. No corner was left unexplored. His rough hands were everywhere, touching every inch of skin I'd never shown anyone else.

Instead of being shy and uncertain like I imagined I'd feel during my first time, I felt myself blossoming under his attention. Callan had always had a way of making me feel like the most fascinating, beautiful woman in the room, and even now, his touch was magic. My skin puckered in the wake of his hands. My eyes fluttered shut and I gave myself over to the delicious feel of him.

"God, Cricket," he groaned, his mouth leaving mine to roam across my jaw with open kisses.

"Just Cricket is fine," I muttered back, feeling like everything in the entire world had turned to golden happiness in the last sixty seconds. I was practically drunk on giddiness.

I felt Callan smile against my neck. "Never *just* Cricket."

And that was Callan in a nutshell. He'd always made me feel safe and loved and cherished beyond measure. Maybe that's why I'd never slept with any of my previous boyfriends. They'd never made me feel even a fraction of what Callan did.

"You need to lose some clothes. ASAP."

Callan pulled back just long enough to shoot me the sexiest, half-lidded, drugged-out look before whipping his shirt over his head and letting it drop to the ground. My hands left his biceps to travel across his torso. How did one man possess so many perfectly sculpted muscles? It really wasn't fair to all the other males who paled in comparison.

I lifted my head to study him as I realized he'd gone still, his hands fisted at his sides. His jaw was rock hard, but his chest was lifting and falling with huge gulps of air. "What?"

"I'm just trying to slow myself down, that's all."

That was so not in my plan for living life to the fullest. Fuck going slow. I wanted Callan unleashed. I wanted to see him express every part of him, not just the parts he thought I wanted to see. I knew, with zero hesitancy, that he'd never hurt me. So I went on a hunch. Little things he'd told me over the years had me theorizing what kinds of acts Callan liked in the bedroom.

"Tell me what to do, Cal. What do you want me to do next?" I trailed a single finger down his chest and over the bumps of his abs.

His chest vibrated with a growl. My pussy clenched.

Fuck, that was hot.

"Take off my pants," he said from between clenched teeth, like the command had been ripped from him.

I nodded, a secret smile forming at the thrill I got from him telling me what to do. Now we were getting somewhere. My hands got to work on his belt, unbuckling it and then lowering the zipper on his jeans. I pushed the denim over the globes of his ass and down his thighs. I sank to my knees to continue my task, my heart thumping wildly at the groan from Callan. Of course, I accidentally took his boxers with his jeans, Callan's cock springing forth and bopping me in the face like he was happy to see me. And God, was I happy to see him.

"Wrap your hands around him, angel." Callan's voice still sounded like he smoked cigars for a living, but his command was stronger. More sure. Like maybe, just maybe, he'd realized I wouldn't break.

I wrapped both hands around his cock, the head still poking free when I couldn't contain his whole length. I looked up through my lashes at Callan. "Like this?"

If I thought Callan could burn me with his gaze earlier, that was nothing compared to what was happening now. If I didn't know Callan to the bottom of my soul, I might have been worried about what his fierce expression meant. But I was safe here. Safe to experiment and explore.

I bent even closer and gave the head of his cock a lick. Callan hissed, but I was too busy cataloguing the musky, salty taste of him. My lips wrapped around him, my tongue now obsessed with tasting him. His hand plunged into my hair, knocking the pins that held back the tiny braid that swooped across the front. He held me to him, slowly rocking me up and down his length, showing me how to pleasure him.

I'd done this before, of course, but it had been almost something I did to placate the guy I was dating, not because it was something I particularly wanted to do. This... Well, shit. This was something else entirely. I was obsessed with Callan's cock. I wanted to do this every day and twice on Sunday. I wanted to feel his cock jump in my mouth as I hit a particular spot. I wanted to hear Callan groan above me. I wanted to feel his fist tighten in my hair. I wanted to smell him, taste him. I wanted my knees to ache and my pussy to drip as I gave him pleasure.

"Fuck!" Callan slipped from my mouth as he jerked his hips back and fisted himself. "You gotta stop, angel."

I pouted. Yes, I knelt there on the ground, spit dribbling down my chin, and pouted.

There was literally nothing better than seeing Callan standing there with his pants down around his ankles, his own hands strangling his own cock because he was too turned on by what I was doing to him to let me continue. I was the most powerful woman in the world, surely.

His eyes gleamed. "Pretty proud of yourself, aren't you, pretty girl?"

I smiled wickedly. "You bet your ass I am."

One hand peeled off his cock to crook his finger at me. "Stand up and come over here."

I scrambled to my feet, pins and needles distracting me momentarily as I stood before him. Then Callan pushed on the front of my shoulder. "Turn around and bend over to take your sandals and panties off."

I bent to obey when he barked at me, "Slowly!"

I hooked my thumbs in my panties and ever so slowly pulled them down my hips, then over my ass. My face had gone hot as I overthought everything. I'd never stripped in front of a guy before and wasn't exactly sure I was doing it right. Usually I just stepped out of my underwear and threw them in the direction of the laundry bin without a care for doing it in a sexy manner. Hell, what if I tripped?

Callan's hand met my back, between my shoulder blades. He pushed gently and I followed, bending over to push my panties down to my feet.

"Mmm. Just like that," he muttered.

Well, I guessed whatever I was doing was good enough for Callan.

"Now the shoes."

I stayed bent over, feeling a little awkward trying to undo the stupid buckles on the side of my sandals. Oh, how I wished for Velcro shoes like I'd worn in kindergarten. There was a distinct draft in places that didn't normally get ventilation. Especially not with Callan standing there watching. By the time I got my sandals off and stood back up, I was pretty sure I would pass out from all the blood pooling in my face.

Callan wrapped his arms around my shoulders and pulled me up against him. His nose nuzzled my neck as he covered me. "Do you have any idea how much I want you? How beautiful I find you?"

He knew just the right thing to say at just the right time. The embarrassment that had begun to creep in fled in an instant. I turned in his arms and wrapped my hands around his neck, smiling up at him. Feeling a surge of that same carpe diem attitude I'd had since the doctor walked out of the exam room, I leveraged his shoulders and jumped, wrapping my legs around Callan's waist. He barely even leaned back as he absorbed my abrupt move. His hands locked on my hips, his eyes softening as we stared at each other.

"Why don't you show me?"

"Gladly, angel."

And then he kicked the pants from his ankles and stalked out of the room, carrying me to his bed and placing me down on the mattress as if I were the most precious thing in the world. Not fragile. Precious. I could finally see the difference as I stared into Callan's eyes and saw myself reflected.

CHAPTER EIGHTEEN

allan

THERE WERE SO many fantasies I'd had about Cricket over the years that I craved to act out, but I kept reminding myself she wasn't ready for that. No, not because of her medical diagnosis, but because of her inexperience. I didn't want to scare her away when we were just getting started together.

"You're doing it again," Cricket whispered, pulling me from my thoughts. She reached up to smooth a finger over my eyebrow. "You keep retreating into your head. Are you debating whether you want to be with me like this?" She tightened her legs that were currently wrapped around me as I lay over her on my bed.

That was so far from what I was thinking, I huffed out a laugh.

"Hell no. The opposite, actually."

Her smile made every part of me feel like it was seeing the sun for the first time. "Then how about you show me what you want? Do you want me on my knees again? Or tied up to your bed?" Her face brightened. "Oh! Are you into spanking?"

My forehead dropped to her shoulder. Absolutely everything she offered sounded fantastic, and was most definitely something I'd fantasized about with her before, but all that wasn't what I thought should be anyone's first time.

She poked me right in the ribs and my head shot up. "Ouch, woman."

She smirked at me and then softened. "I don't want you compromising what you want because you think you'll scare me away, Cal. Tell me what you want."

I leaned down and plucked a kiss from her lips. "I just want you." When she gave me a look that said she was about to argue, I continued. "All the other stuff is just for fun. It can come later. Okay?"

Cricket pursed her lips like she was debating my answer. Quite frankly, I was done debating. Done talking. Done discussing things. I had the woman I'd been obsessed with since senior year of high school naked in my bed. What fool would waste more time talking? Maybe Ethan, but I wasn't about to start thinking about my brothers when I could be fucking Christine VanHunting, my lifelong best friend.

I pushed away from her and slid down her body until I settled between her legs. Her thighs were tense, like she wasn't sure what to expect. That wasn't going to work for me.

"Trust me, angel," I said a little more harshly than I meant to.

Cricket huffed but I felt her legs relax around my ears. I put one hand on each knee and pushed until she was spread open for me. "Don't move."

And then I dove in headfirst, reminding her that anytime I put my head between her legs, she should immediately relax because she was about to be treated to the best orgasm she'd ever had. She was already wet for me which made me screw my eyes shut and take measured breaths. If I didn't watch it closely,

I could make a mess on my sheets before I'd even sunk into Cricket's body.

I worked two fingers into her as I used my tongue to lave her clit. She was already twisting on the bed, making it harder to stay right where I wanted. I pressed a hand down on her stomach and she stilled.

"Good girl," I whispered against her flesh. She whimpered and the next thing I knew she'd clamped her thighs around my head and let out a shout. I let her ride it out, every muscle in her body quivering as she came back down. I waited until her breathing began to even out.

"Knees, angel," I barked.

Her eyes flew open and she immediately opened her legs again. I slid my fingers from her heat and drew a line up her stomach to her breasts, my tongue following the same path, tasting her the whole way. Everywhere my hands had been was a slightly red mark, as if her body held a memory of where I'd touched her. Her heart was thundering in her chest, from the orgasm and maybe from the anticipation of what would come next.

I hovered over her, waiting until she was looking straight into my eyes. Pink covered her chest, up into her neck, and especially in her cheeks. She had that lazy look of a satisfied woman. I never thought I'd get to see that look on Cricket's face.

"Are you sure?"

A faint smile tilted her lips. Her pretty blue eyes blinked slowly. "Mhm. Totally. One hundred percent. Completely. Firm yes—"

"Cricket?"

"Hmm?" She blinked slowly again, that haze not leaving her eyes.

I didn't answer, just reached down to line myself up and thrust the tip of my cock inside of her. Cricket's eyes lost the haze really fucking fast, but to her credit, she never tensed up, just stared into my eyes as I worked my way inside of her inch by inch. She was small, the top of her head not even meeting my collarbone when we hugged. She barely weighed a hundred pounds. I sometimes forgot how small she was because her personality just seemed so big to me. But now that I was trying to fit myself inside of her, I was fully reminded of our size difference.

I told myself to go slow. To let her adjust. To make sure she was comfortable the whole time, but the second I felt her squeeze around me, I was lost. I couldn't think about this being her first time. Or the fact that I was finally making love to the girl who had starred in my dreams for years. I wasn't thinking at all. I was one human-sized bundle of nerve endings that were experiencing the greatest pleasure they'd ever had. Little by little, I was able to thrust in a bit further.

Cricket's arms came up to wrap around my head. She was breathing hot and heavy into my neck. I stilled, finally fully seated inside of her. I wasn't stopping to give her time. I was stopping to give myself time. I was about to lose it like some one-pump chump my brothers would have made fun of. I squeezed my eyes shut and thought through the sequence of actions to take when responding to a vehicular accident.

And then Cricket's heel jabbed me in the ass and brought me back to reality. "I swear to God, Cal, if this is it, I want a refund."

Well, fuck. No woman had ever asked for a refund. At least not that I knew of. And definitely not while I was still inside of them.

I pulled her arms from my neck and reared back to look at her. I was livid and she was smirking. "A fucking refund?"

Her smirk turned to a giggle that I felt more than heard.

I pulled almost all the way out of her and shot her a look that shut her up real fast. "I don't give fucking refunds." And then I slammed back inside and she yelped. I felt badly about treating her so roughly for all of two seconds.

"More, please," she moaned.

And so I gave her more. So much more that she had to reach up and grab hold of the headboard to keep from sliding so far up she hit her head as I continued to slam into her. I'd been worried for nothing. Cricket might be small and inexperienced, but she was also adventurous and far more robust physically and emotionally than I gave her credit for. She met me thrust for thrust, moaning out my name and the occasional, "more."

"There's my angel," I whispered, reaching between us to stroke across her clit. She deserved it for already being so much more than I could have hoped for.

I felt her orgasm before her face registered what was happening. She was so tightly fisting me, I felt that first flutter and everything immediately started to go black around the edges of my vision. Cricket's mouth dropped open on a silent scream. Then she tossed her head back and I thrust into her one more time as I lost all ability to coordinate movement. My muscles locked up and the most intense pleasure-pain shot up my back. I spilled into her as she gasped over and over against my shoulder. My arms gave out completely and I crushed her underneath me, both of us breathing so hard that was the only sound to fill the room.

In the back of my head I knew I needed to move. Needed to give her space to breathe, but my muscles weren't cooperating. Cricket's lips brushed against my shoulder, so apparently one of us could move.

"I take it back."

"Huh?" I was very eloquent post-orgasm, clearly.

"I don't want a refund. I want a do-over. Again and again."

I chuckled, feeling so relaxed and happy I wasn't sure I'd ever move from this spot. Someone would just have to come by every day and feed us. Although I couldn't stand the thought of anyone else seeing Cricket naked, so maybe I'd have to re-learn how to move my limbs after all.

Using every ounce of energy I had left, I rolled to my side, taking Cricket with me. She squeaked and even that I found adorable. "Give me like five minutes and I'll give you that do-over." Fuck that. I'd need at least an hour, but for her, I'd try to shorten the recovery time.

Cricket settled in with her head on my shoulder and her top leg thrown over mine. Her fingers traced a line back and forth across my stomach as we both stared up at the ceiling.

"I know I'm new at this, but aren't you supposed to use a condom so we don't have a little Callan running around in nine months?"

I shot straight up, Cricket rolling away from me in a tumble. "But— You—" I couldn't seem to form a sentence. Panic filled every cell in my body that had been content just a moment before.

Then I heard Cricket's peal of laughter as she pressed her face into the bed.

I pounced on her, pulling her up. "You little devil."

"Hey! I'm your angel, remember?"

"Not with that little trick, you aren't."

She put hands on either side of my face, sobering. "I'm sorry. I was just kidding. I'm on birth control."

"I know. You went on it when we were nineteen. I remember dying a slow death thinking you were getting on it so you could sleep with that guy you were dating then. The one who couldn't grow a beard to save his life. I just assumed you were still on it. I should have asked." I shrugged, the panic receding as quickly as it had come. "Regardless, I want kids with you someday. Just not yet. I want to give you a kick-ass wedding first."

Cricket's jaw dropped. "Callan..."

I snapped my fingers, only half joking. "Keep up, Cricket."

She shook her head, blinking repeatedly. "I'm trying to, but this is all kind of fast, don't you think?"

I pulled her hands from my face and held them tight. "I've loved you as a friend since elementary school. I fell in love with you senior year. You just turned twenty-four last week. If anything, I'd say we're taking this kind of slow."

"But—"

I climbed out of bed and held my hand out for her. There was a warm shower I intended to take with her. "Like I said. Keep up, Cricket."

CHAPTER NINETEEN

ricket

WE WERE RUNNING LATE, so Callan didn't walk me into the salon the following morning. After learning the glorious mechanics of shower sex last night, I'd been too sore this morning to move at my normal speed. Who knew regular sex with a Hellman brother could be all the workout program a girl needed?

Before Kennedy arrived or any of the clients I had lined up for today, I shoved my purse in the back where I kept my closet of colors, hoping to regularly use them one day, and texted my friends. I'd been neglecting them since I moved in with Callan.

Me: Greetings, friends. Thank you again for helping with my birthday party. It was everything I always wanted in a party.

Meadow: Hey! She's alive! With the way Callan's eyes were eating you up at the party, I wasn't sure if you'd still be standing.

Addy: Wait, didn't you have your doctor appointment yesterday? What did he say?

Annie: Leave it to Meadow to focus on the sexy times...

Meadow: Those are the exact times that make the doctor appoint-ments and all that crap worth it. Amiright?

Me: True, my dear Meadow. I have epilepsy. And I'm starting a medication today to control the seizures. That's basically it. Not a big deal.

Addy: Well, it kind of is. I mean, I'm glad you have a diagnosis, but it's okay to also admit that this is life altering.

Meadow: Wow, way to rip the Band-aid, Cricket. Sheesh. PS-what can we do to make this diagnosis easier? Leave you alone so you get more Callan time?

Annie: Just make sure you can communicate frequently with your doctor about those medications. You might need to go through a couple before you find the right one for you. Not that I'm comparing you to a golden retriever, but I had one as a patient who went through five medications before we found one that worked with minimal side effects.

That made my stomach flutter with worry. I hadn't had time to even think about possible side effects from the medication I needed to pick up from the pharmacy after work. Guess I'd be spending my lunch hour Googling it and freaking myself out.

Me: Thanks, you guys. I really am okay. Just one day at a time. It's actually nice to have a name for the spacey episodes I've always had. And just to get your minds off the epilepsy thing, you will be pleased to hear that I've finally gotten rid of my V-card. Ripped it up and burned it to a crisp last night.

There. That ought to get them talking about something other the medical stuff that honestly just drove me crazy.

Meadow: OMG. Why is this via text?? I'm literally in the supply closet squealing before my class files in from morning recess. This deserves a sleepover with a lengthy description.

Me: Speaking of lengthy...

Annie: LOL Our little Cricket made a dick joke.

Addy: Ah yes, another woman falls for a Hellman. Welcome to the club.

Meadow: I feel kind of left out now. Can we make Judd an honorary Hellman?

Annie: Wait. I remember hearing a rumor about Callan.

Meadow: GASP. Yes! I remember that too. It was when he was dating what's her name two years ago. The one with the damaged hair.

Me: Her hair dresser should be fired for not using a hair mask after highlighting...I mean, that's just basic-level stuff.

Meadow: Enough about her hair! She said he was into some kinky stuff. Did he go full daddy-dom with you, Crick?

My cheeks flooded with heat just thinking about Callan telling me to take off his pants. I wouldn't consider that daddy-dom like Meadow said, but I had the sense that he had that in him. And I wanted to bring out that side of him.

Me: Sadly, no. There were a few things that pointed in that direction, but I think he was holding back. It was my first time and all that.

Addy: Hellmans aren't just gorgeous slabs of muscle. They're considerate too.

Annie: Maybe he's waiting to introduce you to that stuff. And good lord, if he does, you HAVE to share!

Me: I'm hoping I get to see some of that soon.

Meadow: I know! Maybe we should take a trip to The Hardware Store and buy a few items to nudge him along in that direction...

Me: I'm in!

"Good morning!" Kennedy's greeting pulled me from my phone, my heart racing. It wasn't like she could see what we were texting back and forth, but it still felt naughty just the same.

Me: Gotta go, girls. Talk soon.

I slipped the phone in my purse and headed to the front of the salon to get my day started. My first client had walked in with Kennedy, a woman with curves to spare, a bright smile, and some gray at the roots of her strawberry-blonde hair.

"Hi, I'm Cricket. You must be Rita Rose."

We shook hands and she beamed even brighter. "I sure am. Just got into town yesterday and decided I needed these gray hairs covered before I do anything else. Wouldn't do to go around meeting new people looking like I'm eighty."

I laughed. She was so far from looking like the Yeddas of Hell that I didn't think she had anything to worry about. At best she was mid-thirties. "Come on over to my chair and I'll get you all fixed up." She sat and I swooped a black cape over her, excited to be using some color again. "What brings you to Hell?"

She smacked her hand down on the armrest. "Well, here I thought I moved to Auburn Hill. Did I take a wrong turn?"

I laughed again. "I forgot Amelia quit tagging the welcome sign. Yes, this is Auburn Hill, but for years, someone was crossing out the Hill and making it Hell. The name just kind of stuck."

"I take it Amelia is one of the teens in Hell?"

I shook my head. "Nope. She's actually the daughter of the town chief of police. Well, he's retired now, but back in the day he had his hands full with five daughters. Amelia is now married to her lifelong best friend and owner of the Peacock B and B."

"Oh, that's where I stayed when I visited here a few months ago and I'm staying there now while my house is being built. Lovely place. That's so nice to hear that childhood friends became lovers." Rita's smile dimmed a bit. "No luck for me in the love department, I'm afraid. How about you, Cricket?"

I nodded, brushing out her hair and getting an idea for which colors to mix to match her beautiful natural shade. "I just started dating my childhood best friend too."

Rita sat forward and spun in her chair to peer up at me. "Oh! Would you look at that? You have the glow of a woman getting good lovin'."

Before I could be embarrassed, a loud hoot had my gaze shifting to the front where Yedda and Poppy were sitting down with iced coffees and a pastry bag in hand. I rolled my eyes. Their appointments weren't until much later, but of course they were here early. Busybodies needed to get around town to collect and spread the gossip.

"She's dating a Hellman. 'Nough said." Yedda took a huge sip of coffee to hide her smile.

"Not nearly enough said if you ask me," Poppy huffed, settling into a chair like she intended to camp out there all day. "I want *all* the details. Spill, Cricket."

I spent the next hour putting color on Rita's roots while getting grilled about my love life. Even Kennedy started in on me and it was four against one. Lucky for them, I was all too happy to gush about how amazing Callan was. There were just so many things he did that were boast-worthy. By the time I rinsed out Rita's hair and cut off all conversation with the blow-dryer, I thought Yedda and Poppy might just melt right off their chairs.

When I spun Rita around to see the final hair results, she beamed at me in the mirror. "I love it! Perfectly blended like I'm twenty again. Thank you, Cricket."

She stood and I took the cape from her. She surprised me by giving me a hug that nearly knocked the breath from my lungs. She was short like me, but surprisingly strong.

"I'll book my next one in four weeks. We should grab coffee sometime too. How about I leave my number with Kennedy so you can text me when you're free?"

She seemed so friendly I thought I just might text her. Hell was a small town after all. We'd see each other all the time, so we might as well be friends.

"Sounds good. So lovely to meet you, Rita."

She walked to the front and all of us watched her go. There was just something about the sway of her hips that was intoxicating. Like she oozed feminine confidence in a way we all envied. I'd definitely be texting her. I'd bet every last cent I had that Rita Rose knew some tricks about how to seduce a man.

Speaking of, even my absent-minded father held the door for Rita as she sailed out, new hair blowing in the wind like a shampoo commercial.

"Hey, Dad. What are you doing here?" I looked over at

Kennedy. "Would you mind taking Yedda back and getting her shampoo started?"

Dad shifted his gaze around the salon like he just remembered I was at work and that there'd be a room full of women around. When his gaze landed on Poppy, who was not at all hiding the fact that she was eavesdropping, he took me by the arm and steered us to the front corner of the shop.

"I've been thinking since you called us last night, pumpkin. I made some calls this morning and got you in to see a specialist in San Francisco."

My heart sank. "Dad. I already have a doctor. A very good one. Everything is under control, I promise."

Dad kept his hand on my arm, as if he was afraid to let me go. "I know Callan seems to like this guy, but I think you need someone from a larger practice. One who specializes in this kind of thing."

"My doctor *does* specialize in epilepsy. And he's close by. I really think I'm good, Dad."

Dad's head dropped and I realized he'd grown a lot more gray hairs since I last looked at the top of his head. When he lifted it, there was concern etched across the fine lines of his forehead. "When I had my heart attack, I didn't waste time. I found the very best doctor and attacked my treatment head-on. I want you to do the same, pumpkin. Please? For me?"

I sighed. I was too tired for this crap. If seeing his precious doctor would make him calm down and not argue with me every step of the way to recovery, it might be worth it.

"Fine. I'll go see him. Simply for a second opinion," I added quickly when Dad looked ready to throw a party to celebrate my acquiescence.

"Okay. That seems fair." He pulled me into a hug. "Now say you'll come for dinner on Sunday or your mother might kill me for not convincing you."

"Sunday's good. I'll bring Callan."

Dad lost his smile pretty quickly. "Fine," he grumbled, turning to walk out the door.

I shook my head at his back. What was his deal with Callan? You'd think he'd want me to be dating the guy who'd always been there for me instead of these guys he set me up with that were total strangers.

"Not sure what he has against Callan, but if my granddaughter dated a Hellman, I'd be celebrating."

I turned to see Poppy had moved seats to be closer to the conversation. That she wasn't a part of.

I sighed. Typical Poppy. Sticking her nose in everyone's business, yet somehow saying things that made you kind of like her anyway.

"I thought your granddaughter was happy with James?"

Poppy brightened. "Oh she is, but if she'd dated a Hellman before James, there's no way I'd have let her break up with him for James. There's just something about those Hellmans. Even their father had it. Like they have an extra Y chromosome that makes them uber-males."

I wrinkled my nose, not sure if I liked her thinking about my boyfriend like that. "You mean alpha males?" Thanks to Meadow, I'd heard a lot of terms I wouldn't otherwise know.

Poppy shrugged. "Maybe. But there's more to it than that. Take Callan. He's a total puppy dog for you, which is the opposite of alpha male, but yet not. You know?"

I nodded along, surprisingly following her explanation. "Annie read a book last month that she said had a cinnamon roll hero. First time I'd heard it said that way, but I think that might be what Callan is."

Poppy got a gleam in her eye that spelled trouble. "I don't know, Cricket. Callan seems like he's sugary sweet on the outside, but hot daddy-dom on the inside."

My jaw dropped open. What were the odds two people would use that term in one morning? "Have you been talking to Meadow?"

Poppy shot me a wink. "I'll never tell."

I rolled my eyes and got busy with Yedda's hair. Poppy would most certainly tell, but what I wished she'd tell is why my father seemed to have a beef with Callan. I needed the two main men in my life to get along now that Callan and I were talking about forever.

CHAPTER TWENTY

allan

"HAVE YOU ALREADY LOST THAT LOVIN' feeling, bro?" Xavier's teasing voice cut through my darkening thoughts. I blinked and looked out the windshield at the darkening sky before turning to my partner.

"Huh?"

We had exactly twenty-three minutes on shift before I could cut out of here and head home to Cricket. Normally I'd be ecstatic to be so close to being in her presence, but my mind had been highjacked by worries about her dad. Dinner at the VanHuntings' last night had been tense. Cricket's mom had kept up a frantic conversation amongst Cricket shooting her dad warning looks and her dad shooting me narrow-eyed glances that held more than a little heat. We hadn't even stayed for dessert. The guy didn't like me, that was clear. And I had no idea what I'd done.

"Nah, dude. I'm still crazy for Cricket."

"Just wait 'til she has you picking out towels," he muttered, then brightened. "I'm kidding. Cricket seems chill. What's the deal with the frown though? I was starting to think your goofy I'm-in-love smile was permanent."

I ran a hand over my face and sighed. I didn't like sharing my troubles, but Xav and I went back a ways. Along with my brothers and Cricket, I knew I could count on him to listen.

"It's her dad," I started.

Xavier slapped his thighs and danced around in his seat. The whole ambulance rocked as he chuckled. "Ohh, shit, dude. Already in trouble with the dad? What did you do? Feel up his daughter at the dinner table?"

I frowned. "No, of course not. I didn't even touch her the whole night."

Xavier calmed down enough to actually think about my situation. "Well, you must have done something. I mean, wasn't he always setting Cricket up on dates with guys? Clearly he doesn't have an issue with Cricket dating someone. Just has an issue with you."

"Thanks, that really sets my mind at ease," I said dryly.

He was only saying out loud what I'd been thinking in my head all day.

"Sorry, man. But now you just have to figure out why he's got a beef with you. Didn't you say her mom likes you? Maybe you could ask her?"

I sat up a little straighter. "You know what? That's actually not a bad idea."

Xavier frowned. "You say that like I usually have bad ideas."

I lifted a shoulder. "Well…"

He punched me in the arm lightning fast. The dude took a boxing class to stay in shape, and given how badly that fucking hurt, he'd been improving.

"Just drive us back to the station, asshole."

I started the engine, all too happy to get home to Cricket. "I'll try, but I think my arm is dead."

"Serves you right. Maybe if you came to class with me more often, you could defend yourself."

I was more of a weights-in-the-gym kind of exerciser, but he already knew that. I took the occasional boxing class with him just to keep my skills up in case a fight ever broke out. Oddly enough, that had happened more than once on a call and several times at The Tavern when my brothers and I had been there.

Ace came out of the fire station when we pulled around back and cut the engine. I grabbed my bag out of the back and Xavier and I climbed out of the rig.

"Hey, Xavier," Ace called out to my partner. Xavier waved and headed for his truck. Ace walked over to join me as I locked up the ambulance. "I'm heading over to Blaze's for a quick beer. Follow me over?"

Well, there went my evening with Cricket. Although he said quick. Maybe I could slam back the beer and get out before Cricket got home from the salon. Today was Kennedy's day to drive her home and I didn't want her getting to my place when I wasn't there to turn on some lights.

I nodded at Ace and got in my own truck to follow him over to Blaze's house that he and Annie shared on the outskirts of town. Ethan and Daxon were already there when we pulled up. They framed the front door, waiting for us, goofy grins on their faces.

"Jesus," I muttered under my breath.

Ace swallowed a laugh and clapped me on the back.

"Is that...oh my God, Ethan. I think that's our triplet, Callan!" Daxon pointed at me, talking way too loud in a falsetto voice.

"Shut the fuck up before the neighbors get angry." I pushed him inside the house as he laughed uproariously. Ethan hugged Ace and then me, keeping his arm around my shoulders, pulling me further into the house.

"Hey! 'Bout time we got us all together." Blaze joined us in the living room with a six-pack of beer, handing us each one.

"Hard to do when Callan's with Cricket twenty-four seven," Ethan muttered before taking a long pull of beer.

I rolled my eyes. "Not my fault your only action is with your own palm."

My brothers all made various noises as the first insult was lobbed. This was typical. We all got together and spent most of the time ribbing each other as if we didn't share a deep and life-long love for each other. It drove our mother crazy, which was probably why we started it in the first place.

Two tan and white fluff balls ran into the room, dancing around in our circle, looking for who would pet them first. Ethan dropped to the ground and scooped them both up.

"And who are these adorable puppies?" They attacked his face, covering him in so much spit it made me grimace.

Blaze stepped forward to tap the ground and they instantly left Ethan to sit where he'd tapped and stare up at us. Their little tails were going crazy, but they stayed seated.

"These are two collies we got from a shelter down in San Jose. I picked them up a couple days ago."

"Let's see if we can guess. Seeing Eye dogs?" Ace made the first stab at what service these new dogs would be trained in.

"More blood sugar sniffers? They have long snouts," Ethan chimed in, standing back up and wiping his face on his shirt sleeve.

"Good guess, but no." Blaze turned to me. "They're usually quite good at sensing when a human has a seizure."

I pulled my gaze from the puppies to lock eyes with Blaze. A question passed between us and he nodded subtly. That bastard of a brother had bought two collies so he could train them and let me adopt them. For Cricket.

Fuck, I loved my brothers sometimes.

"Do you have any that will sniff out hot girls who love a good beard?" Daxon cut the emotional moment just like he always did. "For Ethan, obviously."

We all guffawed and changed the subject, talking about our

jobs, home life, and every little thing that had happened since we were together last. The beer went down easy and I was almost done when the subject of our father came up like it always did with enough alcohol consumption.

"Did you contact Dick?" Ace asked cautiously, shooting me a glance.

Everyone went quiet. I nodded. "Shot him a text yesterday but haven't heard back. For all I know he'll ignore it."

Blaze snorted. "If you could only be so lucky."

Ethan instantly defended. "I highly doubt a simple conversation could cause harm."

"You don't know our father. He's like a sticky web. He likes to reel people in with good looks and charm. Once you're good and caught, he'll fuck you over." Ace looked ready to start a fistfight.

"I didn't fall off the turnip truck yesterday, boys." Why couldn't they trust me to have a conversation with our father and not turn to the life of a criminal in the same breath?

Everyone started talking over each other, but the slamming of the front door had us all shutting up at once.

"Hello?"

"Who invited Mom?" Daxon whispered, eyes wide.

"Not me."

"I didn't."

"Does Mom ever need a formal invite?"

A living, breathing whirlwind of green paisley caftan came around the corner. Mom sported checkered Vans with Mickey Mouse on the front. Not really sure how she thought that matched with green paisley, but for some reason, it just worked on her. Maybe it was simply all the energy that crackled off of her that drew one's attention.

"There are my boys. Come give your mother a hug." She spread her arms wide and we all dutifully came over to give her a hug and a kiss on the cheek.

Her eyes sparkled at the attention and we all had the same

thought running through our heads. *We really should make more time to spend with Mom.*

"I see you left one beer for me, you sweet boys."

Ethan leaped to grab the last beer and pop the top for her. "You know it!"

Mom took a long swig of beer, let out a dainty burp behind her hand, and then turned to me. "I have failed you as a mother, Callan, and I'm sorry."

I looked at my brothers for help, but they remained as confused as me. "Huh?"

Mom hustled to stand before me, her hands clutching my biceps as she looked up. "You had dinner at the VanHuntings last night and I realized I should have invited you and Cricket over to my place for dinner. Why I didn't think of it first, I don't know." She clapped her hands to her mouth, eyes going impossibly wide. "Momagth!"

I gently pulled on her wrists, holding her hands in mine. "What's that?"

She looked positively stricken. "I must be developing dementia!"

Ace stepped over and pulled Mom under his arm. "Hold on there, Mom. You're fine. Just because you didn't get the scoop on the latest gossip first doesn't mean you're losing your mind."

Mom jabbed Ace in the ribs and he let go with an oof. "It most certainly does! Soon Poppy will know all about my own sons before I do! This is unacceptable."

Mom spun in a full circle, her outstretched finger pointed at each of us in turn. Ah, shit. We knew that stern look. We'd been on the receiving end of it our whole lives.

"We're reinstating Sunday night dinners! New rule: if you're dating someone, you have to bring them! And secondly, if you're not working that night, you *have* to come. No other excuses will be accepted." Her eyes narrowed. "Don't think I don't know your work schedules."

"Jeez, Ma." Daxon took his life in his own hands and put his arm around Mom's shoulders. "We'd love to reinstate Sunday dinners. No threats necessary. You make the best tacos in the state."

Mom lifted her nose in the air, looking like she wasn't quite ready to let go of the angry. I wasn't quite sure how it was our fault that she hadn't thought to invite Cricket and me to dinner, but that was Mom for you. Everything had to be a huge drama.

"I think you meant to say that you couldn't wait to be in the weekly presence of the woman who gave you life."

Daxon shot us a look that clearly said "help," but we let him deal with his own bullshit. He and Mom were quite the pair. Both of them drama queens with a deep, untapped reservoir of goodness.

"Absolutely. Exactly what I said, but of course you said it better."

That seemed to mollify Mom as she slid an arm around Daxon's waist and gave him a squeeze.

"Okay, well, this has been fun," I clapped my hands and set my empty beer bottle on the end table nearest the front door. "But I have my girl waiting for me."

Mom looked over Daxon's arm and winked at me before turning to Ethan. "And how come you don't have a girl to go home to, young man?"

As I got to the door, I heard Ethan sputtering. "B-but Daxon doesn't either!"

I smiled and shook my head, closing the door behind me, grateful I could escape Mom's grilling for once. Oh, she'd be back to being on my case soon enough, but this little respite was appreciated.

Before I got back on the road, I pulled my phone from my back pocket and texted Cricket. But first, I looked at the picture she'd sent me earlier in the day. She was in the bathroom at the salon, her reflection in the mirror over the sink making me instantly hard. She'd pulled her shirt up to show herself wearing a sheer lace white bra with the caption, *can't wait to show you this new bra in person.*

If I'd had any idea that Cricket would engage in midday sexting, I would have made my move on her much earlier. Maybe.

Me: Go upstairs and grab something before Kennedy takes you to my place.

Cricket: We were just on our way out the door. Can it wait?

Me: I think it's in your best interest to go grab it.

Cricket: Grab what, Mr. Cryptic??

Me: Your senior year prom dress.

Cricket: What?? Why?

Me: Be a good girl and do as you're told.

I shut off my phone and tucked it back in my pocket, biting my lip to keep from laughing out loud. If she knew what was good for her, she'd take the time to go upstairs and grab that dress even if her first reaction would be to flip me off for bossing her around.

I had a particular fantasy to act out, and tonight sounded like the perfect night to do it.

CHAPTER TWENTY-ONE

ricket

THE GIRLS and I had been going back and forth via text for days, all aflutter with ideas on how to entice Callan to show me his dominant side in the bedroom. Or should I say Meadow was the one instigating most of the discussion. I was perfectly happy with how things were, thank you very much. But if I was being perfectly honest with myself, there was a growing part of me that wanted Callan to show all of himself to me. He was my closest friend, and now lover, and I was a touch jealous. If he'd bossed around another woman before, and enjoyed that kind of thing, I wanted him to share that with me too.

Callan: Be a good girl and do as you're told.

My jaw flopped open and I nearly bobbled the phone from the tremor that started up in my limbs. Was I angry? Maybe right at first, just on instinct. I didn't like people telling me what to do.

Did I?

The tremor turned into a deep quake that felt a lot like a

thrill, not anger. That ribbon of heat in my gut felt like an electric rush that had every sensory on full blast. This was not anger. This was desire on steroids.

"Are you coming, Cricket?" Kennedy called from inside her car.

I put up a finger and then closed the passenger door where I'd been about to climb inside. Instead, I jogged up the side stairs to my tiny apartment over the salon and made a beeline for my coat closet. There in the back was the dress I'd worn to prom, covered in plastic and a light layer of dust. I hadn't looked at the thing since I'd shoved it into the closet when I moved in. Prom dresses were like bridesmaids dresses. You spent your last dime to purchase them, wore them once, and then hauled them around house to house until you begged your own daughter to wear it to her event, only to have her roll her eyes at you and your ridiculous fashion choices.

Except it seemed like this old thing was going to get a second life after all.

I draped it over my arm and jogged back down the stairs, thinking that might count as my daily exercise that the doctor had ordered. So far I didn't have any real side effects from the new medication except for being extra tired during the day. Although that could have been from Callan keeping me up at night, and I, for one, was not going to complain about that.

Kennedy gave me an odd look when I climbed in the car, but didn't question me, thank goodness. She dropped me off at Callan's house and backed out right away when she saw Callan's truck in the drive.

"Thanks again for the ride," I called, waving to her. Dropping her boss off a couple days a week was above and beyond the call of duty for a receptionist. I'd have to find a way to bring her food or coffee to make sure she didn't quit on me.

When I went through the front door, I didn't see Callan at first. Blood rushed through my veins and filled my ears with white noise. I swore if he jumped out at me, I'd go through the roof. My nerves were shot with anticipation of what was to come.

"Cal?" I called out, dropping my purse and kicking off my shoes before venturing into the house.

I found him on the chair in the living room, just sitting there, watching me as I walked in. His chin was in his hand as he leaned on the armrest, one ankle crossed over the opposite knee. He'd changed out of his work uniform. A collared shirt was open at the neck, the crease in his dress slacks fresh.

What the hell was going on here? Did we have a fancy event to go to that I didn't know about?

"Hey."

Callan ran his thumb across his lower lip as his eyes took me in from my bare toes to the top of my head where my hair lay piled in a messy bun.

"Go put on the dress. Heels."

His velvety voice washed over me. I was too tired to want to go anywhere tonight, but if Callan kept talking to me in that voice, I'd agree to just about anything. I opened my mouth but he shook his head, cutting me off before I even had a chance to speak. I snapped my jaw closed and decided to just go with it. I trusted Callan completely.

I turned to walk into the bedroom with the dress, my footsteps faltering when I heard him mutter just loud enough for my ears to pick it up, "Good girl."

I'd never been one to get off on praise, but just hearing the purr of that phrase off his lips was doing something to my breathing. The air had gotten thick and sucking in enough oxygen to keep walking was proving difficult.

I threw the dress down on the bed and stripped out of my clothes in a hurry. Back when I went to prom with Logi, I'd fought with my mother over wearing a bra. She'd said it was improper not to wear one, but I hadn't wanted any lines to show beneath the lacy top. We'd settled on stickers to keep my nipples from poking out, but today I was going without anything.

Where was the joy in having small boobs if you had to wear bras?

The long skirt with the slit up the one leg went on without an issue, though it was a bit snugger than I remembered across my hips. The burgundy was deep, darker than anything I'd wear these days, but it did leave my pale skin looking like porcelain. Pulling the matching lace top over my head, my hair fell out of the bun, spilling across my exposed shoulders. I'd worn it up for prom, so I found some pins in my makeup case and piled it up there as well as I could on short notice. I had a feeling Callan wanted me to recreate that night.

I didn't have the same heels after six years, but I had a pair of black barely there stilettos I'd worn for an ill-advised bachelorette party for Meadow. The party wasn't ill advised, just these damn shoes that left my toes tingling after just twenty minutes of wearing. I had a feeling I wouldn't be wearing them for long tonight. That settled, I looked in the mirror and paused. I looked like teenage Cricket had morphed with adult Cricket. Hopefully all those insecurities I'd harbored as a teen wouldn't come rushing back just because I donned the clothes.

If there was one person who could soothe my nerves and make me feel like an angel on earth, it was Callan Hellman. And he was waiting for me in the living room. I spun on my heel and marched out, careful not to trip in the heels.

He was waiting for me all right. He stood there in the living room where he'd pushed the furniture back, leaving the center of the room clear. He held a box in his hand, looking more handsome than any date I'd ever had in my teen years. Hell, more than any date I'd had in my adult years too.

His eyes practically ate me up, taking in every detail. As I walked toward him, his eyes seemed to dart from my bare leg poking out of the skirt to my face, and back around again, as if he wasn't sure where he wanted to stare.

"Damn, Cricket," he muttered, looking down into my eyes as I came to stand before him.

"You look pretty good yourself, Mr. Hellman."

The side of his mouth hooked into a smile. "I nearly killed Logan for taking you to prom senior year. You'd told me you wanted to break up with him and then you said yes when he asked."

I tilted my head, remembering those events that had seemed so important back then. "Well, I couldn't break up with him before prom or I wouldn't have had a date."

Callan's hand came up to cup my face. "I would have asked you."

I sputtered out a laugh. "You were dating some transfer student, weren't you?"

Callan shook his head like I was being ridiculous. "I would have broken up with her in a heartbeat if you'd shown even the slightest inclination of wanting to go with me."

My head rested in his hand. "I didn't know how you felt," I said quietly.

And I wasn't sure if that would have changed how I felt in return. I wasn't sure if I'd have developed feelings for Callan back then. Maybe him telling me at that point in our lives would have ruined everything.

Callan's thumb stroked my cheek as he stared at me. Then he released me and put the box he was holding between us. "Will you go with me to prom now?"

"What?" I laughed, looking down to see a wrist corsage of deep red roses and baby's breath in the box. I gasped.

He pulled the corsage out of the box and slid it over my hand. "Yes or no, angel?"

I peered up at him, my pulse hammering under my skin. "Where'd you get this?"

"Shelby helped me out even though she was trying to close up for the day. Once she knew what I wanted it for, she happily obliged."

"Oh my God, Callan." That was the sweetest thing anyone had ever done for me. Then again, he was always doing sweet things. So many that my heart was constantly under attack. He wanted my whole heart and I wanted to give it to him. Forever.

Callan tossed the empty corsage box on the coffee table and hit a remote. Music flowed from the speaker set up by the television. "Say You Won't Let Go," a song by James Arthur that had always been my favorite, filled the air.

"Yes or no?" Callan held his hand out to me.

I'd never been more sure of an answer before. I slid my hand into his. "A thousand yeses."

He tugged me close and slid his hands to my hips. I wound my arms around his neck and nearly shivered at the heat radiating off his body. He dipped his head and kissed me, his lips soft, gentle, careful. Our hips moved us to the music, a natural swaying that only two humans on the same page can do. Callan and I, well, we'd always been in the same book. Now that he'd made his move, we were definitely on the same page. Same word. Same breath.

"You and me, Cricket. Until we're old and gray," Callan murmured.

"Mhm," I answered, sliding my fingers into the hair on the back of his head that I hadn't lightened. Tears pricked at the back of my eyelids. "I think it's always been you and me."

Callan's arms banded tightly around me and he picked me up. This time his kiss was not soft. There was nothing gentle about the way he invaded my mouth and kissed me until my head was spinning. And just as abruptly, he put me down and stepped back. I nearly stumbled at the loss of him.

He kept his gaze locked with mine, stepping back until the couch hit the back of his legs. He sat and sprawled there, the king of his kingdom. One arm hooked around the back of the couch. His eyes went hooded as he stared at me. The quake in my limbs was back, in an unsteady rhythm with the blood rushing through my veins.

The music shifted to another song, but I couldn't have picked out the singer or the song title. I was wholly focused on the man before me. The way his entire countenance had changed. The way he looked like my familiar Callan, but there was an edge to him that I'd never seen before.

"Lift your skirt."

I blinked, not quite sure I'd heard him right. "What?"

His gaze snapped to my face, a censure in his eyes that made me feel like I'd let him down. "Keep up, Cricket. I only ask once."

Pretty sure he hadn't *asked* anything. I was also pretty sure now was not the time to be pointing that out.

My fingers curled into the slick fabric of my skirt, scrunching it upwards until I held a handful of the material. His finger, the one lying on the back of the couch, lifted and circled to urge me to keep going. I tugged, pulling the material up until the black thong I'd put on this morning was exposed.

Callan grunted, the sound as much of a confirmation that I'd done something right as I'd be getting just then.

"Panties off."

Without hesitation, I hooked my thumbs in the material at my hips and tugged them down, stepping out carefully so I didn't teeter off-balance in the stilettos. Once the thong was at my feet, I lifted my leg and kicked it in his direction. For once, the coordination gods were on my side. The scrap of lace sailed through the air and landed on his lap, as if I practiced such a move in my spare time.

Callan looked surprised for a split second before his eyes became even more hooded. He leaned forward, that arm coming off the back of the couch to prop on his knee. "There's my angel," he cooed.

He sat back abruptly. "Now come show me how much you wanted to go to prom with me and not that douchebag."

CHAPTER TWENTY-TWO

allan

IF I EVER HAD THE thought in the back of my head that Cricket wasn't a woman I could one hundred percent be myself around, I squashed that ridiculous lie when she kicked her panties into my lap, raised her skirt above her waist again and walked over to me with the confidence of a Victoria's Secret angel. The roses on her wrist completed the picture that exceeded all my fantasies.

Cricket lifted her leg, the one that had been tantalizing me with flashes of skin through the slit in her skirt, and put her heel up on the couch right next to my leg, exposing herself to me. My arms trembled there on the back of the couch. I wanted to reach for her so badly, but something in her eyes made me hold back.

"As of tonight, this is the only prom I remember. And I most definitely want to be here with you, Callan. Only you."

Then she straddled my lap and let her skirt go, reaching up to pull me down for a kiss. Her tongue took the lead, telling me without the words that she was putting everything she had into this kiss. With a mighty groan, I realized I needed both. Her words and her enthusiasm. Together, they pushed away any doubts that had plagued me. The doubts that came from wanting a woman for so long and not having her. From getting a glimpse of heaven and wondering if it would be snatched away. My arms left the back of the couch and banded around her torso, holding her to me with a fierceness that was probably hurting her.

Cricket gasped into my mouth. The sound made my brain click into gear just long enough to release her the tiniest bit so she could breathe. I'd kick my own ass if I ever hurt her. She let go of my hair and pushed on my shoulders. I let her go, settling my hands on her hips, ready to apologize for crushing her. Instead, the words dried up as she reached down and whipped her top over her head.

Cricket wasn't wearing a bra. All that was left of her outfit was the burgundy skirt bunched up around her waist and stilettos that I might never let her take off again. My head fell back against the cushions taking her in. If I could have taken a picture of her right then without her kicking my ass for documenting it, I would have. Something to keep on my phone and look at whenever I wasn't with her.

"Fuck, Cricket."

She smiled. "Yes, please."

Her skirt might have been twenty yards of material which made everything more difficult, but we got my pants undone and shoved down to my ankles while she still straddled me. A few of the buttons on my shirt flew off, never to be found again, but I wasn't complaining. Cricket somehow knew what I needed.

"Let me do it," she whispered in my ear, guiding my arms to the back of the couch.

And then, with the look of an angel but the smile of the devil, she lifted up and positioned me at her opening, sliding down so slowly I felt my eyes roll back in my head. I forced them back, not wanting to miss a moment of Cricket, still wearing her skirt from prom, fucking me on the couch while I couldn't touch her. I liked calling the shots, but maybe just this once I could let Cricket take the lead. By the time we collapsed in a heap, slumped over on the couch breathing harder than the horses at the finish line of the Kentucky Derby, I was all for letting Cricket have her way with me every single day.

"Now do you believe me when I say I wish you would have taken me to prom senior year?" she whispered against my chest.

I peeled an arm off the back of the couch and pushed the hair from her face. "Ask me later when the blood has returned to my extremities and I can think straight."

Cricket started giggling, the sound uninhibited and happy. I stroked her hair, promising her silently to always give her reasons to laugh like that.

I THREW an envelope in the mail basket at the fire station the next morning, hoping I was doing the right thing. I believed in Cricket and it was time everyone else knew how incredible she was. There were no guarantees she'd be picked to be one of the contestants at the hair competition thing in New York, but she should at least try. I didn't even know hair competitions were a thing, but when I called Addy yesterday to ask about it, she confirmed that it was indeed a thing and that secretly applying for Cricket was sweet and thoughtful, not underhanded.

My phone vibrated in my back pocket. I waved to the boys just getting off shift before pulling out my phone and heading for my rig to wait for Xavier.

Richard/Father: I can meet next week. Say Friday?

Pretty sure the fact that I'd listed my own father under his first name in my phone was a testament to what kind of relationship we had. Which was why I'd reached out to him in the first place. I wanted to understand it. Why had he left? Why did he continue to stay away? What kind of father didn't want to acknowledge his own children?

Ace and Blaze remembered him well and did not have anything favorable to say. Ethan, Daxon, and I had been too young to remember much beyond hazy memories that may have been the kind of built-up stories little boys made over the years to fill in the gaps. I wanted cold, hard truths for once.

Me: How about Crazy Beans just south of Blueball? I can get there by 3.

I'd have to leave my shift a little early, but Xavier wouldn't mind picking up my slack. He'd give me shit about it, but then cover me no matter what. He reminded me a lot of my brothers, actually, which is probably why we got along so well.

Richard/Father: See you then.

No "can't wait." Or "looking forward to it." But I suppose expecting any enthusiasm would be crazy. He'd never expressed interest in getting to know any of us as teens or adults. I scrubbed a hand over my face and tried to let the hurt roll off my back. Shit, he and I hadn't even met yet and I was already regretting reaching out. What if I discovered a truly despicable man? How could I reconcile the fact that my own father was an asshole? Did that mean I carried his genes? That one day I'd morph into the same type of asshole simply because of biology?

"You look like my girl when I told her I didn't like curtains."

I whipped my head to the right and saw Xavier standing in the open passenger door of the ambulance with a piping hot coffee in each hand.

"Blinds are clearly better."

His smile was blinding. "That's what I said, dude!" He handed one of the coffees to me. "You would have thought I said I hated puppies or some shit."

He climbed in and we officially clocked in by turning on the rig and letting dispatch know we were ready for any calls. It was a busy day, which was good for me, bad for everyone trying to avoid medical emergencies. I stayed so busy I didn't have time to worry about the meeting with my father. Not until I got home and Cricket sensed something was on my mind.

"Okay, out with it, mister." Cricket pulled the dish towel from my hand and set it on the counter. She tugged me out of the kitchen and into the living room, sitting us both on the couch that I would never look at the same way.

"You've been quiet all night. I even dished about the latest place Yedda lost her dentures and you barely chuckled. What's going on in your head?"

I smiled at her, hoping to just forget about Friday's coffee meeting. "I'm fine. Just tired, I guess."

Cricket narrowed her eyes. "Bullshit. This is not tired Callan. This is worried Callan. So spill or I'll have to tickle you to death. You know I have ninja hands. I'll find all your ticklish spots."

Cricket's hands all over me? Sign me up. "I'll show you my ticklish spots," I answered suggestively.

She burst out laughing. "I know everything that annoys you, Cal. I could make your life miserable."

I scoffed. "Like what?"

She counted off on her hands. "I'll play that one Coldplay song you hate on repeat. I'll crack my knuckles just when you're drifting off to sleep. I'll text you in all caps until the day we die. I'll one-up you in every conversation. I'll put the empty Cheez-It box back in the cupboard for you to discover when you're starving and little cheesy crunchy things are the only thing that will do."

I gaped at her. I wasn't sure whether to laugh or run away. "You are diabolical."

She shrugged. "I'm friends with Meadow. We come up with these things all the time. She even has a spreadsheet so she remembers them all."

Now I was horrified. "Remind me to stay away from Meadow."

"Tell me what's going on in your head." Cricket nudged me with her elbow.

I sighed and burrowed deeper into the couch. There was no use hiding it from Cricket. If there was one person in the world who knew me inside and out, it was her.

"Fine. I heard back from my father this morning."

Cricket sat up straight. "You did? What did he say?"

"Just agreed to meet me. We're going for coffee at a neutral spot on Friday afternoon."

"Isn't that what you wanted?" Cricket laid her head down on my shoulder and snuggled against me.

I stroked my thumb across the soft skin of her arm. "It is. But now I'm wondering what will happen if I find out he truly is the asshole my older brothers say he is."

"What do you mean? What could possibly happen? You just go your separate ways like you've been doing."

My head flopped back against the couch. I'd rather be called out to a multi-car pileup than talk about this crap. "I don't know. I guess I just wonder what the father's actions say about the son, you know? Like, what if he's a horrible man, which means I'm destined to be a horrible man?"

Cricket took a deep inhale, not responding for a full minute. The seconds ticked away, each one making me more nervous. What if my fears were confirmed? What if Cricket didn't want to be with me, knowing later on down the road I could walk away from her just like my father did to my mother?

Then she took my hand and laced our fingers together, sitting up enough she could see my face. "I have this one client who comes in every other week to get his hair trimmed. He still drives himself in from Blueball but he shuffles so slowly I finally asked him how old he is. Eight-four years young, he said."

She paused to take a breath while I wondered where the hell she was going with this story.

"Get this. To keep his dexterity up, he plays the piano every single day."

I frowned, truly lost. "He used to be a pianist?" Far as I knew, my father wasn't into music or playing an instrument.

Cricket grinned. "Nope. His granddaughter got engaged last year and he's sewing her veil by hand. Sewed tiny flowers into the material around the bottom edge with a silk thread. Now he's sewing on the little white ceramic flowers to the clip at the top. He brings me an updated picture every appointment. It's gorgeous. Like, the kind of thing a celebrity would wear. Anyway. That's the definition of a man. He takes extreme care of those he loves. Even if it means playing the piano every day to make sure your fingers still work."

Cricket squeezed my fingers. "That's why I love you, Cal. You take extreme care of those you love just like my client. That's the kind of man you are. Meeting the guy who donated his sperm over two decades ago won't change that."

The back of my eyes started to burn. Fuck. Leave it to Cricket to say exactly what I needed to hear in a way that would make me actually listen.

"Angel..." I whispered, pulling her into me and kissing those lips. I didn't stay long, just long enough to get a taste of her. Just to tide myself over until I could pick her up, lay her down on my bed, and show her what she meant to me.

I'd be exactly the man she loved because I wouldn't let myself be anything else.

CHAPTER TWENTY-THREE

ricket

WELL, that was a waste of an afternoon. And to think I'd moved my appointments around just to appease my father.

"Thanks for driving, Dad."

He nodded and waved, not quite looking at me. It was weird seeing my normally overconfident father looking sheepish. He'd had high hopes for this doctor he'd picked out, but from the moment he'd stepped in the room, I'd known he wasn't right for me. That had become abundantly clear to my father when the doctor literally talked right over me the second I opened my mouth. It didn't matter how many degrees you had framed on the wall if you couldn't even listen to your patients.

I slammed the door shut on his Mercedes and headed up the walkway to Callan's house. At least I had a peaceful evening with Callan to look forward to. His truck was in the drive, so I knew he was already home. My dad took off with a toot of his horn. I rolled my eyes. He'd been doing that since I was a little girl. Not so cute when he was dropping me off at school and everyone turned to look at who was honking in the drop-off line.

"Honey, I'm home!" I sang as I entered the front door and immediately kicked off my shoes.

Callan poked his head out of the kitchen, a towel slung over his shoulder. "Hey, you're home early. I thought you said you'd be with your dad into the evening?"

I shrugged and came over to throw my arms around Callan. Every worry floated away when I was in his arms. "I cut the appointment short."

Callan stiffened and pulled back. "Appointment?"

I tugged on the edge of the towel and used it to wipe a spot of red from his cheek. "Yeah. I didn't tell you about it ahead of time. Didn't want to worry you, but you know my dad. Never quite happy unless he's got his hands in the middle of everything. He made me an appointment with a doctor in San Francisco to get a second opinion. The guy was a jerk though. I don't care if he has the cure to all diseases. I don't want to work with him."

Callan folded his arms across his chest, a move that finally sent a warning clanging through my tired brain. His jaw was clenched harder than Poppy's lips when she was trying to keep a secret. He didn't say a word, just stood there looking like a thunder cloud.

"Say something," I said quietly.

He dropped his hands on a frustrated sigh and retreated into the kitchen. I followed, not wanting him to stay mad at me. I'd rather just discuss it and move on.

"I'm not sure what to say, Cricket."

Definitely mad. He didn't call me angel.

"Listen, I didn't want you to worry. Besides, I had no intention of making this guy my doctor. I like the one you picked out for me."

Callan spun around again, throwing the towel down on the counter. "It's not about you picking the doctor I chose, Cricket.

It's about you always falling in line with whatever Hank wants. You're an adult now. He doesn't dictate what you do."

I frowned, feeling wrongly picked on. "I'm aware of that. But what's the harm in considering his suggestions? He wanted me to get a second opinion. I didn't have an issue with that. It's just prudent."

"Then why didn't you tell me?"

I threw my hands in the air. "I didn't want you to worry!"

Callan leaned in, his brown eyes skewering me in a way that made me feel naked. "I doubt very much that was the reason. You didn't want to tell me you were following your dad's suggestion. You knew I would call you on it."

I didn't even blink. He was trying to box me in a corner and he knew me better than that. I would fight back. Guaranteed.

"Maybe you're just mad because there's a man in my life other than you that I listen to. Maybe you're just mad because it's my dad and it's no secret he doesn't like you!"

Callan flinched back like I'd physically slapped him. I immediately wished I could take that back. It wasn't Callan's fault the two didn't get along. That was squarely on my dad's shoulders. Throwing it in Callan's face was just mean.

I sighed and put a hand on his chest. "I'm sorry. That was uncalled for." I tilted my head. "The last part at least. The first part I think has some truth behind it."

"I've done everything I could over the years to gain his favor," he said quietly.

"I know you have. That's on him for not giving you a chance."

Callan put his hand over mine, squeezing it there against his chest. "But you may have a point with the other thing."

My lips were begging to smile. "You mean the comment about another man?"

Callan cringed. "Ugh. Don't say it like that."

I lost the battle with my lips and full-out smiled. Even arguing with Callan, I found myself falling deeper in love with him. "I know your mother is important to you and I'd never make you choose between us. You have a great relationship with her and yet still make me feel like a priority. I'll try harder to do the same for you."

Callan put his hands on my hips and pulled me in close, dipping down to prop his chin on the top of my head. "You know, there for a few years I tried really hard to make your dad like me. Specifically because I didn't have my own father. I stupidly thought he could be my father figure."

My heart nearly tore in two hearing the vulnerability in his voice. I'd spent my whole life watching Callan act like nothing was wrong when other kids had fathers pick them up from school, or there on the sidelines when their high school team won the football game. He'd endured a lot without a father, and I wanted to slap some sense into my own dad for not giving him even a split second of attention.

"I know that's a loss for you, but it's an even bigger loss for my father. He doesn't even know what a great man you are. What a beautiful human you've become. He'll never know why my heart will always be yours. Why I'll always put you first."

I slid my hands around his neck and pulled him down so I could kiss away his pain. He let me too, the kiss slow and lazy. There was a level of passion that burned between us that sometimes felt too hot to handle, but we were also still best friends. If Callan was hurting, I'd make it all better. And vice versa. If anything, I was happy to know that dating each other hadn't changed the fact that we were rooted by an enduring friendship.

"Come snuggle with me on the couch," I whispered against his lips.

He nodded, his lips plucking one more kiss before backing away. "The pizza should be just about done. Let's take it in there and watch a movie."

I grinned. "Damn. Hot boyfriend, homemade pizza, and a movie? I should make you mad more often."

Callan glowered at me. "The pizza was actually for me."

I gasped. "You'd deprive me of pizza?"

Callan smiled evilly. "It's my mom's handmade dough too. Too bad there's not enough for you."

I crossed my arms over my chest. "Oh really? I might just call Nikki, then, and see if she has enough left over for me. If I recall correctly, she always made more batches of dough than she could possibly use herself."

"If you'd rather spend the evening with my mom, go right ahead..." Callan shrugged and turned to the oven.

I took the time to check him out in his jeans, the ones that were so worn they fit his body like a second skin. The T-shirt he wore was one of my favorites. It was soft and hugged his biceps perfectly. Not enough to look like a wannabe weightlifter, but just enough to make a woman want to see him without the shirt on.

"Ugh, fine," I sulked, marching over to the fridge and opening it. "I'll make a sandwich for myself."

A clank echoed through the kitchen as Callan set the wire rack on top of the stove. "I actually have two pizzas," he muttered.

I spun around, triumphant smile in place. "I knew you did!"

Callan looked like he was fighting a smile. "Just shut up and get the plates, would you?"

I came up behind him instead and hugged him, my cheek pressed against his back. "I really am sorry, Callan."

He patted my hands. "I know. I'm sorry too. Now let's eat or I'll get hangry and who knows what kind of fight we'll have then."

I snorted and went to grab the plates. He wasn't kidding. Callan without food was not a good thing for anyone.

CHAPTER TWENTY-FOUR

allan

IN SOME WAYS I was grateful for Cricket's seizure. I'd never been more scared than when I saw her hit the deck right in front of me. Meeting with my long-lost father who abandoned his family paled in comparison. Sure, I was still nervous, but mostly because I knew I didn't have the full approval of my two older brothers. Ace and Blaze wanted nothing to do with Richard Hellman and they were usually spot on in their assessment of people.

Xavier kicked me out of the ambulance early saying I was making the patients we were transporting nervous with my facial expressions. He was full of shit but I took him up on his offer and showed up at Crazy Beans fifteen minutes early. The second I opened the door and heard the loud moo of a cow in my ear—Crazy Beans' way of alerting their baristas to a new patron—I spotted a fellow Hell citizen sitting at the corner table with a baseball hat pulled low while she inhaled what looked to be a bear claw the size of her head. Izzy Waldo.

She owned the only bakery in Hell, having bought it from old lady Monroe who owned it before her. Izzy had made massive improvements, the most important one being that she didn't yell at the kids when they pressed their faces against the glass. I'd been on the receiving end of a verbal blistering from Monroe one too many times growing up. Once I gave her the charming smile I was known for and offered to clean the glass, her disposition would always change. Izzy, on the other hand, just shrugged and made sure the littles got free samples, which meant every mother brought her kids to Baked Goodness and bought copious amounts of high-priced coffee. Genius, really.

But what was she doing here? And why did she look shiftier than a guy in a ski mask leaving a bank?

I ignored the bored barista inspecting her nails behind the counter and headed to the corner.

"Hey, Izzy."

Her dark head snapped up, eyes bugged out and cheeks full of sugary pastry. She put down what was left of the bear claw and chewed vigorously. Once she swallowed the huge bite, she smiled up at me.

"Hey... What are you doing here, Callan?"

She was doing a weird thing where she was talking while still smiling, showing a lot of teeth. Kind of creeped me out to be honest. Her older sister, Amelia, was flat-out dangerous. I'd been called out to more than one event where Amelia had caused injury to herself or others, but that weird smile on Izzy had me on high alert too. You always have to watch out for the quiet ones.

"Buying some coffee. But based on the way you inhaled that bear claw, I may have to get one of those too."

Izzy finally lost the grin, her pale face turning positively ghostly. "You don't see me."

I frowned, folding my arms across my chest. "I don't?"

One dark eyebrow lifted and suddenly I was standing in front of a woman who could eviscerate me with a single glance. Shit, did women come out of the womb knowing how to do that? I'd take that weird smile over the eyes of death and destruction.

"If you know what's good for you, Hellman, you'll forget you ever saw me. *Capisce?*"

I found myself nodding, even though I didn't like getting pushed around by a Waldo sister. "Only if you tell me why you're here looking guilty as sin."

She breathed fire through her nose for a beat. Then she dropped the mother-of-dragons vibe and tossed me a sheepish smile. "I, uh, was here undercover. Heard they made incredible bear claws and I had to see for myself. Market research, if you will."

I couldn't help the grin. "The hat nearly threw me off. Might want to ditch the cupcake earrings next time though."

Her hands flew to her ears, twin spots of color on her cheeks. "Ah, yes. The juvenile earrings always give me away, but Daire likes them, so I single-handedly keep Claire's in business at the mall."

I knocked on the back of the chair. "Enjoy your undercover pastry tasting and we'll both pretend we didn't see each other."

Her dark eyebrows screwed together and she opened her mouth to ask what the hell I was hiding from, but a cow let loose at the door and her gaze flew in that direction, same as mine. Richard Hellman, all six foot four of him, came through the doorway. He glanced around before laying eyes on me and staying there, wariness coating him like a physical thing.

"Ah. My lips are zipped," Izzy said quietly. "And good luck with that."

I didn't glance back at her, keeping my gaze firmly on my father, like I feared he might just turn on his heel and run out of here before I got a chance to ask him anything. "Probably gonna need it."

I met him in the middle of the shop, both of us stopping at a random table and staring at each other like strangers. He had

Blaze's penetrating eyes, but Ace's dark hair. If he ever cracked a smile, I might see Ethan and Daxon in him too. Wasn't sure I wanted to see any of myself in him though.

"Been awhile," I said with no small amount of censure in my voice.

The man didn't even blink. "Two coffees. Black," he called out over his shoulder. I saw the barista freeze, wondering if the new guy was actually calling out his order instead of stepping up to the counter like a normal person. She shrugged and got to making the two coffees.

I grabbed the back of the nearest wooden chair and pulled it out. My father followed suit, having a seat and folding his hands together on top of the scarred table. He was far older than I expected, the deep grooves around his eyes telling his age more assuredly than a driver's license. I suppose the father I'd seen in old photographs was frozen in my mind, forever early thirties without a single gray hair woven through the black. The icy gray suited him, however, making him less distinguished and more cold.

"Thank you for meeting me," I started, wondering how quickly I could leave again.

"Sure," he said, his voice deep and not at all one I recognized. "Wondered when one of you would contact me."

"We were wondering the same thing," I shot back. How many years had to pass before a father reached out to his own kids and tried to make things right?

The barista arrived with two cardboard cups of coffee. She set them down and looked between us, picking up on the tension in the air. "Uh, that's four seventy-five."

When my father didn't reach for his wallet, I did, handing the girl a ten-dollar bill and shaking my head when she muttered something about getting change.

"Why am I here, Callan?"

I let the sound of my father saying my name wash over me. I

thought it might bring me comfort, or perhaps closure, or maybe even disgust but it did none of those things. It was like hearing a stranger say your name. A total non-event.

In a sudden flash of insightfulness, I realized what Cricket had been trying to tell me. The genetics didn't make a father. The enduring love that would accept no distance between a father and a son was what gave a man the title of father. And the guy sitting in front of me had no clue what that title meant. He'd never earned it. Had walked away two decades ago, forever forfeiting his right to the title.

I sat forward and shoved my coffee cup out of the way. Time to get what I came here for and get back home to Cricket. "I wanted to hear from your own mouth why you left us."

Richard did blink then. He suddenly found his coffee cup fascinating, running his thumb around the edge repeatedly. After all this drama and lead-up to this meeting, I was afraid I wouldn't even get an answer to that one basic question. When he finally looked up at me, there was only a disinterested coldness staring back at me.

"When you realize you've made a mistake, you have to be mature enough to walk away from it. That's a lesson you'll learn soon enough, son."

Perhaps it was the flippant way in which he'd just called me and my brothers and my mother a mistake. Or perhaps it was the way he tossed out the word son, as if he had any right to familial ownership after turning his back on me years ago. Whatever it was, I was done with this meeting. Done with this man. And most certainly done with trying to build a bridge across the years. Sometimes you just had to light a match and watch that shit burn to the ground. At least then the past couldn't traipse across the bridge and kick you when you least deserved it.

I scraped my chair back and stood so fast I heard Izzy gasp from the corner of the shop. My voice shook but I got the words out. "No. When you realize you've made a mistake, you have to be man enough to own your actions and the consequences. Children are never mistakes. Perhaps you never matured enough to learn that lesson."

I turned on my heel and stomped out of the coffee shop, fueled by an anger I wasn't used to. I was the happy-go-lucky guy around town. The glass was always half full, and if things didn't go my way, I knew the next day would bring a new chance to make things right. But this...shit, this man was something else. He made me so angry I couldn't see straight. A fact I didn't realize until I ended up walking around the block and down a couple of streets, completely unsure where my truck was parked.

A throat clearing had me lifting my head from staring at the pavement and wondering if patricide was ever warranted. Izzy stood there with something like pity on her face. She lifted her arm and held out a white pastry bag bulging at the seams.

"Bought out all the bear claws." She hitched her lips into a smile. "When I'm feeling anything other than happy, I turn to pastries. Thought you could use a bear claw or seven."

Despite myself I cracked a smile. I took the bag, feeling all kinds of grateful for a friendly face. "Izzy Waldo, you are a lifesaver. Now, if you could point me in the direction of my truck, I'll name my first kid after you."

Izzy took my arm and turned us facing left. "Down that way two blocks." She peered up at me. "Shouldn't you check with Cricket though before promising me a little bundle of Izzy joy?"

I nodded. "You're probably right. If Cricket lets me have babies with her, I'm gonna let her name them whatever she wants. I'll put in a good word for Izzy though."

"It's all I ask." Izzy squeezed my arm, lowering her voice. "And don't let the asshole get you down. I've got a shovel and four sisters who are strong enough and devious enough to drag a body. You need us, you just call. Okay?"

My battered heart turned to look at this woman whom I'd never been particularly close with. She was older than me and we ran in different circles, but she was from the same small town. This woman had my back when I needed it most.

Which was a hell of a lot more than I could say for my own father.

"Thanks, Izzy."

CHAPTER TWENTY-FIVE

ricket

IF A STORM CLOUD could take on the shape of a man, Callan was it. I'd never seen that line between his eyebrows dip in so deep. He'd gotten home early, and so had I, purposely getting here so I could make him dinner, knowing that the meeting with his father had probably been emotional. But I hadn't even gotten the salad fixings chopped and he'd slammed through the front door like the crack of a lightning bolt. A black cloud of fury hovered over him as he dropped his keys on the table and stalked into the living room. I trailed after him.

"Can I get you something to drink?" I asked the back of his head. He just stood there staring out the back window, hands on his hips. I looked in that direction and only saw a wilted plant in a pot and the normal patch of green grass.

When Callan only grunted in response, I knew I had a problem on my hands. Callan didn't grunt. And he certainly didn't ignore me. Not ever. I approached him as one would a wounded animal, keeping my voice low and my touch soft. He tensed the second my hand grazed his shoulder blade.

"Why don't you have a seat and I'll get dinner ready? Then you can tell me all about it."

If anything, his jaw just clenched harder, reminding me of Blaze when he got angry. "I'm not hungry," he bit out, still not looking at me.

Time to retreat and regroup. "Okay." I stepped back and then fled into the kitchen to find my phone.

Me: Hey, Ace, sorry to bother you, but Callan just came home from meeting with your father. He's...angry? Not talking. Just grunting. I'm not sure what to do.

It didn't take long before I saw the bubble that said Ace was texting me back. I heaved out a sigh. Normally I could talk Callan down from anything, but I felt like this situation required a group effort. Callan needed his brothers.

Ace: Shit. I didn't know that was today. I'll call the boys and we'll convene at your place as soon as we can get there.

Me: Perfect, thank you.

Ace: Don't let him leave. Richard Hellman brings out the bad side of anybody. I don't want Callan around town with a head full of steam.

Me: Oh, I won't let him, trust me.

Ace: Hang tight.

I put the phone back in my pocket and slid the frozen pizza into the oven. If Callan wouldn't eat, maybe his brothers would. Then I left the kitchen, only to find Callan still staring out the window. My stomach was in knots.

This was worse than the day that kid Johnny had taunted Callan about not having a dad for Dads and Donuts day in fourth grade. Callan had shoved him into the sand at recess, which got out most of his anger. When he got assigned after-school detention, I organized a bunch of us to do detention with him. It had become a party, especially when the teacher assigned to oversee detention was one of Nikki Hellman's friends and didn't care for what Johnny had said either.

"Hey," I said softly, running my palm up and down his rigid back. "Whatever that guy said, it was probably bullshit."

Callan scoffed, so I knew he heard me. He didn't take his gaze away from the yard. I didn't know what had happened at that meeting, but I could guess. Assholes didn't change their stripes. Or something like that.

"Should I order a man-shaped piñata? You could beat the shit out of it." No answer. "Oh! Or how about we buy out the grocery store's supply of toilet paper and go pay him a late-night visit?" We'd done that a couple of times when we were teens. Callan had always gone back the next day to help the victim of our TPing clean up. We gave him shit for it, but he couldn't help himself.

When that didn't even get a flicker of a smile, I dug deep to remember some of the items on Meadow's revenge list. Thankfully a knock on the front door interrupted my next suggestion which involved a weasel. I wasn't sure where one could find a weasel around here.

"I'll get it." I spun around and jogged to the door, opening it to find Blaze standing there with a six-pack of beer and a grim smile.

He held it up. "Reinforcements have arrived."

I opened the door wide and gave him a wide-eyed look that I hoped conveyed an SOS. He swooped in and called out to Callan. Before I shut the door, I saw Ethan's beat-up truck pull up to the curb. I waved and waited for him. He gave me a hug and came inside too, smelling of man glitter—AKA sawdust. Ethan had always been my favorite Hellman brother. He was sweet in a way that not even Callan could beat. He had such a soft heart I wanted to protect him from the world. His brothers did too, though they gave him enough shit he didn't feel like they were having to look out for him.

When I took the pizza out of the oven to cool, Blaze and Ethan had Callan seated on the couch, shooting the shit. Callan's color was even off. He was normally tan all through the winter, having that healthy glow that set off the highlights I gave him. Tonight though, he took on a ghostly hue that had me worried Richard Hellman had done irreparable emotional harm.

"Did you know there's a bag of bear claws in the driveway?" Blaze asked, pulling a beer out, twisting the cap off, and handing it to Callan. Callan took it, but just held it like he wasn't even aware what was going on.

"That's weird. Did you bring it in?" I hadn't bought any pastries, nor ordered any delivered. Far as I knew, Izzy Waldo didn't make bear claws down at the bakery.

"I put them in Callan's truck. Didn't want the animals getting to them."

"Pastries make everything better," Callan said absently, then took a swig of beer. "Least that's what Izzy said."

Now I was confused. "You saw Izzy today?"

Callan finally looked at me for the first time since he'd been home. "No. I didn't see Izzy."

I folded my arms across my chest. This was like talking to Yedda. "Okay..."

Another knock on the door sounded and I got up to get it. Ace poked his head in and came into the house with Daxon.

"The gang's all here." Ace came over and gave me a hug, whispering in my ear. "Thank you for texting."

Then he went into the living room and pulled Callan roughly off the couch.

"Dude, relax," Callan snapped, slamming his beer bottle back on the coffee table. "What's your deal?"

Ace punched him in the arm and I winced. "That's for not telling us it was today."

Callan grabbed his arm and looked ready to knock skulls together. "I didn't realize you cared."

Ace looked as pissed as Callan. "I said I didn't want to go."

"Exactly."

Ace cocked his arm back like he planned to hit Callan again.

Ethan grabbed his fist and tried to calm him down with some softly spoken words.

Ace dropped his arm and patted Ethan on the back. "I didn't want to go, but I sure as hell cared, Callan. You're my brother. Of course I wanted to know about it and be able to support you. But no. I had to get a text from your girlfriend that my little brother was falling apart."

Callan's gaze swung over to me and I shrank closer to the wall that led to the kitchen. I probably shouldn't be here. Clearly this was a family affair. I turned to walk through the doorway, but Callan's voice cut in.

"Stay, Cricket."

I turned back around, still not sure if I should go. Callan's face was finally flooding with color again. Maybe that punch to the arm had woken him up.

I nodded. Of course I'd stay if that was what he wanted.

Blaze made everyone sit down. I perched on the side of the couch where Callan was sitting. "Start from the beginning. Where did you meet? What did he look like?"

Callan sighed, but he told them all the details of the meeting, his voice getting stronger with each minute that passed. When he got to the part about his father calling these boys a mistake, I jumped to my feet, more incensed than I'd ever been in my life.

"Where the fuck does this asshole live?"

Daxon jumped up too. "I'm with Cricket."

Ace stood and put his hands up. "Listen, guys. Richard Hellman is not worth it. He walked away from the best family— no offense meant, Cricket—in Hell. That's on him. Stirring up old shit might make you feel like you're doing something, but you'll still end up covered in shit."

We all stayed quiet, thinking it through. I, for one, was still pissed. We couldn't just let that man get away with being an asshole, could we?

"I don't want to be covered in shit," Ethan finally said in the silence, sounding so put out by the idea it broke the tension.

"You already smell like shit," Daxon grumbled.

"Shut the fuck up, shithead," Ethan shot back.

"Boys!" Blaze stood and all the boys settled down. "I think what we've all learned here today is that Dick is a bad guy. He's not looking to change his ways, so we need to stop letting him hurt us. Can we agree that we're done with him?"

Ace immediately answered, "Hell, yes."

Ethan and Daxon nodded.

Everyone turned to look at Callan. He ran a hand over his jaw, scraping the whiskers there that needed shaving.

I leaned over the back of the couch and put my hand on his back. "You deserve so much more than Richard Hellman."

"I know you want to see the best in everyone, Callan, but some people just don't deserve your optimism." Ace came to sit on the coffee table in front of Callan, getting in his face like only a big brother can. "I hate seeing you like this, man." His voice caught and my eyes instantly welled up.

It was a thing of beauty to behold. Five strapping men with attitudes, cut jawlines, and enough testosterone floating through their veins to light the Empire State Building. But they loved each other. Their father was the one who lost out by not being in their lives. They didn't need him any more than a fully potty-trained toddler needed a diaper. It was time to move on. I just hoped Callan could see that now.

Callan dropped his head and sighed. Blaze, Daxon, and Ethan all came around him to put a hand on his back and his head, anointing him with brotherly love.

"Okay," came his voice, soft at first. Then Callan lifted his head to look at his brothers. "I'm done too."

They all dog-piled on top of him with hugs, whispered encouragement, and then digs to get a rise out of each other until they were laughing and pushing everyone off of each other. They grabbed the beers that were getting warm while I wiped my face.

Callan looked over his shoulder at me, saw the tear tracks,

and reached out to pull me over the couch and onto his lap. "Thank you, angel," he whispered.

Then he kissed me, his lips sending relief through my whole body. He was okay. Then he let out a light groan and coaxed my lips open for a kiss completely inappropriate for an audience of his brothers.

"Jesus," Ethan muttered.

"Get a room!" Daxon called.

"This kind of *is* their room," I heard Ace say.

I lifted my hand and waved them away to the kitchen. I pulled away from Callan just long enough to call over my shoulder, "There's pizza and more beer in the kitchen."

And then I was back to kissing Cal, letting his lips and tongue and hands reassure me that the man I loved was only stronger after taking an emotional beating today.

Richard Hellman was a fucking idiot.

CHAPTER TWENTY-SIX

allan

THE FOLLOWING week had to have been the best week I'd ever had. Cricket and I fell into an easy rhythm of living together, being best friends, and yet exploring this new slide into lovers. I knew I came on strong at the beginning, pushing her faster into a relationship than she was comfortable with, but I knew Cricket. If I didn't push, she would stay stalled out forever, waffling between staying comfortable and taking a leap.

I even bought an engagement ring the night she was out with her girlfriends. Not that I was going to tell her about it. She'd freak out and say it was too soon. I wasn't planning to propose until I knew I'd get an immediate yes. Until then, I'd keep it tucked away in the back of my closet inside an old bag of gym clothes I knew she wouldn't go near. Just having it, and knowing I was working toward making her mine forever, made me feel better.

Well, that and giving up on my father finally. I hadn't realized that I'd tucked away a small glimmer of hope that he'd one day come to his senses and want a relationship with his boys. Our meeting had shattered that hope, and while it had hurt at the time, I now felt free. Free to live my life the way I wanted without his dark shadowy past hanging over my head. He'd been a coward, holding a part of himself back from his family. It probably made it easy to walk away when the going got tough with five little kids. Unlike my father, though, I was going all in on Cricket. I'd give her all of me, knowing she was doing the same for me.

"You getting up anytime soon, sleepyhead?" I swatted what I thought was her ass, a cozy lump under all the covers. I'd been up for an hour already and she was sleeping away our Sunday, the one day we both always had off. Wasn't my fault she'd been looking all cute last night and I'd been forced to keep her up late.

"Ftmph," was my answer.

I cracked a grin and decided to pull out the big guns. "Too bad, really. I packed a whole picnic lunch for the beach, just for us. Guess we won't get to go now."

Cricket immediately threw back the covers and squinted at me. Her hair was a tangled mess and she'd been drooling on her pillow again. She was fucking gorgeous.

"Really?" Her voice, still thick with sleep, made me want to dive back under the covers with her and hear it chant my name while I did wicked things to her body.

"Angel," I warned, warming up to the idea of forgetting about the picnic.

Her eyes widened. "Don't you do that sexy voice thing! You promised me a picnic lunch!" She threw a pillow at me, making me laugh.

"Fine. But hurry up and get out of that bed or I'll make sure you never leave."

She paused.

"Angel..."

"Okay, okay, I'm going!" She tossed back the covers and climbed out, wearing my old paramedic T-shirt. "But you toss out these ultimatums like they're some sort of punishment when, really, I kind of like the punishment."

I squeezed my eyes shut. "Please stop talking."

If she asked for sexual punishment, I couldn't be held responsible for ruining the picnic. She was still adjusting to her new epilepsy meds. There was no way I could do the things I wanted to do to her when she was still not feeling one hundred percent. But asking for punishment? That might be my undoing.

We made it out the door fifteen minutes later. Cricket insisted on a swimsuit, even though the water would be way too cold for swimming. She bundled up in a sweatshirt and shorts, her hair piled on top of her head and the largest sunglasses I'd ever seen perched on her nose. Her beach bag was packed to almost overflowing.

I parked by the cliff the whole town went to, knowing the place wouldn't be too crowded this late in the season. "Did you bring sunblock?"

Cricket was so pale she'd fry in twenty minutes.

"Oh shoot!"

"That huge bag and no sunblock?"

Cricket stuck her tongue out at me.

I sighed, knowing full well she'd have forgotten. "I brought some in the picnic basket." How many times did we go to the beach as kids and she forgot sunblock? It only took one bad burn before I started bringing sunblock everywhere with me just in case. Hell, I'd gotten teased in elementary school for having sunblock in my backpack like some kind of helicopter mom, but I didn't want Cricket's delicate skin to get ruined just because she was forgetful.

"My hero!"

I rolled my eyes at her teasing and got out, getting the basket out of the bed of my truck and grabbing the blanket I'd stuffed there this morning. Cricket grabbed my free hand and swung our arms back and forth as we descended the cliff on the well-worn path. The ocean crashed below, the sea spray already coating our skin. Everything about the beach reminded me of my youth. And of Cricket. She was in at least half of all the memories I had. I hoped she'd be the star of all the memories I'd make going forward.

"Oh, Chief and Susie are here!" Cricket pointed to a couple off in the distance, her beach bag nearly sliding off her arm.

I got us down to the sand and found a secluded area to place our picnic. As I spread out the blanket and Cricket got busy unloading all kinds of things from her bag, Chief and Susie had turned around on their walk and were headed in our direction.

"Callan! Cricket," Chief called out in that booming voice of his.

We waved and waited for them to walk up. Susie came over to give us each a hug. She and my mom got along well, both of them mid-level gossipers of the town, compared to Yedda, Poppy, and Lucy. Chief shook our hands, looking slimmer than usual.

"Looking fit, Chief," I said with a smile.

He hitched up his shorts and shot a wink at Susie. "Been working out again. Retirement has given me some time back. Plus I gotta be limber enough for all the grandkids, you know?"

"Is it true Vee is expecting?" Cricket asked, clearly more in tune with town gossip than me as I hadn't heard that one.

Susie clapped, looking like she might just pee her pants. "Yes! Isn't that amazing? Brant finally has his PhD and they've decided it's time. I'm hoping for a boy."

Chief shrugged. "Don't matter to me, I just want a healthy grandkid." He leveled a bushy eyebrow at me. "Maybe one of your brothers will be giving your mama a grandbaby soon?"

"Whoa, I don't know about that. Ace just got married and Blaze is still planning his wedding with Annie. Might be a touch early on the baby stuff."

Chief stroked his impressive mustache. He'd been growing that thing long before it was popular again. "I don't know, Callan. Babies are always a gift, no matter when they come."

I flashed back to my father and his reference to us boys as mistakes.

"Some men don't see it that way, but they're not much in the way of men in my estimation. They're cowards. Better off without cowards in our lives, wouldn't you say, Callan?"

I squinted at Chief, wondering just how much he knew. He was certainly talking as if he knew I'd met with Richard. Maybe Izzy hadn't kept her mouth shut after all, but I couldn't fault her for it. "I think you might be right."

Chief nodded, smiling. "'Course I am. We'll leave you two with your picnic." He clapped me on the shoulder and shot me a wink. "You ever decide to have babies of your own and need a god-grandfather, I'm your man. You understand me, son?"

My intake of air was shaky. "Yes, sir, I do."

Chief nodded again, took Susie's hand, and the two walked off together, their two gray heads close together as they chatted.

"That might just be the sweetest thing I've ever witnessed," Cricket whispered, sounding like she was about to cry. "And I've seen your brothers in a group hug."

I looked out at the blue ocean, feeling like everything had come full circle this week. My chest felt tight, not from nerves but from feeling the love of everyone around me. Father figures were everywhere if you just looked and kept yourself open to the possibility. Putting my arm around Cricket's neck, I pulled her in and kissed the top of her head. "This town fucking rocks."

"Yes, sir, it sure does."

I turned so her body was pressed against me. "Did you just call me sir?"

Cricket sputtered and tried to step back. I held her tight, wishing we weren't out in public right now.

"No, don't go, angel. I fucking loved it. Say it again."

"No! It was a figure of speech!"

I rolled my hips against her stomach, making sure she felt just how much I loved it. "Say it," I whispered, suddenly desperate.

She let out a surprised squeak and went up on tiptoes to wrap her arms around my neck. "Only if you accept my gift."

I frowned, not following. "What gift?"

She tilted her head. "The one I have in my beach bag. You accept it and use it, I'll call you sir tonight."

I wasn't one to negotiate terms, but there wasn't much I wouldn't do to hear her use that term while I had her naked in my bed. "Sure."

She squealed and let go, turning and lunging for her bag. I let her go and shook my head. Cricket was always surprising me. She had us sit down on the blanket and then she presented me with a medium-sized box, wrapped in plain brown paper.

"What's this?" I shook it but nothing rattled.

"Open it, silly!" Cricket clasped her hands under her chin and couldn't seem to sit still. Whatever it was, she very much wanted to see me open it.

I tore off the paper to see a plain gift box without any markings. I lifted the lid and would have had to sit my ass down if I wasn't already seated. There, on a bed of velvet, lay a pair of steel handcuffs and a wound strip of Nubuck leather. I ran a finger across the leather, my pulse quickening.

"Cricket...is this...?"

She came up on her knees and pulled out the handcuffs. They clinked together, sparkling in the midday sun. "They're restraints from The Hardware Store!"

I closed my eyes and reminded myself I was taking things slow with her until she felt better. "Angel..."

Suddenly the box was taken from my hands and my eyes flew open. Cricket sat half on my lap and grabbed my face between her hands.

"Callan, I swear to God if you say we have to take things slow, I will break up with you right now. I. Am. Fine! I love you, but you need to get that through your thick skull. Stop treating me as if I'm fragile. Please?"

She had no idea how much I wanted to believe that. "I just..."

Cricket got real still, her hands slipping from my face. "You keep saying you're doing it for me, but I'm telling you right now that I'm ready. I'm good. I'm healthy. I trust you. If you still don't want to go further, then maybe you ought to look at yourself. Maybe you don't trust yourself, and I can't help you with that."

She went to stand, but I pulled her back, my fingers bracketing her wrists so she couldn't pull away.

"Cricket." I waited until she looked in my eyes. Her cheeks had gone red and I knew her well enough to know she wasn't embarrassed. She was pissed. And she had reason to be. Maybe I was holding back due to my own issues, not hers. But either way, I'd let all that shit go earlier this week. She bought me restraints for God's sake. She was clearly ready. "Pack your shit up. We're going home."

She narrowed her eyes, assessing my expression. "Because..."

"Because we're using that gift you got me."

Her face broke out into a smile. "Yes!"

I clucked my tongue, keeping the smile I felt in my heart and away from my face. "No, angel. It's yes, sir."

Her eyes went wide and I grew so hard I'd have a hard time standing up in these jeans.

CHAPTER TWENTY-SEVEN

ricket

"I DON'T TREAT you this way because I think you're fragile, you know." Callan put me down in front of his bed, having carried me into the house when we got home from the beach. "I treat you like an angel because in my mind you are. You're the most precious person in the whole world, and if I can do something to make your life easier or happier, I'm going to fucking do it."

My heart melted right there in my chest. Callan had always been right by my side, helping me, guiding me, and looking out for my best interests. I'd always thought maybe he believed me to be incapable of doing these things myself, but I knew now that he just loved me and wanted to spoil me.

I pulled my sweatshirt over my head and let it fall to the ground. "What would make me happy right now is you. Teach me everything you like."

Callan's gaze dropped to take in the bright red bikini top I'd previously only worn to the pool with my girlfriends and not out in public. It left little to the imagination but made for the best tan. And believe me, I needed all the help I could get in the tanning department.

His arm lifted and a single finger came out to trace along my collarbone. My breasts instantly felt heavy. Every single nerve ending in my body sat up and took notice of his touch.

"That's the thing, angel. I don't care what we do in this bed. It's not the moves or the positions or the toys. It's about being one hundred percent with you." He stepped closer and his other hand came around to tug at the strings against my back that held the bikini top together. "To know that I'm all you can think about." The top loosened all at once and fell to my feet. "To possess every single thought you have." His hands cupped my breasts, his warmth seeping into me. "To give you everything you've ever wanted." He stepped closer again, and I let my head drop back to hold his intense gaze while I hung on his every word. "To know that I'm the only man in your life that you depend on. That's what I need."

"You're the only man I need, Callan," I whispered, meaning every single word. It was true. I could lose everything around me, including my health, but as long as I had Callan by my side, I knew I could face anything and be happy.

His eyes flared at my words, the warmth in the room cranking up by several degrees. "Then be a good girl and get naked. I'll teach you a position we haven't tried yet."

With my pulse hammering in my throat, I stepped back and slid my shorts down my legs, pulling the swimsuit bottoms with them. I kicked them to the side, reaching for Callan.

"Uh-uh." Callan lifted a finger and shook it at me. "Fold your clothes nicely like a good girl."

I lifted my chin, instantly wanting to tell him to go to hell, but then remembering I said I wanted this. I wanted to see Callan lose himself in his element. And if that meant folding my goddamn clothes for an odd cleanliness fetish, then so be it. Thinking about it though, Callan had always been neater than me, his clothes always put away after he washed them, as opposed to me who mostly just got clothes out of the dryer when I needed to wear them.

I stooped down to grab my clothes, folded them nicely, and set them in a stack on the single chair in the corner of his room. I could feel him watching me the whole time which only ratcheted up my nerves. My hands were shaking, not from fear but from anticipation of what he'd do next. When I turned back around, he was adjusting himself, his eyes taking in every inch of my body.

"Now what...sir?" I whispered, unsure of rules in these situations but knowing he'd quite liked when I called him that at the beach. And a deal was a deal. My gift was on the bed, waiting for us.

"Take my clothes off." Callan's voice was rough, the scrape of it sending a flare of desire across my skin.

I approached, going for his shirt first. I could barely get it over his head because he was so tall. Not because I was short. I was just right, thank you very much. He wasn't helping much either, which was a departure for him. As he said, he usually jumped in to help me before I could ask for the help. But this was a different side of Callan I was seeing right now. The side that barked orders and would hopefully repay me in spades for being a good girl.

Pulling down the zipper on his jeans, I accidentally brushed against his impressive erection. Okay, it wasn't accidental, but you can't blame a girl for copping a feel.

"Not yet," Callan hissed.

I nodded meekly and got busy getting the jeans and boxers off his feet. Walking over to the chair again, I folded his clothes as best I could and enjoyed the view as I walked back to him for my next instructions. A naked Callan was a thing to behold, but a naked, aroused, and commanding Callan was enough to make me feel faint.

"Good girl." Callan pointed to the bed. "Now go sit on the side of the bed."

I hurried over, excited to get to the really fun part of this lesson. Callan followed me, stopping in front of me as I sat. He nudged my feet apart and came closer, putting his erection right in my face.

"Show me what you know how to do with your mouth."

I lifted my hands and wrapped them around his erection, my tongue darting out to lick my lips.

"Uh-uh."

I looked up at Callan, confused.

"I said use your mouth, not your hands, angel."

I wanted to smack the smug look off his face. But a deal was a deal.

"Um...sorry?"

"Sorry what?"

"Sorry, sir." The words didn't want to leave my throat, but the second they did, Callan's eyes burned hotter. If he truly loved being called sir, I was actually happy to do that for him.

"If you can't follow directions, then I'll have to help you. Put your hands in your lap."

My lips pouted, but I peeled my hands off of him and put them in my lap. Callan reached around me and came back with the soft leather restraint I'd gifted him. He wound it around my wrists, tight but not overly restrictive. Out of nowhere, the first trickle of nervous fear hit my gut.

"You okay, angel?" Callan asked, his hands pausing.

I swallowed and analyzed the situation. Sure, being tied up was a new experience, but in truth, I trusted Callan completely. It was time to put action behind those words.

"Totally fine," I said softly, looking up at him and seeing genuine concern behind the hooded eyes.

Callan cupped my chin, taking his time looking at me to see the truth of my answer. "You're my brave angel, aren't you?"

I smiled, soaking in his praise like sunflowers turning toward the sun. He continued tying my wrists together and then tying the other end to the bed post. My arms were stretched to the side, but not uncomfortably so.

"Now show me what your mouth can do."

And so I did. Eagerly. And with every stroke inside my mouth, his inhales and exhales got shakier. His taste filled my senses, my tongue lapping up everything he'd give me. When my jaw began to ache, I took him further down my throat, egged on by the way his shallow breaths had turned to moans. When my eyes began to water and I had to focus on dragging air through my nose, he pulled back abruptly, breathing harder than me.

"Apparently, you learned that lesson all too well. Jesus, angel."

I grinned up at him wickedly, feeling quite smug that I could make such a strong man feel out of control. Callan narrowed his eyes at me, a smile tugging on the corners of his lips.

"Lie down."

I tugged on my wrist restraints. "How do I do that with my hands tied?"

Callan's whole face dropped the grin. "I'll have to show you, then."

He leaned down and picked me up as if I weighed nothing, turning me and then placing me facedown on the bed. My arms stretched out overhead. I could hear Callan walking around the bed but I couldn't see him with my face in the comforter. His warm hands grabbed my ankles, surprising me. Then he tugged, spreading my legs and pulling me further down the bed. A soft squeal left my mouth, swallowed up by the cotton. The restraints pulled tight, spreading a slight burn to my shoulders at the stretch.

"Mmm." Callan's hands left me and I wondered what he was doing. I felt the need to squirm, stretched out on the bed with my legs wide open, no idea what he planned next. It was not a comfortable position to be in. "Don't move," he barked. I stilled instantly.

Several seconds ticked by, the silence stretching out so long my cheeks began to heat with embarrassment or anticipation. I wasn't sure.

"Do you have any idea how beautiful you look right now, angel?" Callan's reverent voice finally broke the silence, floating over my skin like a physical touch.

Before I could decide if he wanted a response, he was in motion. The bed creaked as he put his weight on the area between my feet. And then he was mounting me, his hands pulling at my hips, angling my ass up in the air. He didn't give me even a second to know what was next before he positioned himself at my opening and pushed his way in with a single thrust that rocked the bed and had my insides clenching.

All the air was pushed from my lungs, from both the thrust and Callan collapsing his weight on me right after. He was everywhere, his chest pressing into my back, his legs on top of mine, his face buried in my neck. Hot breaths and open-mouth kisses rained down on my shoulder and neck as he began to rock inside of me. I was moaning, unintelligible words dropping from my lips and becoming lost in the comforter. I was tied up and smashed into the bed by a person much bigger than me. There was no way to put up a fight. Not that I wanted to.

I wanted Callan to keep rocking his pelvis into my ass, his thrusts firm but shallow in this position. Every time his skin slapped against me, he pushed me further into the mattress. I rolled my hips as much as I could from a position that gave me zero leverage, not-so-silently begging him for more. And more is what I got. His thrust became more forceful, his ragged breaths becoming grunts that should have been off putting, but weren't. He was losing all control, all finesse. He was taking what he wanted from me and I was rejoicing in it.

"Fuck, Cricket," he muttered against my neck, our skin sliding together as the heat turned to liquid.

"Yes, please. Yes, Callan. Please."

I was begging and I didn't care.

Callan slammed into me on a grunt. "Please what?"

I pulled on the restraints and turned my head to see him. "Please, sir, let me come!"

He grinned, a bead of sweat dripping down the side of his face. He kissed the side of my mouth and then picked up the pace, slamming into me over and over again. I traveled across the bed, the comforter and sheets a tangled mess around us. Then he reached a hand under my hip and found where I needed him most. It took one stroke across my clit and I was exploding, my shouts muffled as I buried my mouth against my shoulder.

Callan was not far behind, ramming into me one more time before grunting my name in a way that only made me pulse around him that much longer. We lay there smashed together, our lungs heaving in tandem as we tried to recover. When the sweat between us began to cool, Callan finally pulled out with another grunt and got to his feet. The restraints gave way and then there was Callan, rolling me over and picking me up.

He sat back down on the bed with me in his lap. His hands rubbed up and down my arms, sending off a flurry of pins and needles. I hissed and he kissed my forehead, my cheeks, and then finally my lips.

"I want to hear it," I whispered against his mouth.

He pulled back just a bit to stare at me inquisitively. "That I love you? That you're the most beautiful woman I've ever seen? That you completely rock my world and make me want to be a better man?"

That made me smile, of course. I wanted to hear those things too, but there was one phrase I'd just found out that I liked hearing even more.

"Tell me I'm a good girl," I said coyly, not quite believing we were actually having this conversation.

A smile grew on Callan's face. The kind that said he was proud of me. The kind that promised all manner of pleasures in my near future.

Callan ran his fingers through my hair and rubbed the back

of my scalp, his forehead touching mine while we stared into each other's eyes. "You're a good girl, angel. *My* good girl."

And then he kissed me, his tongue invading my mouth to show me just how pleased he was with me. We didn't end up using the handcuffs, but I knew it was just a matter of time before Callan was ready to teach me a new lesson.

The whole trip to The Hardware Store with my friends had been a selfish endeavor to see what sweet Callan was like with an edge to him. But what I'd ended up with was a new understanding of what made Callan unique. He had a huge heart. He wanted to give more than anyone I'd ever met, and doing so made him feel good. He wanted to take care of me, and come to find out, his care made me feel loved.

It also went to prove that you never knew what you'd be into until you're with the right person to awaken those desires. The right person who made you feel safe to explore. And Callan was most definitely the right person for me.

CHAPTER TWENTY-EIGHT

allan

"What about a trip out of town to a fancy hotel? I could put the ring on her pillow when she wakes up the next morning."

Daxon snorted. "Does she even care about fancy hotels? She doesn't seem the traveling type."

I frowned at his ugly mug. "Not all of us got to travel around to fancy locals for photoshoots like spoiled models when we were teens."

"Oh shut up. That happened, like, once." Daxon threw a peanut at me.

The Tavern was trying out free peanuts as a draw to get people to drink more beer at their establishment. I thought it was nuts. Pun totally intended. There were peanut shells all over the floor and all I wanted to do was get a broom, not drink more beer.

"Sorry I'm late." Blaze slid into the empty chair at our table. "I was training a puppy that Poppy might adopt and she nearly bent my ear in half with all of her gossip."

Ace grimaced. "I had a call out at Yedda's cat place today. She was trying to set up a fire pit so her cats can go outside and roam at night this winter. Of course, one of them got too close and singed his tail. Hence the call to the fire department. These old ladies in town are a menace."

Blaze huffed. "No kidding. Poppy was trying to tell me that Cricket was on a lunch date with someone other than Callan. The woman has done lost her mind."

That sure as hell caught my attention. "Say what, now?"

Blaze swatted his hand through the air. "She said Cricket was having lunch with some guy—who wasn't you, as she told me at least five times—and according to Poppy's sources, she looked rather cozy with him. Maybe the woman needs glasses. Like Cricket would be out with some random guy. I've never seen a girl crazier about a guy. Well, except maybe Annie. She's pretty crazy about me."

"Jesus," Ethan muttered, taking a long swig of his beer and looking around the bar for somewhere better to be.

I didn't even hear most of what they were saying. Instead, I was wracking my brain for what Cricket had told me her plans were today. She hadn't mentioned anything about a lunch. I'd have to ask her about it tonight, but I wasn't worried. Cricket and I were good. Stronger than ever. That little tidbit from Poppy was just idle gossip not founded on truth.

The Tavern got busier as the night went on, as it typically did on a Friday night, but the crowd was packed by the time the live band took the rickety stage, proving that maybe the peanuts were a good draw after all.

I promised my brothers to stay until the band took the first break. I had no interest in dancing if Cricket wasn't here. They weren't half bad, so the time passed quickly. The minute the band announced their break, I headed for our table in the back to down the rest of my beer and head out. Instead what I got was a mass of bodies in the way of my quick exit.

"Dude, did you see that new guy in town today? He was

picking up groceries this afternoon. I swear to you, he picked up a bottle of wine that was almost fifty bucks! I introduced myself to him, but he didn't ask for my number."

Some woman, who might have graduated with Blaze if I remembered correctly, was gushing to her friends about a guy. I tried to step between them to get to the table. "Excuse me."

Apparently they didn't hear me or didn't care because they kept on talking as if I wasn't standing right behind them.

"Of course he didn't get your number. He's already dating Cricket."

I froze, my ears straining for the rest of the conversation.

The first girl gasped. "Seriously? I thought she was dating that one Hellman brother. Jeez. Can't she leave some for the rest of us?"

"I know, right? I mean, the new guy has only been here one day and she's already making out with him at Forty-Diner. Slut much?"

Steam was practically pouring out my ears. I clenched my fists to keep from striking out and turned around, marching toward the exit, pushing people out of my way not-so-gently, and tried to make sense of what I'd heard in my mind. I wasn't sure if I was pissed about those girls calling Cricket a slut or if I was more angry that Cricket herself hadn't told me she'd had lunch with some guy.

I pushed open the door and stepped outside, nearly gasping for air that didn't smell like stale peanuts. Before I got to my truck, I had my phone out, calling Cricket. When she didn't answer right away, I tried again.

"Dammit!" I yelled, wrenching open the door to my truck and climbing in. My brain was spinning. What the fuck was going on here?

"Hey! Callan!" I turned to see Ethan jogging out of The Tavern toward me. "Wait up!"

"What do you want, Ethan?" I loved my brother, I really did, but I didn't have time to deal with him right now. I needed to find Cricket and get to the bottom of what happened today before the rumors got even more blown out of proportion.

He stopped at my door and held his phone out to me. "This is circulating. I'm sorry, bro."

I looked down to see a picture of my Cricket and some man at our favorite booth at the diner. She was laughing and he was looking at her as if she hung the fucking moon. He was dressed in a fancy collared shirt with a wrist watch I couldn't buy even if I sold my truck for the necessary cash. The picture was the type you saw on TMZ of celebrities caught with someone they weren't supposed to be with. The kind of photo we all gawk over and laugh, not realizing that someone's life was shattering. I just sat there staring at it until the screen went black. Seeing Cricket with another man, whether it was innocent or not, was like throwing gasoline on a bonfire in windy conditions. Shit was getting dangerous now.

"Dude, take a deep breath. Go talk to her. There has to be an explanation."

"Step aside," I said between clenched teeth. Ethan blinked at me and opened his mouth to argue. "Step. The fuck. Aside."

Ethan sighed, but stepped back, letting me slam the door shut and crank the engine. I peeled out of the parking lot so fast I left some of my tires on the pavement. I knew I needed to calm down, but I couldn't seem to manage it, no matter how many deep breaths I forced on myself. By the time I got home and saw the light on in the living room, I had at least ten possible scenarios in my head, each progressively worse than the first.

I threw the truck in park and climbed out, storming into the house with the devil on my heels.

"Callan?" Cricket called out from the bedroom.

I stood there in the living room and made my feet stop in their tracks. I couldn't go in there like this. Like a wild animal, completely out of control. Cricket deserved a chance to tell me what had happened. So I stood there, deep breathing and counting to ten over and over again, until she came down the hallway and into the living room. She had on her normal pajamas of one of my T-shirts and a pair of tiny shorts that gave me a peek at the curve of her ass when she walked.

"Hey, what's wrong?" She rushed over to my side and put her hands on my cheeks when she saw my face. "What happened?"

I inhaled, letting the familiar scent of her calm me down. It did, but it also made my chest ache.

"Where have you been?" I asked quietly, trying like hell to keep the anger from my voice.

Cricket frowned. "I just got out of the bathtub, why?"

I took a second to really take her in. Little strands of her hair in the back were wet and curling, a sure sign she'd been in the bath. That's why she missed my calls. See? Everything was making sense. Everything had an innocent explanation.

"Did you have a nice lunch today?" I asked calmly.

Her face froze and so did my heart. An innocent lunch would not make her freeze. She snatched her hands back and backed up. I braced myself, having an out-of-body experience. It was as if I was watching this whole thing from the ceiling. Guy catches girl. Girl gives ridiculous excuse they both know is a lie. Guy must decide if he wants to believe the lie just to make things go back to the way they were before.

"I see the Hell rumor mill is alive and well," she said dryly.

"Just tell me about your fucking lunch, Cricket." My voice was rising, try as I might to keep calm.

She glared at me, having a seat on the couch and gesturing for me to join her. I stayed standing. She rolled her eyes at me. "I will tell you, but you need to calm down first."

"Really, Cricket?" Telling me to calm down? How many times had I tried that line on her and she always railed on me to never say that to a woman.

She huffed out what could have been a laugh under different circumstances. "Yeah. Not possible, huh?"

I folded my arms across my chest and she rushed to explain.

"Dad called and wanted to take me to lunch. I sat down at the booth, but he was there with another guy. He introduced me to Sam and then Dad launched into why he'd invited me to lunch." Cricket scooted forward, clearly excited. "Dad wants to buy me one of the new condos that are going in just outside of town."

Now I was really confused. "What? Why? You live here."

Cricket tilted her head, shooting me a smile I did not like at all. "Do I, though? I'm just staying here until the doctor says I'm stable on my new meds. I can't just live with you forever, Cal."

My mouth dropped open. My brain was spinning super speed now. There I'd been, planning how to propose to her so we could be together forever, and Cricket had been planning her exit.

"So, Sam's the real estate guy overseeing the sale of the new units. Dad got a phone call though and had to leave early. Sam and I stayed for lunch so he could tell me about the condo amenities. Isn't that amazing?"

Dear God, was she really that naive? Her father hated me. Had tried setting her up with men over and over again. Did she really think this stunt was anything more than a way to get her away from me? How did she go from promising me last week that I was the only man in her life to accepting a condo from her father and a lunch date with a realtor her father set her up with?

My arms dropped to my side. All that anger that had driven me here in a frenzy left my body in a flash. "Are you serious?"

Cricket smiled, nodding slowly, still not getting it. "Yeah, I think he's really going to buy it for me. I mean, at first I said no, because jeez. He's always trying to buy me things and I want to stand on my own two feet, you know? But then as I thought about it, and Sam described the opportunity, I really feel like I can't turn it down. I could get in when it's cheap, live there a few years, and then sell it for a nice little profit."

It hit me with sudden clarity: Cricket wasn't on the same page. Maybe not even the same book.

I wanted forever with her. White picket fences. Babies.

Matching ugly Christmas sweaters and fights over whose turn it was to make dinner. Movie marathons and her drooling on me when she fell asleep before the credits rolled.

I'd pushed her too fast. I knew she was taking longer to get where I was, but I'd been so head over ass in love with her I hadn't seen that she was lagging that far behind. She was talking condo profits and years of living apart.

Given half a chance I would have married her tonight in front of a judge in his robe and slippers.

I took a step back. Figuratively and literally. She'd made her choice and it clearly wasn't me. Her father threw out a hare-brained offer and she jumped at the chance. And this wasn't even the first time. Was I fooling myself to think she'd ever put me first? She clearly wasn't ready to be with me the way I wanted, so I needed to give her the space she needed.

I inclined my head toward the front door. "I need to go chat with someone. Why don't you head to bed? I might be a little late."

Cricket frowned, clearly lost. That made for two of us. Without her, I'd be lost too.

I didn't wait for her to respond. I just turned my back on her and headed for my truck. Not one damn thing penetrated my brain the whole drive over to Mom's house. I probably was in no shape to drive, but I got there okay, sitting in the driveway long enough that Mom poked her head out the front door to peer at me like I was crazy. She must have seen something on my face through the windshield because next thing I knew, she was flying across the pavement to open my door and wrap her arms around me.

"Come inside and tell me what's wrong, honey. Whatever it is, we'll find a way to make it right."

I followed her into the house, welcoming her fussing but knowing she was dead wrong.

Nothing would ever be right again.

CHAPTER TWENTY-NINE

ricket

EERIE SILENCE FILLED MY EARS. My fingers and toes felt cold as ice. I blinked repeatedly, taking in Callan's bedroom as if in a fog. I'd woken up here for weeks now and it had begun to feel like home. The couch was empty and the bed hadn't been slept in. Waking up this morning without him, knowing he never came home last night had my head spinning. Had that actually happened? Had we had a fight so severe he just left?

My phone pinged and I checked it, thinking it might be Callan and that this whole fight might be just some vivid dream I'd had.

Dad: Don't forget to take the condo tour at nine. Sam will be waiting there for you.

I bit my lip, my eyes beginning to sting. It was real. The condo, the offer, Sam the realtor guy. I shook my head, going over and over every line of our argument, wondering where in all that had I gone wrong. I knew Callan liked taking care of me, but like it or not, I did have a father in my life. Just because

Callan didn't, didn't mean I should ignore mine to spare his feelings.

Right?

I hopped off the bed and grabbed the first clothes I found that looked like they might be clean. I wasn't going to sit here crying. I had a condo to look at and then I'd find Callan and straighten this out. We'd had arguments before and we'd always found our way back to each other. This would be no different.

I pulled up to the new condo complex a little early, seeing that only half of the complex was built. The other half was crawling with construction workers and trucks and hard hats and cranes. I climbed out of my car and gazed up at the four-story structure. It was the tallest condo building we had in the area. It was amazing, but also a little bizarre. I wasn't sure how I'd feel living that close to so many other people.

"You should make an offer and just see what they say."

I turned away from the construction to see two ladies around my age or a little younger staring at the completed section of condos. The brunette laughed.

"I can't afford it. They'd laugh me out of the building."

Her friend put her arms around her shoulders. "You never know unless you try, Audrey."

I froze, eavesdropping like a total creeper. I knew of an Audrey, but what were the chances I'd run into her here? Callan had told me all about how he'd helped her and her friend on the side of the road. She'd had no idea who he was. Didn't even realize she was flirting with her half brother.

"I know exactly what they'll say when they see my minimum wage paychecks and the lack of zeros in my bank account." Audrey rolled her eyes. I studied her, cataloguing all the similarities. That smile. That shade of brown hair that caught the sun. She was clearly a Hellman.

"Why don't you ask your dad for the down payment? He'd give it to you, you know."

Audrey snorted, sounding as stubborn as Callan. "Hell no.

His help comes with strings. Remember my first car? He paid half and then felt like he had the right to ask me where I was going every second of every day. If I let him buy me a condo, he'd be monitoring who came and went. No, thank you."

Her friend laughed. "You're right. Can't let daddy run your life forever or you'll be one of those sorority girls who jumps from daddy's bank account to a man's, marrying for money." She sighed. "These condos are hella cute though..."

Audrey laughed and pulled her friend away, nodding hello to me as they passed. "Stop looking at them. We'll move here one day, but it'll be on our terms, right?"

"Damn right, girl."

I watched them walk away until they climbed in the car and headed out of the parking lot. My brain was back to spinning, this time because I was having an epiphany. And it wasn't a very pleasant one.

"Hey, Christine. Hope I didn't keep you waiting."

I turned, seeing Sam stride across the parking lot in his fancy shoes and slicked-back hair. He didn't even know my name. No one called me Christine. He shook my hand and pulled me in to kiss my cheek, a cloud of cologne hitting my nose. What the hell? I stumbled back and he held my elbow, steering us toward the front door of the complex. His touch made my skin crawl.

"I'll give you the grand tour. You won't be able to say no after you see the kitchens."

I needed to get out of there. Black dots danced around my vision. If I was going to pass out or have a seizure, I wanted Callan with me, not this sales guy who clearly had the wrong idea about me. All the epiphanies kept triggering, whacking me upside the head until I felt the physical effects. I didn't want to be here. I didn't want to be a sorority girl going from one man's wallet to another. I didn't want anything but Callan.

"I have to go," I said faintly, wrenching my arm from his grasp and running across the lot.

"Christine?" I heard Sam shout from behind me.

I picked up speed and nearly rammed straight into my car. After fumbling with the lock, I climbed inside, started the engine, and tore out of the lot. I only made it one block before I pulled over to the side of the road and slammed on my brakes. My lungs were heaving like I'd run a marathon.

I held up my hands to see them shaking. "I'm such an idiot," I said out loud.

Needing to fix things, I grabbed my phone out of my purse.

Me: Can we talk? Please?

I sent it before I could talk myself out of it. I'd phrased it as a question, but it wasn't. I'd find Callan and make him listen to me. He had to listen to me. Just had to.

Callan: I think it's best we take a break.

I gasped out loud in the car, re-reading that same line over and over again. He had to be joking.

Me: Callan. Please. Let me talk to you.

Callan: Fine. I have that training out of town over the weekend. Let's talk after that.

He wanted to wait? For the first time since last night, I realized the gravity of the situation. Callan wanted to take a break. From me. From us. My hands began to shake so hard I could barely type a response. As it was, it took me three tries to get it right.

Me: Okay. I love you.

There was no immediate response. And as I sat in the car staring at the screen, the first tear fell. More came after, each one keeping time with each minute that passed. Each minute that did not bring a response from Callan.

By the time the tears stopped, my eyes were swollen and I'd had another epiphany. I was that girl. The one Audrey had made fun of. The girl who couldn't stand on her own two feet. Dad bought me the car I was currently sitting in. The one I shouldn't even be driving right now due to my epilepsy, but without the watchful eye of Callan to stop me, I immediately became irresponsible. Dad had put the down payment on my studio and the apartment above it.

Now he was trying to buy me a condo so I'd move out of Callan's place. And apparently trying to set me up with the realtor too. Even Audrey, who was younger than me, understood that lesson.

My heart still felt like it was breaking, but now I felt the first trickle of anger. Anger at my dad. Anger at myself for always taking the easy route. Callan had asked me to make him my priority and I had. At least until dear ol' Dad made me a generous offer involving money. No wonder Callan had been pissed.

I sat there for at least another hour, just staring out the windshield at the poppies growing like weeds on the side of the road. I had some growing up to do and I wasn't going to waste another minute. Callan, though extreme in his delivery, was right. Partially. I couldn't jump from my dad's safety net to Callan's. I needed to stand on my own two feet before I could then rely on him. Starting right fucking now.

I wiped my face, put the car in gear, and headed to the used car dealership on the outskirts of Blueball. What I really wanted to do was go over to my dad's and let him have it. Instead, I was taking that finger and pointing it at my own chest. This wasn't my father's fault. This was my fault.

THE UBER DROPPED me off at my parents' house four hours later. My stomach let out a growl that probably startled the wildlife four counties over. I hadn't eaten all day, which wasn't good for my epilepsy, but I did what I had to do.

"Honey?" I looked up to see Mom standing at the front door. She looked happy to see me, which brought tears to my eyes. I'd held it in the whole time I'd been at the car dealership, but seeing kindness brought it forward again.

"Hey, Mom. Dad home?" I pulled the purse strap higher up my shoulder.

Mom gave me a funny look, but put her arm around me and pulled me into the house. "Sure. He's in his office, but I'll go get him."

I sat on the couch and listened to the familiar ticking of the grandfather clock. The hours at the car dealership had given me time to calm down. Time to think about exactly what I needed to say.

Dad came into the living room and sat across from me, a smile on his face. "Well, what did you think?"

"I didn't look at the condo, Dad."

He frowned. "I don't know why you'd leave Sam waiting like that. I pulled in a favor, you know."

Anger flared in my chest. "I didn't ask you for that favor, Dad. I didn't ask you for the condo. I certainly didn't ask you to set me up with Sam."

His gray eyebrows drew together in a hard line. "Of course you didn't. But I am your father and I like to provide you with things I didn't have growing up."

I put my hand up. "I get it. I do. But I'm asking you to stop. I want to stand on my own two feet for once and I can't do that if you're paving my path with gold and diamonds. Just let me do things on my own."

Dad let out a huff. "You were just in the hospital, pumpkin. Now is really not the time for this silly rebellion."

I nodded, rage propping me up when what I really wanted to do was collapse to the floor and cry. "Oh, I know. The time was several years ago when I was a teenager, but I somehow skipped over that phase. Listen, Dad. I'm in love with Callan. I'm sorry you're not on board with that, but that's how it is. And now your meddling has put all that on pause."

"Oh no," Mom gasped, turning to level a glare at Dad.

I took a deep breath. "So, I'm taking a break from you."

He leaned forward to grab my hand, the first sign of actually listening to me. "Pumpkin..."

I shook my head. I gave his hand a squeeze and then let go. "I mean it. Please stay away until you can let me live my life. I appreciate all you've done for me, but I'm asking you to stop. When you can do that, I'll be happy to see you."

I climbed to my feet and headed for the door, stunned silence in my wake. Silence except for that damn grandfather clock. Just as I hit the front door, I heard Mom's sandals slapping against the hardwood as she came after me.

"Cricket! Wait, honey." She slid in front of me, moving faster than I thought she had in her. Her hands landed on my shoulders, her eyes filled with tears. "I'll talk to him. I'll get him to make this right. I can't live without you in my life, honey. I just can't. Whatever it takes, I'll make sure he does it. You hear me?"

I sagged under her grip. "I know, Mom. It's not you. I'm not cutting you off, just Dad's heavy-handedness."

She nodded, gulping back her tears. "Okay. Okay, good. I'll deal with your dad, you deal with Callan. Get him back, honey. He's crazy about you, and I see how happy he makes you."

Now my eyes were watering. I could barely choke out the words. "He really does."

"REINFORCEMENTS HAVE ARRIVED!"

Annie's shout broke me out of my thoughts. I was back in my little apartment over the hair salon. Callan had asked for space and I was giving it to him. For now. There was a deflated dick balloon in my kitchen that made me cry all over again. If only I could go back to the day and do things differently with Callan.

"Oh lordie, you look terrible, babe," Meadow said with a wince, plopping down beside me on my tiny couch.

"Thanks so much," I said dryly, clearing my throat when it came out as little more than a croak.

"What she meant was we brought ice cream. Nature's pick-me-up." Addy pulled pints of ice cream out of her tote bag, one by one, filling my coffee table with more ice cream than the four of us could ever eat in a night.

"Nature, huh?"

Addy grinned. "Okay fine. Natural...with a little assist from Ben and Jerry."

Annie came from the kitchen area with spoons. "Pick your favorite." She sat down on the other side of me, leaving the chair by the door for Addy. "Also, I grabbed your mail. When was the last time you checked it, girl?"

I looked at the hefty stack she put on the kitchen counter. "I'm not sure, to be honest."

"She's been getting Hellman dick. Can you blame her for blocking out everything else going on?" Meadow shot me a wink.

My eyes filled with tears.

"Oh shit. I'm sorry!" Meadow threw her arms around me, which only made me cry harder.

Between bites of ice cream and blowing my nose until it was raw and red, I told them everything. I felt like an asshole, seeing clearly now that Callan had every right to be disappointed in me. And that's what gutted me most. He wasn't mad. He was hurt. Disappointed. Let down by the one person who should have had his back. By the time I got done talking, I wasn't sure if my friends should comfort me or be disgusted with me.

"Oh, honey," Addy said quietly, rubbing my back.

"You made a mistake. I'm sure Callan will forgive you once he's done being angry," Meadow said with more than a little false hope on her face. "He never stays mad long."

I shook my head, feeling worse than I ever had before. "No, that's just it. He's not mad. He didn't make me leave his house, *he* left. Even when I'm an idiot he's still a nice guy. I let him down and I feel awful."

We sat there for some time, trying to brainstorm ways to apologize. So far, we hadn't come up with a plan that felt right. Nothing felt like it was enough. Callan deserved more than words. I needed something weightier.

"Hey, Cricket, did you see this?" I looked over to see Annie holding up a black envelope with gold writing.

I really didn't care about the latest credit card company that wanted me to spend their money so they could then charge me an arm and a leg in interest. I shook my head and went back to wracking my brain for a proper apology.

"Oh my God!" Annie screamed and waved a letter in the air.

"What is it?" Meadow asked, jumping to her feet to investigate what had Annie so excited.

"You've been selected to compete in our thirty-second annual International Beauty Exhibition in New York City!" Annie read aloud as Meadow began to jump up and down.

I was lost, and quite frankly, just wanted to climb in my bed and spend the rest of my night crying myself to sleep. "Huh?"

Addy grabbed my hands. "Callan entered you into that competition in New York. He asked us a month ago if it was a good idea and we encouraged him to do it."

I shook my head to clear the fog. "What? Why? Why would he do that?"

Annie came over, dropping the letter in my lap. "Because he believes in you, silly."

"Damn. We better help you pack." Meadow leaned over my shoulder, reading the letter. "You need to book a flight. It starts in two days."

"What?" I pulled my hands from Addy's and finally looked at the letter. It was an invitation to compete in the very competition I watched every single year growing up. It's where my love for crazy colors came from. I'd always envisioned being there one day, seeing a grown-up version of myself taking New York by storm and wowing the world of hair fashion.

"I...I can't go to this," I stuttered. I wasn't ready emotionally. I wasn't prepared. I wasn't good enough.

I must have said that last part out loud as Meadow looked ready to punch me. "Are you fucking kidding me? You've always been good enough! You're wasting your talents in this tiny town. Get your ass to New York City and make us proud, Cricket."

I thought about it. Really thought about it. Could I go? Could I go to the mecca of style and fashion and not fall flat on my face?

"Babe. You have to take chances. Fate doesn't open doors like this very often. You say no now, you might not get another chance." Addy's soothing voice was everything I needed to hear. "Go spread your wings, Christine VanHunting."

I had just told myself today that I was going to be the adult I knew I could be. Callan deserved a fully grown-up woman by his side. I'd been handing over responsibilities to my father because it was easy. I was done hitting the easy button.

"I'm fucking going," I said with more determination than I felt.

The girls cheered and then it was a whirlwind of packing.

Sheer terror didn't have a chance to settle in. Not until I was on the plane and leaving the coast that held everything dear to me. I didn't know where I was going, or if I'd be laughed out of the competition. My heart was in my throat. If this is what adulting felt like, I wasn't sure I was up for it.

But for Callan, I'd do anything.

Including running off to New York and leaving him behind.

CHAPTER THIRTY

allan

HEADING out of town was the smartest thing I could have done. Staring at my empty house without the sweet scent of Cricket in the air was straight torture. Everywhere I looked, I saw her. Where she sat with her legs pulled up under her. Where she'd lay her purse down when she came home from the salon. The spot where I almost kissed her that time she dyed my hair. She was everywhere and I didn't quite know how to carry on without her. Even in San Francisco for the training, Xavier had to nudge me constantly to get me to focus on what the instructor was saying.

I threw my duffle bag on my bed and swore I'd unpack it before I went to sleep that night. It was a lie I told myself every time I returned from out of town and didn't want to do laundry. Cricket would have given me shit about it and then sweetly done my laundry for me even though she hated folding clothes. But Cricket wasn't here, was she? Because I'd pushed her away.

God, sending that text about taking a break had nearly broken me.

Time out of town had given me space to think maybe I'd made a huge mistake. Xavier had congratulated me on being single again, but that was truly the last thing I wanted. I wanted Cricket. Plain and simple. But only if she wanted me just as much. If I was being honest, there was a mismatch there that I'd been ignoring. I felt like maybe I'd been wanting her for so long, it led to me being the one putting in all the effort, or at least a larger share of it. I wanted—no *needed*—her to need me just as badly as I needed her. I wanted both of us all in.

"You decent?" I heard Daxon shout from what sounded like my front door.

I let out a sigh and stared at the ceiling. He wouldn't go away if I ignored him. Sadly. Couldn't the guy just give me five seconds to wallow in my misery before showing up at my place uninvited?

My door burst open and there was Daxon, his shoulders filling the doorway like they hadn't even just a year ago.

"Dude, you have to lay off the creatine and protein shakes. You're about to bust out of your shirts."

He shot me the middle finger and strode over to clap me on the shoulder. "I heard you and Cricket broke up."

Wow. Okay. Guess we were going straight at it, then.

"Not broken up. Just...paused."

Daxon's face scrunched up. "What the hell does that mean? You're either getting pu—"

"I'll stop you right there," I interrupted. "Before you really piss me off."

"I told him to wait for me, but he never listens." Ethan's voice broke the stare-down Daxon and I were having. He walked into my bedroom and looked back and forth between us. "Oh great. He's already pissed you off."

"Doesn't take long," I drawled.

Daxon opened his mouth to say something else that would probably have me ready to punch him in the nose, but Ace and Blaze walked through my doorway, busting us boys up like they always did.

"We're here to help," Ace said, widening his eyes at Daxon before coming back to me with a look of pity.

There wasn't enough room left in my bedroom to fucking breathe. "Can y'all get the fuck out of my bedroom?"

Blaze scoffed and then pushed Daxon and Ethan out the door. "Let's head to the living room. I didn't bring beer, seeing as how it's just past noon, but if this takes awhile, I can run out and remedy that."

I shook my head, but followed them out. They thought I was some sort of basket case. Which I probably was, but they didn't need to say it to my face, the bastards.

They all sat on my couch and then stared at me, like they expected me to just spill my guts at their feet. I didn't invite them here. This was their show, not mine. Let them be the first to speak.

"If you have something to say, say it." I crossed my arms over my chest and leaned against the wall.

Ethan leaned over to address Ace. "He's in denial."

My lip settled on a snarl. "I'm not in fucking denial. And this isn't some shrink session."

Ethan shot me a friendly smile. "Hey, no disrespect meant, brother. I actually saw a therapist last year and she was amazing. I can give you her number."

We all turned to Ethan, shocked. "When did you see a therapist? And what for?"

Ethan didn't look fazed. "A healthy mind leads to a healthy life. I went because I had some things to work through and I did. You should all give it a try sometime."

Blaze put his hand up. "We're going to come back to that later, but first, Callan. What the hell happened with Cricket?"

I knew they wouldn't leave until they knew every last detail. They were worse than Poppy with needing to know every last bit of gossip. So I told them what happened and why. Maybe that would get them to leave sooner so I could go back to bed and sniff Cricket's pillow just to get a whiff of her shampoo.

"This is about Dick, I just know it," Blaze growled. Ace ground his teeth so hard we all heard it.

I sighed and sat down on the chair I'd gotten from a yard sale. "Maybe. Maybe not. I just need Cricket to need me."

"Ahh," Ethan interjected. "Because if she needs you, she won't just up and leave you suddenly like our father did. Right?"

We all stared at him again.

"Well, shit, Ethan. Maybe you're onto something," Daxon muttered.

Ethan smiled smugly. "Told you therapy is the bomb." Then he turned to me, all serious again. "But I gotta say, bro, I think you're going about this all wrong. In a relationship, there's two people's needs. What does Cricket need?"

I frowned. "To be taken care of?"

Ethan tilted his head. "Really? Or is that, once again, what *you* need from the relationship?"

"I don't know, man. Why don't you just tell me since you seem to know so much about this shit?" He was starting to piss me off.

"How long has Cricket been living on her own?" Ethan asked patiently.

"Is this going to take awhile, because I'll be honest. I'm tired. I'm mentally and emotionally exhausted and I just want to grab some food out of my fridge and go to bed and hope tomorrow is better than the last few days."

Ace stood up and came over to my chair. "I think maybe we should hear Ethan out. He's going down a good path."

Ethan sat forward. "I'll speed this up since you were so kind at sharing space when we were all growing in Mom's torso."

Daxon flinched. "Why you always gotta bring that up? It's weird, man."

Ethan bit back a smile. He knew how to rile up Daxon. "Okay, so Cricket hasn't been living on her own very long. Maybe six months before her seizure? And even then, her dad bought the salon and the apartment, right? Who bought her car?"

I felt my jaw clench just thinking of it. "Her dad."

"Exactly! Dad paid for everything. So here she is, newly twenty-four and feeling like Daddy is still funding everything. And then you come along and sweep her off her feet, only to try to force her to be dependent on you instead of Daddy. Am I getting close?"

A trickle of shame diffused some of the anger I was harboring in my gut. "Well, when you say it that way..."

"She has to stand on her own before she can depend on you," Daxon said quietly. Then he looked up at me, his eyes more serious than I'd ever seen them. "She has to be able to trust herself before she can place that trust in you."

Ethan clapped Daxon on the shoulder. "Exactly. So the only question is...can you give her the space to do that?"

Comprehension dawned on me inch by slow inch. I didn't know why I hadn't seen it before. Didn't know why it took my brother—younger by two whole minutes—to open my eyes to what had been under my nose this entire time. I finally saw the situation clearly, and not just from my side of the story.

I stood up, energy flooding my veins for the first time in days. "I have to talk to her."

I DID NOT, in fact, get to talk to Cricket.

I went to her apartment, which was empty. The salon was dark and locked, which made no sense since it was a Monday and Cricket always worked Mondays.

So I did what a desperate man does, I texted the hell out of her, and when she didn't answer, I drove to her parents' house. I was willing to deal with the devil himself to fix this thing with Cricket.

But first, I went back home and pulled the ring I'd bought

her out of that dusty workout bag in the back of the closet. I put it in my pocket and promised myself that at the soonest opportunity, I'd make things right and slide that ring on her finger. Not to make her mine, but to show her that I was all in. For the rest of our lives. However long she needed until she felt she could place her trust in me.

I was seriously second-guessing my plan when Hank answered the door and not Debbie, like usual. He instantly frowned upon seeing me and stayed in the crack of the doorway, as if to fend off a robber from entering.

"Callan," he said cautiously.

"Mr. VanHunting. Nice to see you." Lies, all lies. "I'm looking for Cricket but I can't find her. Do you know where she is?"

Hank inhaled through his nose the way people do who think they're better than you. "I do."

"Okay... Can you tell me?"

"I'm not sure that I should."

I was the town's nicest human. I was voted Mr. Nice Guy in our senior yearbook in high school. I rescued people on their worst days. I was kind. I was gentle. I was caring.

But right now, I was fucking done.

"Listen, I don't know what your issue is with me, but you might try pulling your head out of your ass long enough to see that I love your daughter, Mr. VanHunting. I want the best for her, and if Cricket decides that's me, then you and I need to try to get along. For her sake."

The door swung open and Debbie stood there beaming. "I was wondering when you'd get the courage to say that."

Hank shot his wife a stunned look before turning back to me. If looks could kill, he already had his shovel ready to bury my body. "Excuse me?"

I threw my arms out to the side. There was nothing left to lose here. Cricket and I were on shaky ground and her father already hated me. "You've hated me since day one. I've done everything to show you that I'm a good guy, but you have no interest in seeing who I really am, do you? So, let's put it all out there for once. What is your deal with me?"

Hank huffed, his face turning a dark red. Debbie put her hand on his back. "Just tell him, Hank."

He stared at his wife, but finally controlled himself. Then he looked back at me, a resignation of sorts in his eyes. "Fine. You're right. I've never liked you. When we first moved to Auburn Hill, we were looking for some investment property in Blueball also. Gosh, Cricket must have been just six or seven years old. We were at an open house and Debbie had gone upstairs to check out the master bedroom."

"No, no. I was checking to see if they had a bathtub. Because it's the most important part of a home. I can't live without soaking in a tub on a regular basis," Debbie interjected, clearly wanting the story to be right.

"Which I told her had nothing to do with a rental, but it's like talking to a brick wall sometimes. A beautiful brick wall," Hank said quickly when Debbie stiffened.

At this rate, I'd be here all night and still not get to talk to Cricket.

"Anyway, I brought Cricket upstairs ten minutes later to find a tall, dark-haired man with his hand on Debbie's back. She was edging away from him, but he just kept getting in her face. I instantly knew something was wrong."

Debbie kept the story going. "Hank barreled in there and shoved the guy away from me. It became a shouting match and then the guy just walked off." Her hand fluttered up to her hair. "It was disconcerting. You think you're safe in an open house, but you just never know who's there."

"I followed the asshole, of course. He went back downstairs to his wife or girlfriend or whatever and left. His woman was downstairs the whole time while he was upstairs flirting with my wife, making her uncomfortable. Who knows what he would have tried if I hadn't come up there when I did." Hank looked highly agitated, which I kind of understood. If that had been Cricket, I would have gone a little nuts too.

Debbie put her hand on my arm, a soft expression on her face. "So we checked the registry on our way out to see who it was."

They both paused and the silence extended into something uncomfortable. The kind of silence that makes the pit of your stomach clench. I was familiar with the feeling and there was only one person who made me feel that way.

"Let me guess. Richard Hellman," I said, deadly calm.

Hank looked at me and I could have sworn all he saw was my father's face. He finally dipped his head in confirmation.

I turned away and ran my hands through my hair. The neighborhood spread out in front of me, but I didn't see the big houses and their expensive properties with perfectly manicured grass. How many times and in how many ways could one man try to ruin my life?

But I'd learned a few things this last month. I absolutely was not my father. He had been part of my life once, but no longer. I turned back to Hank and Debbie.

"I would say I'm sorry, but I'm not responsible for my father's actions. I used to try to take on that responsibility, but I realized recently, with your daughter's help, that I'm only responsible for me. I'm nothing like my father. While my father only looks out for himself, I'd take up piano lessons for the rest of my life for Cricket."

Hank frowned and Debbie just smiled at me, proud that I was sticking up for myself, even if what I was saying made no sense to her. "What the hell does that mean?" Hank groused.

My heart began to race. "It means I love your daughter more than anything or anyone on this planet. And I really need to speak to her. Could you tell me where she is?"

Debbie held her hand up and jingled her keys. "You're in luck, son. I was just on my way to go pick her up from the airport."

Now it was my turn to be confused. "The airport?"

"Come on. Let's not be late." Debbie turned me around and hustled me to her car. Hank followed, but she put her arm up to bar him from the car. "She didn't want you to come, remember?"

My jaw nearly hit the pavement. Debbie had never stood up to Hank before. That was one of the things that drove Cricket crazy about her parents.

"Deb, honey. I'm sorry, okay? I'll apologize and beg her forgiveness. Just let me come pick up our girl, huh?"

Debbie narrowed her eyes at him. "Fine. But you sit in the back! Callan's up front with me."

I slid into the front seat before they could get into an argument about it. I wasn't sure what was going on, but it sounded like Hank and Cricket were in a fight. For the first time ever, I felt some sympathy for him. Being on Cricket's bad side was not the best place to be.

We were halfway to the airport before Hank piped up from the back seat. "You know she refused the condo."

I swallowed hard. "I didn't know that."

"Says she loves you."

I closed my eyes and breathed that in. I let the words settle the anxiety and doubt that had taken root around my heart.

"She even sold her car!" Debbie chirped, chuckling. "Which is why we have to pick her up. I didn't think an Uber would be safe at night."

I nodded, but didn't understand. "Why'd she sell it?"

Hank sighed. "Said she didn't want anything I bought her. She even emailed me a spreadsheet with projected payments so that she could pay off the down payment I made on her salon and apartment. Can you believe that?"

A smile began to tug at my lips. "She's standing on her own two feet."

Debbie took a hand off the wheel to pat my knee.

Hank sighed again. "I suppose she is."

Silence stretched out again until we hit the exit off the

freeway for the airport. Hank leaned forward and put his hand on my shoulder.

"Don't be an idiot like me and lose Cricket."

And there it was. The olive branch from Hank. The first time he seemed to actually care about me. It felt nice.

Debbie swung into a parking space and cut the engine. "Neither one of you lost her. She's just growing up and figuring out what she wants and needs. You can either let her grow up and be part of her life, or you can dig your stubborn heels in about how you think she should be living and miss out on her life entirely. Your choice, boys."

She got out of the car and Hank and I looked at each other.

"Ready to grovel, son?"

I nodded, tucking away the experience of Cricket's dad calling me son. "Never been more ready."

CHAPTER THIRTY-ONE

ricket

I'D HAD the worst best weekend of my life.

The second I blinked my eyes open and stared at the familiar ceiling fan above my bed—the one that needed dusting but I had yet to actually do it—I was flooded with such opposing emotions, I felt rooted to the spot. Moving would have been impossible with the emotional elephant sitting on my chest.

My chest ached for Callan. Sadness joined in for where we were because of my careless actions. Anger at my father for constantly interjecting in my life. Guilt for being mad that Dad constantly showered me with gifts. Joy and hope from connecting with fellow hairstylists in New York. Shock and jubilation at the positive feedback from the competition. It was a lot and it was all hitting me at once.

I turned my head and stared at the framed picture of a group of us from high school. I was on Callan's back, my arms wrapped around his muscular yet smaller shoulders, a broad smile on my face. Callan was looking up at me, oblivious to the other ten people crammed around us. Wholly focused on me.

There was so much I wanted to tell him. So much to explain. So much to apologize for. I couldn't imagine living more days on this planet without having him to turn to and share it with. But I also knew I had more soul searching to do.

When I overheard Audrey last week, it had burst some kind of bubble that I'd been existing in. Her flippant comment had made me wonder who I was without my parents, Callan, or my friends. I'd been just bumbling along in life, taking hits like my epilepsy diagnosis, but knowing I had backup. Which wasn't wrong. I didn't need to push people away to stand on my own two feet, but I couldn't constantly lean on them either. Not when I could do the standing myself.

Which was why I texted Mom not to come pick me up from the airport last night. I didn't need her to drive all that way in the dark when I could simply take an Uber home. It was a small thing, but it made me feel like the adult I was supposed to be. I planned on making more choices like that. I'd stand on my own and prove to myself that I was capable. Then I could lean on Callan like he wanted me to, knowing it was a gift for him and not a necessity for me.

My stomach let out a growl that shook the rafters. With a groan, I pushed back the covers and sat up. Part of being responsible for myself meant that I had to get something to eat. Low blood sugar could trigger a seizure. I'd been doing so well on this new medication that I didn't want to have a setback.

As I found the one yogurt container in the fridge that wasn't expired, I thought about having to live in Auburn Hill if Callan didn't eventually take me back. Because that was definitely a possibility. I'd hurt him immensely. Thinking of the look on his face that night was like a punch to the gut. It was like finding out you were the monster that kicked a sweet puppy when it was hurt. Suddenly I wasn't hungry again.

"Okay, Cricket. Come on." I marched back into my room to

get dressed. I couldn't sit here all day wallowing. I had to search for a new town (a new country?) to live in, just in case. I needed to take a look at my schedule this week and check in with Kennedy. And then I needed to sit down on my laptop and make up a budget for myself. Eventually I'd need my own car, which meant I needed to save up for one, something I'd never had to do before.

Once I found some clean clothes, I brushed out my hair. One of the other stylists I'd roomed with in New York had given me rose-gold highlights that were to *dye* for. The corny hairstylist jokes had been flowing all weekend, that was for sure. I looked at myself in the mirror, and while the shadows under my eyes were a clue to my heartache, there was also a glow to my skin. Even in heartbreak I could find purpose.

Besides, Callan hadn't broken up with me. He'd said we needed a break. I intended to show him that not only was I sorry for my previous actions, but that our break could come to an end. I was ready for forever with him. But I knew words wouldn't cut it. I needed to take solid action to prove it to him. Which is why I needed to get my business together so I could make a shit ton of money and pay back my father for the down payment he'd made on my salon. Then I'd truly be standing on my own two feet.

I gave myself a wink in the mirror and went looking for my phone, only to realize I'd forgotten to charge it last night and it was dead. I went looking for a charger, finally found one under my bed—yes, cleaning my room was top of my be-an-adult list too—and started to charge it. In less than a minute, it sprang to life, pinging and ringing with a dizzying array of notifications.

I realized with horror that Mom hadn't gotten my text message and had driven to the airport, only to miss me. Her last text message had come in around one in the morning, saying that Callan was coming to check on me, and if I wasn't at my apartment, she was calling the police.

My heart thumped heavier in my chest. There weren't any

messages from Callan though. My shoulders slumped as I tried to piece together what that meant. My phone pinged in my hand, making me jump.

Kennedy: Hey, Cricket, welcome home. Still up for coming in early today? I was thinking of getting us coffees so you could tell me all about New York before your first client.

I frowned. I purposely cleared my schedule for today, knowing I'd be exhausted after my trip.

Me: Um, yes, I'd love coffee and to chat, but I shouldn't have any appointments.

Kennedy: Oh yay! Okay, I'll head out now to get coffees. You do have appointments though. Like five of them. Back-to-back.

I wanted to throw my phone. Shit! I didn't have time for that today. I needed to get my life back on track so I could get Callan back. There was nothing to do though but to get my ass in gear and do what needed doing. I yanked the phone charger out of the wall and took it with me. As my feet hit the cold wood outside my door, I realized I needed shoes. Jesus.

After going back inside for proper footwear, I headed down the stairs to the salon. This life epiphany, while super unfortunate with the fallout with Callan, really did come at the right time. I was a mess.

It was early enough that most of Hell hadn't woken up yet. The sidewalk was empty. I had my head down looking at my phone and all the notifications I'd missed overnight. My arm lifted and my hand reached for the gold handle I'd special ordered for the front door of my salon. I pulled on the cool metal and the door swung open.

It was the scent that hit me first. The scent of being in a field of wildflowers when I should have been smelling perm solution. I looked up, eyes wide, nose already inhaling another heady scent of blooms. All around my salon was bouquet after bouquet of every flower imaginable. Every surface was covered in flowers and greenery, turning my salon into an exquisite arboretum.

And in the middle of it all was Callan with a single long-stem red rose in his hands.

"Cal?" I asked breathlessly, forgetting all about my phone, and my plans to wrestle this day—and this life of mine—into submission.

He was beautiful. More precious to my eye than the thousands of flowers surrounding us. His hair looked like he'd been running his fingers through it. He had matching shadows under his eyes, but the familiar brown irises made my heart melt. That little soft smile that made the blood in my veins rush around in excitement. He was home to me. Always would be.

In stunning clarity, I knew that if this didn't work out, I'd definitely be moving. It wasn't me being a drama llama. I simply couldn't exist in a Hell where Callan and I weren't together.

"Angel," Callan said softly, stepping forward and sending my heart rate into the stratosphere. He only called me angel when he was into me.

"Wh-what are you doing here?" I stepped fully into the salon and felt the door hit my backside as it swung closed.

He was in front of me now, so close I could reach out and touch him. And good lord, how badly I wanted to touch him. His shirt stretched across his chest, highlighting how wide his shoulders were now that he was all man. If there was one man I could trust, I knew it was him, but even so, I had to trust myself more.

"I'm here to apologize," he began, gesturing to the flowers all around us. "And to beg you to forgive me for pushing you. I pushed you so hard I pushed you away. I asked you for something you weren't ready to give, and I'm sorry for that. If you'll give me another chance, I promise to give you time. To give you the space you need to grow into who you want to be. No more pushing, Cricket."

Hope flooded my chest. The kind that makes you feel like you're floating on air. "I kind of like it when you push me, Callan."

His eyes heated, that golden brown turning into a pool of

melted chocolate as I watched. He leaned in closer, extending the rose to me. "I came to your apartment last night and used my key to get in. I had to make sure you were home and alive, even if it was probably creepy that I broke in. I just...I can't stop myself from wanting to look after you. I promise I'll give you space this time around. Please say you'll give me another chance."

Ah, Callan. The sweet boy who'd been my friend all through school had turned into a man so devoted he'd look after me even if we were broken up. Or taking a break, I should say. I was going full-stalker-mode and declaring that he could never fully break up with me. I simply wouldn't allow it.

I shook my head slowly, not daring to break his heated stare. A little line formed between his eyebrows, so I rushed to explain. "I will only forgive you if you'll forgive me first. I wasn't ready. Not like you needed me to be. But your half sister smacked me in the face and I got my head screwed on straight. I promise."

Now he was really frowning. "Audrey? She hit you?"

I put my hand on his chest before he flew right out of here to avenge me for some perceived aggression. "No! No, I overheard Audrey talking— You know what? It doesn't matter right now. Just know that I got the message loud and clear and I'm doing things to be independent. I see now what my father was doing, and I won't let him run my life. I promise."

Callan's hand came up to cover mine on his chest. "I know. Your dad and I talked."

Now I was surprised. I scanned his person for cuts and bruises. "You did?"

He nodded, his lips hitching to the side in a wry smile. "Yes, we did. He explained why he never liked me and we worked through it. He also told me you sold your BMW. Why'd you do that?"

I shrugged. "I didn't need my daddy buying me a car. But get back to the important part. Why didn't he like you?"

Callan's lips tightened. "Some stupid shit in the past with my father."

My mouth dropped open. Oh shit. That would make a lot of sense though. I knew it couldn't be something Callan had done. He was the nicest guy I'd ever met.

Callan's hand tightened on mine. "So, what do you say? Will you give me another chance?"

I smiled up at him, plucking the rose from his hand. "How about we do this the way we've always done everything?"

Callan looked as hopeful as I felt. His hand settled on my hip, pulling us together. "And how is that?"

I lifted up on my tiptoes and got as close as I could to his lips. "Together, silly."

He didn't waste a single second before swooping down to kiss me. With a sob of joy and relief palpable enough to make me shake with need, I opened my mouth and let him back in. Living without Callan wasn't even a possibility.

He lifted me off my feet and I wrapped my legs around his waist. My hands wouldn't stop moving, exploring every inch of him, as if I needed the reassurance that he was here, he was mine, and we were back together. My back hit a vase and the thing went crashing to the floor. I gasped and Callan growled. He swung me around but only sideswiped another bouquet.

"Dammit," he muttered. "Not one fucking surface is free."

I looped my arms around his neck and tossed my head back, laughing. His sweet gesture had backfired on him. When the laughter finally settled down, I saw Callan smiling down at me with all the love he felt for me in the softness of his eyes. I could stay lost in them forever and be perfectly happy.

I ran my fingers through the back of his hair. "I do have an apartment right upstairs, you know..."

Callan froze and then let out a whoop. He spun us around and literally ran out of the salon with me clinging to him, bouncing and laughing so hard I had a momentary worry about peeing my pants.

This was life with Callan. Perfect. Crazy. Wonderful. Mine.

EPILOGUE

allan

THREE SHORT MONTHS later

"WHY DID we think we could pull off a town-wide fundraiser all by ourselves in three short months? And right after the holidays?" Cricket was running around our house—I'd quit calling it *my* house the second we made up and she told me flat out that she wasn't living without me ever again—looking adorable in leggings, furry boots, a blue scarf that matched her eyes perfectly, and a knit hat with some kind of fuzzy ball on top of it. Her blonde hair streamed down her back in long waves that came from the curling iron that I burned myself on pretty much on a weekly basis. Girls' tools were dangerous.

"It'll be great. Once we roped in the moms, things were pretty much out of our control anyway." I sat on the couch and waited patiently. I'd been ready twenty minutes ago and I'd learned it was better if I just stayed out of her way.

Cricket had her first follow-up appointment with her doctor and he'd adjusted her meds two months ago. While they'd been controlling her seizures well, they'd made her tired every single day. The new meds also controlled the seizures, but she was back to her normal peppy energy. I was happier than I knew was even possible, seeing her healthy, motivated, and in my bed where she belonged every damn night.

She skid to a stop in front of me and did a slow turn, modeling her outfit like she did most days. She liked to show off her style and I liked to watch her. It was a mutually beneficial habit.

"You're gorgeous," I said gruffly, wishing we didn't have to get to the fundraiser early and I could pull her back into our bedroom.

"Why, thank you, sir." She shot me a wink and then grabbed my hands to pull me off the couch. "Come on! We don't want to be late!"

I should have been nervous. Not because she and I were basically the emcees for the whole fundraiser, but because I finally planned to pull that ring out of my pocket and put it on Cricket's finger this afternoon. I wasn't nervous, though, because it felt like the most right thing I'd ever done. Going any longer without the ring on her finger made me nervous. A life without the possibility of together forever and babies and houses and in sickness and in health was the only reality that made me nervous.

We got to the park just as the sun was peeking over the pine trees, and even so, Mom, Debbie, Poppy, Yedda, Rita, Susie, and Grandma Donna were already there, decorating all the booths that my brothers and I had assembled last night. Cricket had put the whole thing together, going to each of the small businesses on Main Street and roping them into the charity event. Shelby would be teaching multiple flower arrangement classes. Cricket would be doing haircuts right there in the park. Izzy Waldo would be selling baked goods. Dante from Coffee would supply the caffeine. There were ten more booths planned, but I couldn't remember all the details. All I knew is that they'd pledged to give all their proceeds to the Pediatric Epileptic Foundation. Cricket didn't want one more child to go undiagnosed like she had, feeling like they were different from all the other kids in school and not knowing why.

With a toot of their horn, I saw that even Jackie and Neil, Addy's parents, had driven their RV to Auburn Hill for the event. Which meant my number one priority would be keeping an eye on Neil to make sure he didn't sneak away with the teens of Hell and get them all higher than a kite on his stash of marijuana. The man could put Snoop Dog to shame.

Cricket reached up and pulled me down for a quick kiss before running off to help the moms (or Hell Moms as we affectionately referred to them) finish things up. Hank appeared and clapped me on the back after she left. He handed me a coffee.

"She's amazing, isn't she?" he said absently, watching Cricket charm everyone while simultaneously getting most of the decorating done while the moms shared the latest gossip.

I nodded. "That she is." Hank and I had become almost friends over the last few months, putting the past behind us and focusing on the future. A future in which both of us were lucky enough to have Cricket in our lives.

"You got the ring, son?" He glanced over at me, a secret smile on his face.

"I've had it on my person every day for close to three months." I patted my leg. "But I made triple sure it was there this morning."

Chief Waldo swaggered up to us, stroking his handlebar mustache. "Mornin', Callan. Hank. Nice to see you figured out what the rest of us already knew about Callan."

Hank kicked at a rock by our feet, looking mighty sheepish. "Yeah, Debbie's always told me I'm hardheaded."

Chief hooted. "Sounds like she's been talking to my wife."

The two older men chuckled. I found their banter hilarious,

but I also couldn't wait to be their age, teasing about my wife but everyone knowing I loved her to the depths of my soul.

"In all seriousness, I'm glad you and Callan patched things up. He's a good man. All those Hellman boys are." Chief turned to me and gave me a nod.

It occurred to me that while I'd never hear my father say he was proud of me, it meant even more to hear it from Chief. He wasn't expected to be proud of me like a blood relative, and yet he was. That squeeze in my chest felt new and unfamiliar, but also nice.

"That they are," Hank confirmed. "I couldn't have picked out a better son-in-law for my daughter."

Chief hooted again. "Oh, it's like that, huh? Guess the town gossip is a little slow this morning."

I put my hand up. "Keep your voices down, gentlemen. I haven't yet asked the lady. Stick around though and you might hear the answer the same time I do."

Chief stroked his mustache again. "Well, damn. That's a mighty good reason to skip my afternoon nap. Good luck, son." He clapped me on the back harder than you'd expect from a retired guy and sauntered off to walk around the booths.

Before I finished my cup of coffee, the rest of the town had shown up to either support Cricket and her mission, or to simply see what everyone else was up to. I didn't care why they came, I just cared that they spent money and put more dollars in the coffers. I made sure Cricket stayed fed while she ran around and in between haircuts. I talked with nearly every single Hell citizen before the event wound down.

I got Cricket's attention and tilted my head. She lifted her finger and wrapped up the conversation she was having with Penelope Fines. I stepped over to grab the bullhorn we'd positioned by the last booth like we'd planned. I flipped the switch on and winced at the whine it let out before going silent.

"Thank you all for coming today and supporting the Pediatric Epileptic Foundation." I paused for the spattering of applause and for everyone's attention. "We appreciate you supporting a cause that's near and dear to our hearts." Cricket rushed over to my side and beamed at the assembled crowd. "We also appreciate all the Christmas gifts you donated to get into the fair. All those extra toys you found you didn't really need will light up a child's face when they need it most."

Cricket took the bullhorn next and announced the total dollar amount of funds that had been raised today. "The check we'll hand off will go directly to the care of children who are receiving a tough diagnosis. Your money will help pave their way in a new life that includes testing, doctor visits, medications, and possibly surgeries. Thank you so much for caring and coming out today."

Her voice choked up there at the ending and I took that as my cue. We absolutely had not planned the next part. I took the bullhorn from her as everyone clapped and I got down on one knee right there in the grass while our whole town looked on. A hush fell over the crowd while I dug in my pocket.

"Cal?" Cricket hissed. "What are you—"

"Angel," I said into the bullhorn. She jerked back—to be fair, it was kind of loud having a bullhorn in your face—and looked at me like I'd lost the plot. And I had. The very second I realized I was in love with my best friend our senior year of high school. "I can't remember a day of my life when I didn't love you. And I can't imagine a day of my future without you in it, by my side, in front of me, dancing around your salon...wherever you want to be is all right by me. Please make me the luckiest man in all of Hell and say you'll be my wife."

I held up the ring, the sun reflecting off the surface of the diamond and sending little rainbows of color to the ground. Cricket had her hands over her mouth, her eyes wide and already leaking with tears. She looked frozen, stunned I'd asked her to marry me in front of everyone, so I put the bullhorn on the ground.

"Let's not waste any more time. Let's get married, angel. Let's have a whole house full of miracles together," I begged her.

She dropped her hands and looked down her nose at me, though I wasn't that much shorter than her, even on one knee. "I was wondering when you'd hurry up and ask me to marry you. My answer is yes. A thousand yeses."

I grinned from ear to ear, shaking my head. "You mean I've been carrying this ring all this time and you would have said yes awhile back?"

Cricket put her hands on my face, tossing me a wicked smile that made my insides melt. "You think I didn't know about that ring in that smelly gym bag? I've just been waiting for you to do the deed."

My jaw dropped and that's when she kissed me, hard and fast. She lifted her head and addressed the crowd I'd forgotten about. "I said yes!" she shouted.

Everyone erupted in cheers and then I was on my feet, picking my girl up and spinning her around. She held on tight, and when the world stopped spinning, I lost myself in her kiss. It was just her and me, like it had always been. Her tears were the first of many happy ones in our future. Even if they were sad, I'd kiss them away and do everything in my power to make it right. I'd always been looking out for Cricket, but now she was looking out for me too.

"If they'd come up for air, I could congratulate them." My mother's voice cut through the kiss that I could have gladly let go on for a lifetime.

I pulled back just enough to press my forehead to Cricket's. "I love you, angel," I whispered, needing just one more private second with her.

She grinned back at me. "And I've always loved you, so that's mighty convenient."

My brothers chose that moment to dog-pile us, throwing their arms around us both, forming a ring of out-of-control congratulations. Then Cricket's friends—most of whom were my sisters-in-law—joined in, their high-pitched squeals making me wince even as I laughed.

"Congrats, brother," Ace said ruffling up my hair.

Blaze punched me in the shoulder. Daxon gave me a knowing smile and said something sleazy about just wanting in on the married-sex thing the others kept harping about. Ethan, being the best of the bunch, had tears in his eyes as he hugged me hard.

"She's a lucky lady, bro," he said roughly before pulling back and receiving ribbing from Daxon for being emotional.

"If you don't mind, boys," Mom's voice cut in.

Right on cue, everyone backed off and there was Mom, looking at me like a beauty queen eyeing the crown before it was placed on her head. "You make me proud, son." She put her arms around my waist and I hugged her back. This woman had put up with a lot raising five boys on her own. She deserved to be front and center to our happiness.

Next, Hank and Debbie squeezed in to hug us both. They'd known about my plans for today, so they weren't shocked. They were just happy, giving us their blessing.

I gave Mom a kiss on the head and patted her back. She was still squeezing the life out of me. "You're just happy because we might be the first to give you grandkids," I teased her.

"Well..." Ace said out of the blue.

Addy giggled and snuggled into his side. Stunned silence hung in the air.

Mom let go of me so suddenly I felt the breeze. Her attention was laser focused on Ace and Addy. Like a hawk circling above roadkill.

"Ace? Addy? Do you have something to announce?"

The two of them shared a look. "Well, we don't want to overshadow Callan and Cricket," Ace hedged.

"Please," Cricket encouraged, ducking under my arm and squeezing in close to my side now that Mom had moved on. "Overshadow away!"

Addy nodded up at Ace, who placed a quick kiss on her forehead before addressing the group. "Addy and I are pregnant."

Mom let out a shout, her arms flinging wide before she ran straight for the happy couple. It was quite the performance because it was real. Mom had been talking about us giving her grandbabies before we even had our first girlfriends. If there was one woman who would spoil grandkids like it was her job, it was Nikki Hellman.

Neil and Jackie were next, surrounding Addy and Ace, suggesting all kinds of natural childbirth methods that had me wincing. In all the times I'd thought of Cricket and I having kids together, I hadn't actually thought about what happened to a woman's perineum, and quite frankly, I never wanted to think about that again.

We all eventually got a chance to hug the expectant couple. Then Mom was back to drilling Addy about her prenatal care. Addy just laughed and assured her that she was taking only the purest of medicinal tinctures. Mom looked like she was gearing up for some old-fashioned harassing before Neil wrapped his arm around her shoulders and pulled her away, saying he had something she needed. I rolled my eyes, hoping Mom was smart enough not to smoke a joint with Neil. Then again, this was Nikki we were talking about. She'd probably help him roll it *and* smoke it.

"This is the best day," Cricket whispered, laying her head on my chest as we watched our families chatting together.

I pulled her closer and leaned down to kiss her. "Nah. All our best days are in front of us, angel."

SNEAK PEEK

Sneak Peek

Daxon

Two years earlier

Fuck, I hadn't been this drunk in a long time.

The bottles behind the bar all blurred together in a delightful collage of colored glass. I lifted my shot glass in the air, signaling for another. One more wouldn't hurt. Hell, nothing hurt right now. Even the tip of my goddamn nose was dumb. No, not dumb. Numb. Whatever. I was no English major.

"You got a ride lined up, honey?" The bartender had a voice only a mother could love. She'd clearly been smoking a pack of cigarettes since the day she was born. I liked her though. She was skinny as a rail and didn't take no shit. I owed my life to a bartender just like her in another town and in another lifetime.

"Got my Uber app all ready, sweetheart." I wiggled my phone at her. Her eyebrow lifted, but she poured me another one.

As she moved away to help someone else, I inhaled as deep as my lungs would go, feeling the burn there and imagining that one particular face that haunted me. I lifted my glass and exhaled all the bullshit.

"Cheers, motherfucker." Then I tossed the liquid back. Like it always did, the burn erased the memories. Took away the shame that liked to creep into my veins and poison my mind.

I pushed back from the bar, stood on my own two feet and let the room settle into a gentle rocking instead of a full tailspin before I made my way to the bathrooms. Music filled my ears from the live band still playing for the folks out on the dance floor but I ignored it all. I pushed the wooden door open and let it swing shut behind me as I came to a stop. There in the mirror was a woman putting on lipstick. I watched the column of red make a full circle, painting her lips as her gaze found mine in the mirror.

"You lost, handsome?" she asked, her voice reminding me of a rose petal. All soft and sweet and something I wanted to touch.

"Not anymore," I answered, taking another step into the bathroom. Somewhere in the back of my brain I registered that I was in the wrong place, but the alcohol didn't seem to care.

The woman spun around and threw her lipstick in her purse. Her jean skirt was short, made more so because her hips were so curvy the material bunched up there before leaving most of her thighs exposed. I thanked the heavens for making a woman with hips like that. Her muscular legs ended in red cowboy boots that matched her lips. Breasts spilled out of a black tank top.

"Found the prettiest girl in the whole place," I said, taking yet another step and rejoicing when she didn't look scared. I didn't want to harm her. I just wanted to touch her. See if she was as soft as her voice.

"Girl, huh?" She inhaled and those breasts had a life of their own, expanding in front of my eyes. "I'll have you know I'm all woman."

I reached her boots, the proximity giving me a whiff of her flowery perfume. If the alcohol wasn't playing tricks on me, she smelled like a goddamn rose. "And I'm all man, so aren't we the pair?"

Thank God for all these years of flirting every chance I got. I could probably flirt the skirt off a girl while I was asleep. And I really wanted to see this one without that skirt. See if my fingers would meet if I wrapped my hands around her tiny waist like I suspected.

Those lips curved up into a smile. I couldn't seem to look away from them.

"Does that line actually work for you?"

My gaze traveled up a few inches to lock with pretty blue eyes that held my attention even more than her mouth. "Only a small percentage of the time. You could help me up that percentage though."

The woman let out a laugh and pushed away from the counter. Her breasts were now brushing against my stomach. "You drunk?"

"No," I lied instantly.

"Because I don't like drunk sex. I like a man to know what he's doing or why waste my time, you know?" She tossed a lock of strawberry-blonde hair behind her shoulder.

Hot fucking damn, she was offering? I could sober up faster than being caught drinking behind the bleachers during a football game in high school when the principal came looking for me with his flashlight.

I reached up and traced my thumb along her jawline. Fuck. Soft as a rose petal. I knew it.

I dipped my head and softly bit her earlobe. "I know what I'm doing, believe me." I pulled back to see if I had permission.

Her tongue darted out to wet her lips. Her hand grabbed my belt buckle and tugged me into all her soft curves. "Show me."

I dipped my head again. "Gladly, sweetheart."

I grabbed those hips and set her up on the counter so I could reach her lips better. She spread her legs and let me press into her hot center. Before I had a chance to lay another cheesy line on her, she grabbed the front of my shirt and tugged me down to kiss me. The woman devoured me whole, taking command of the situation. I was too drunk and happy to care. She could use me over and over again.

Things got hot and hazy from there, but when I woke up the next morning facedown on my couch with the world's worst hangover, I still smelled like roses.

Present time

"Where the fuck did I put it?" My voice was drowned out by the compressor nail guns and circular saws my crew had going from sunup to sundown. This was my largest build to date and I was losing my goddamn mind.

As I exited the shell of a cabin my crew and I had been laboring on for over a month already, I threw my hard hat into the stack of my personal belongings. The stack that did not contain my sweatshirt. I'd worn it here, so how could it disappear? Sadly, it was not the first item I'd lost recently.

"Fuck," I muttered, reprimanding myself mentally to keep better tabs on things. The wealthy aristocrat who'd hired me several months ago was paying big money for a state-of-the-art home that was more mansion than cabin. How could I provide a mansion when I couldn't even keep track of my own damn clothing?

"You kiss your mama with that mouth?" came a voice behind me.

Namely, my mother's voice.

I spun around and saw Mom standing amongst the pine trees, her bright turquoise shirt, pants, caftan—whatever the hell women called the tent of material she was wearing—standing out like a lighthouse during a storm. Her fur-lined boots matched the rugged environment though. For once, Nikki Hellman had made an effort to wear something practical.

As much as her outfits mystified me, my mother was, and would always be, the most important woman in my life. I didn't let word get out that I was a mama's boy, because believe me, I was a ladies' man too, but this woman held a special place in my heart.

"Hey, Mom. What are you doing here?" I came over to pull her into a hug and kiss her forehead. I eyed her little sedan behind her. There was ice on the roads this time of year and I didn't care for her being so high up the mountain in that stupid car. I kept trying to buy her a truck, or at least a four-wheel-drive SUV but she rejected my offer every time, saying I'd done enough.

"Just checking on my favorite son," she said with a wink.

"Uh-huh. You only say that because the other four aren't here."

She waved away my comment. "You're my favorite because you have that nice ass that got you a billboard over the I-5 freeway. You remember that?"

Of course I remembered that. I'd been trying to forget it ever since.

"You got that ass from me, you know," Mom kept going. "You might not be able to tell now, but back in my day, I had the nicest ass in all the county."

I grimaced. "Okay. That's great, Mom. Is there a reason you came up here to see me? Other than to gross me out?"

Mom fluttered a hand to her chest and I braced myself for the theatrics. "Does a mother need a reason to check in on her own children? I just want to see how you're doing. You've been working so hard on this new project I haven't seen you much."

"Mhm." If I waited her out long enough, she'd eventually get to the real point of her visit.

"Now I know that your brothers all getting paired off can be a bit of a shock to the system. Ace and Addy having that sweet baby soon. Blaze and Annie getting married in two weeks, Callan and Cricket engaged. It might make a single man start to wonder what he's doing with his life. You know?"

I rolled my eyes and she swatted my arm. "Mom..."

"Don't you 'mom' me, young man. You need to stop with your womanizing ways and start thinking of settling down."

I gaped at her. "Womanizing ways?"

She swatted that comment away too. "Whatever you want to call it. Those ladies you've been dating are barely old enough to be legal, son. It's time to find you a *woman*. Find one with ample hips and a mind for settling down."

I couldn't seem to pick my jaw up off the forest floor. Mom had always been over the top, but she was reaching new levels today. "Okay, I'm going to pretend you didn't just tell me to find a woman with childbearing hips. Thank you for your concern about my dating life, but I'm good. Why don't you go harass Ethan? He's still single too."

Mom stomped her boot. "I already talked to him earlier. He said he has a date tonight that looks real promising."

That was a flat-out lie, and as much as I wanted to rat his ass out to our mother, I wouldn't. The brother code and all that shit. We had plans to get beers tonight, so I knew for a fact Ethan didn't have a date lined up.

"Well, good for him. You'll have to call him tomorrow bright and early to get all the details."

Mom's face brightened. "Oh, that's a good idea. Maybe I can give him some second-date advice to keep things moving along."

I nodded, wishing I could be a fly on the wall for that conversation as Ethan lied like a rug.

"Awesome. Now I hate to cut things short, but I still have a crew to lead here." I pulled her into a hug before she could protest, then turned her around and opened her car door for her. "Take it nice and slow out of here. Roads are a bit unpredictable."

Mom looked over my head, her eyes going all glassy and weird as she stilled. "Kind of like life, huh?"

Dammit, she creeped me out when she did that. Got all serious and spooky out of the blue. It was like she had the sight, seeing something in the future that no one else sensed. I patted her back and made sure she put her seat belt on before shutting her door.

I stood there until she was headed down the road again, shaking my head at her antics. Wasn't it enough that three out of her five boys were married off? Did she really need to harass me about it too? I loved my sisters-in-law, but as far as I was concerned, marriage was for suckers. And I'd quit being a sucker the year a picture of my ass hung there over the freeway.

A flash of gold fur out of the corner of my eye had my head snapping to the left. A sleek animal, not much bigger than a house cat darted behind a large bush we'd been able to keep when we cleared this land for the new build. Stepping as quietly as I could in steel-toed work boots, I crept over in that direction.

"Hey, boss! It's Friday, yeah?" one of my crew called from the second story where he was belted into the frame we'd managed to put up this week. He looked down with a cheesy smile under his hard hat.

Whatever wild animal had been hiding in the foliage was long gone after that shout. "Congrats, Javier. You know the days of the week."

"Ah man, come on, boss. Don't be like that," he whined.

I rubbed the back of my neck. It *was* almost quitting time. And they'd been working their asses off this week to get back on schedule. We'd lost a week when a freak storm had come through and delayed laying the foundation.

"Yeah, yeah. Get to a stopping point, clean up, and get out of here, you lazy assholes."

A cheer went up and a frenzy of activity ensued. My crew was the best. I'd been working with a few of them from day one of starting my business. I'd had to add a few more to the payroll when I scored this project. We might give each other shit on the daily, but there was even more mutual respect.

"See you Monday, boss!"

I waved them away before putting my hard hat back on and jumping up onto the foundation. I was always the last to leave a jobsite. I didn't leave anything to chance when it was my name on the sign out front. Hellman Log and Timber Homes meant quality and trust.

Everything looked buttoned up tight for the weekend. I was almost back to the front of the cabin when I heard a car door slam. Thinking one of the guys must have come back for something they left, I called out, "What did you forget, asshole?"

The only response was the wind whistling through the pine trees. I came out from behind what would eventually be the front living room and stared down at the most beautiful woman I'd seen in a long time, her arm around a preteen girl who looked a lot like her mama.

"You forgot your manners, clearly," she snapped, fire in her baby-blue eyes.

Her very *familiar* blue eyes.

Scan the QR code below to join my newsletter and get a FREE novella set in Hell!

ALSO BY MARIKA RAY

All Steamy RomComs Set in Hell:

Grumpy As Hell - Hellman Brothers #1

Bro Code Hell - Hellman Brothers #2

***

Ridin' Solo - Sisters From Hell #1

One Night Bride - Sisters From Hell #2

Smarty Pants - Sisters From Hell #3

Ex Best Thing - Sisters From Hell #4

***

Love Bank - Jobs From Hell #1

Uber Bossy - Jobs From Hell #2

Unfriend Me - Jobs From Hell #3

Side Hustle - Jobs From Hell #4

Man Glitter - Jobs From Hell Novella - Grab it FREE here!

***

Backroom Boy - Standalone

Steamy RomComs:

The Missing Ingredient - Reality of Love #1

Mom-Com - Reality of Love #2

Desperately Seeking Househusbands - Reality of Love #3

***

Happy New You - Standalone

Sweet RomCom with Delancey Stewart:

Texting With the Enemy - Digital Dating #1

While You Were Texting - Digital Dating #2

Save the Last Text - Digital Dating #3

How to Lose a Girl in 10 Texts - Digital Dating #4

Sweet Romances:

The Marriage Sham - Standalone

***

The Widower's Girlfriend-Faking It #1

Home Run Fiancé - Faking It #2

Guarding the Princess - Faking It #3

***

Lines We Cross - Nickel Bay Brothers #1

Perfectly Imperfect Us - Nickel Bay Brothers #2

Steamy Beach Romance:

1) Sweet Dreams - Beach Squad #1

2) Love on the Defense - Beach Squad #2

3) Barefoot Chaos - Beach Squad #3

* Novella - Handcuffed Hussy

4) Beach Babe Billionaire- Beach Squad #4

5) Brighter Than the Boss - Beach Squad #5

* Novella - Christmas Eve Do-Over

ACKNOWLEDGMENTS

Thank you so much for reading Friend Zone Hell!

Special thanks to Jennifer Olson for the incredible Cover Design and for the hours cover model searching that were so incredibly tedious. lol Thank you to Judy Zweifel for triple checking this manuscript and making it shine as usual.

To my Rays of Sunshine: you give me life. <3

ABOUT THE AUTHOR

Marika Ray is a USA Today bestselling author, writing small town RomCom to make your heart explode and bring a smile to your face. All her books come with a money-back guarantee that you'll laugh at least once with every book.

Marika spends her time behind a computer crafting stories, walking along the beach, and making healthy food for her kids and husband whether they like it or not. Prior to writing novels, Marika held various jobs in the finance industry, with private start-up companies, and then in health & fitness. Cats may have nine lives, but Marika believes everyone should have nine careers to keep things spicy.

If you'd like to know more about Marika or the other novels she's currently writing, please find her in her private reader group called Marika Ray's of Sunshine on Facebook.

If you want to take your stalking to the next level, here are other legal-ish places you can find Marika:

Join her Newsletter -
http://bit.ly/MarikaRayNews

Amazon - https://www.amazon.com/author/marikaray

Goodreads - https://www.goodreads.com/author/show/16856659.Marika_Ray

Bookbub - https://www.bookbub.com/authors/marika-ray

TikTok - https://vm.tiktok.com/ZMJvnQ2Cv